all Best Wishes!

PRAISE FOR *THE DESECRATED*

"John Gray announces himself as a major voice in modern literary horror with his debut novel *The Desecrated*. Surgically precise suspense, breakneck pacing, and a brilliant narrative arc that gets under the reader's skin are all in full force here. At the heart of this tale, though, is a taboo that spans generations and asks big questions about death, life, good, evil, and all the scary stuff in between. A remarkable debut, and highly recommended."
—Jay Bonansinga, New York Times bestselling author of *The Walking Dead: The Rise of the Governor*; *The Walking Dead: Road To Woodbury*

"John Gray's *The Desecrated* is a spine tingling page turner."
—Harlan Coben, #1 New York Times Best-Selling Author

"Suspense and horror fans will love this deeply atmospheric thriller that twists and turns its way to a shocking end!"
—Lisa Gardner, New York Times bestselling author of *One Step Too Far*

"This is a hell of a book. I was dragged in on the first page and couldn't get out again. The writing is both spare and rich – a character-driven horror/crime thriller, set in a Gothically-authentic New York City."
—James P. Blaylock, World Fantasy Award-Winning Author, Co-Founder of the Modern Steampunk Genre

"A realistic look at the darker side of human nature . . . a compelling horror story."
—Kirkus Reviews

THE
DESECRATED

JOHN GRAY

THE DESECRATED
John Gray

Ellysian Press
www.ellysianpress.com

The Desecrated
© Copyright John Gray. All rights reserved.

Print ISBN: 978-1-941637-80-7
First Edition, 2022

Editor: Maer Wilson, M Joseph Murphy
Cover Art: M Joseph Murphy
Many thanks to Jonathon Clayborn for special services

Thank you to the artist Surang for the use of the Anubis Graphic.

DEDICATION

To Melissa Jo Peltier, Wife, Partner,
Forever Heartthrob

PROLOGUE

New York City, 1908

"This one's been dead too long."

Otto stared at the dates on the gravestone in the dim glow of the lantern, doing the math. Jacob, already soaked from the relentless rain and wanting this night to be over, stood beside him.

"Are you sure?" Jacob whined, shifting his weight off of his sore leg.

Otto glanced at him with disdain and thrust the lantern into his hands. He shouted to be heard over the stinging downpour. "Dead no more than a week. How many times do I have to tell you?"

Grabbing the wheelbarrow containing their tools, he pushed it through the mud toward the newer graves. Another flash of lightning lit up the night sky. "Try to keep up," Otto shouted over his shoulder at Jacob, but he was drowned out by the thunder as he trudged on. He passed under a looming angel statue – one of the many marble sentries that stood guard over this ancient cemetery. All were seemingly lost in thought as they stood in eerie silence. He gave it a nod for luck, but when he saw the statue's blank gaze in a flash of lightning, he knew that no angel would side with him tonight.

The muddy graveyard was home to a microcosm of the city's nineteenth century population. Notable bankers, politicians, and society matrons all rubbed cold shoulders with laborers and shop owners in the democracy of death. Some of the wealthiest dead lay under a cage of crisscrossed iron bars – *mortsafes* – put in place to save a loved one from grave robbers and, even more reviled, the unholy body snatchers.

Body snatchers. Like Otto and Jacob.

Otto had to catch his breath. It was hard enough dragging his rusty wheelbarrow through the cemetery on any ordinary night; in the mud and rain it was agony. Pausing to ease his stinging muscles, he looked up, and had to admit that even in the rain the cemetery was beautiful. Maybe even more so. Otto knew nothing of architecture and even less about nature. Still the sloped roofs and columns of the mausoleums shining with rainwater, the intricately-carved monuments and headstones, and the weeping trees bent with age and sorrow – all made him want to cry. Otto loved it. It felt like home to him.

He had almost forgotten about Jacob. He stopped, straining to turn around in his heavy raincoat, barely able to see through the driving downpour. Halfway down the slope, the dim lantern glowed as his corpulent partner pulled his great bulk through the mud, two dented shovels slung over his shoulder. Otto had known Jacob since prison days – that was nearly fifteen years before. Jacob had not remained thin but had remained stupid. Nevertheless, he was reliable,

2

strong, and malleable, three things Otto needed in a colleague.

At the top of a small hill, Otto stopped, impatiently waiting for the lumbering Jacob to catch up to him. Pausing only made him feel the rain soaking through the shoulders of his coat even more. His tobacco-stained teeth ached with pain; his back molar had been bothering him for a while now, but the idea of seeing a dentist filled him with dread. It was barbaric, what they did, and Otto avoided them at all costs.

Jacob, wheezing, finally came beside him. His face was a pincushion of whiskers, and his breath fouled the air as he panted. Surveying the ocean of graves nearby, Jacob shouted to be heard over the downpour. "How 'bout that one?"

Otto followed his gaze to the new-looking granite headstone. Squinting to see the date, he counted on his fingers. "No. Been dead two weeks."

Jacob grimaced, revealing the blackened stumps of his dozen or so teeth, forcing Otto to think about dentists again. "Does it really matter?" Jacob asked. "I mean on a night like this?"

Otto again stared at Jacob with contempt. He hated laziness. "Yes," he snarled, "it matters. We're paid to do a job."

Otto's coat squeaked as he turned and pulled the reluctant wheelbarrow out of the mud and deeper into the cemetery. Jacob grudgingly followed. Otto took his work seriously. Any man who referred to him as a "grave robber" was in for a beating. Otto did not *steal* from a grave; he did not take jewelry or other possessions. Otto was a "resurrectionist." *Procuring* bodies was a time-honored profession dating back to the 1600s. A necessary profession. Maybe, in Otto's view, even a noble one, for Otto and others like him provided a vital service to science.

The Desecrated

As the number of medical schools in the city grew, the need for cadavers to study grew along with it. An attempt had been made to address the need legally by attaching certain capital crimes with post-mortem "dissection" penalties, where executed criminals were offered to medical schools for study. Unclaimed bodies were also sent to medical schools. However, the rapid proliferation of these schools quickly outpaced the legal supply of corpses, which is where professionals like Otto came in. Commissioned by local medical schools, they were charged with providing fresh cadavers for their students to carve and study. Although the schools knew full well where these bodies came from, they preferred not to dwell.

Otto sniffed at the mortsafes he passed – even in death the rich were given special treatment. No matter. It was far better to take the body of a poor person whose family would have no recourse. Stopping at another new-looking headstone, unencumbered by an iron cage, he bent over to see the carved date through the rain. Jacob leaned over him with the lantern to help him see. There was a smell of stale tobacco and some vague fish odor emanating from Jacob that made Otto's stomach turn.

Jacob spoke. "Died October ninth. This is the fifteenth." His face pinched with the sheer mental effort. "So, dead for five days."

"No you idiot," Otto replied. "Learn to count. It's seven days."

Jacob shifted his considerable weight. "Either way, it's fresh enough," he reasoned.

Otto, wet and tired, his toothache throbbing, agreed. Setting down the wheelbarrow, he caught one of the shovels Jacob tossed at him, and they began their work. As they dug, Otto glanced at the name on the gravestone. *Adelina Baraket.* Very exotic. Arabian maybe? Who knew, but not from New York, in any case. One less foreigner in his city, he thought with a tight smile.

Otto's palms were raw, and Jacob's back was on fire when, after twenty minutes of intense digging, they heard the familiar sound of metal hitting wood. They straightened up, their sopping wool coats and ragged leather boots sloshing with water. They exchanged glances. The hardest part was done. Otto, fully in the grave, watched as Jacob set the wheelbarrow alongside the opening in the ground.

It wasn't necessary to fully expose the coffin. All they had to do was scrape enough dirt off the top of the lid to chop a hole through it. They would then use the long metal hooks they carried in the wheelbarrow to drag the corpse through the opening in the coffin and out of the grave. The clothes and any jewelry would be removed and put back into the casket – another point of pride for Otto – *he was no thief.* There was also the matter of severe penalties for stealing, while mere body snatching was a slap on the wrist.

Otto scraped the dirt off the top of the coffin. It was new, dirty and muddy but not too damaged yet. It was much easier dealing with older graves; the coffins came apart with a lot less effort, and a dried-out corpse was a lot easier to handle. Then again, it was much easier to dig through the loose dirt of a new grave. Be that as it may, the school would not pay for an old corpse; they needed fresh. Intact. A nice new corpse would bring them $9.25. Or $5.00 as far as Otto told Jacob; no need for the overfed hulk to bother himself with facts and figures. Besides, Otto was the brains of the operation, only fair he should be better compensated.

Otto gripped the handle of his shovel with both hands, tightly so his hold wouldn't slip in the rain, and raised it above his head. Slamming the shovel into the coffin lid, he watched it splinter and crack. Two more assaults on the coffin, and the lid exploded, splitting right down the middle. Otto shook his head. "Cheap bastards. These coffins might as well as be cardboard," he said, disgusted at the corners cut by loved ones to save a few cents.

"What *is* that?" Jacob shouted down at him. Otto followed his gaze into the coffin. The corpse was visible. A young woman, maybe just out of her teens. Her pale blue face still held some beauty, in spite of the visible veins at the surface of her skin, and the half-open eyes that stared in two different directions as if she were vaguely interested in what was happening on either side of her. Otto saw what was drawing Jacob's attention - the round swell of the corpse's belly straining against the already decaying death gown.

This dead body was pregnant.

"I never seen that before," Jacob grunted.

Neither had Otto. Staring down at the corpse's belly, he was only a little ashamed by his first thought: perhaps they would be paid for two corpses? Or maybe a smaller payment for the child? Surely there must be some medical value to the body of an unborn human?

Jacob spoke again. "What's that shiny thing?"

Otto let his gaze drift back up to the corpse's face and neck. Yes, there was something shiny around her neck. He bent over and studied the gold disc – an amulet of some kind. On it was the blank outline of a dog – one of those Egypt-type dogs, Otto thought. Ah! That explained the weird name. The woman must've been Egyptian. The dog icon itself had been pried off of the amulet, leaving only the shape behind.

"Is it gold?" Jacob asked, barely audible over the rain.

Otto nodded his head. Ignoring the fresh jolt of pain from his aching tooth, he cleared the rain from the amulet with his fingers; it was smooth and cool to the touch. Otto briefly debated his code: a true resurrectionist does not steal belongings – but this – this was *gold*. It could change his life.

"Let's take it," Jacob suggested. Otto struggled with his

conscience – and his conscience won.

"We're not taking it."

"Bastard," cursed Jacob.

Otto glared up at him, the rain pelting his face and eyes. "Shut up and get me the hooks." As Jacob sulkily turned to the wheelbarrow, Otto heard a faint cry. Staring down at the corpse in the broken coffin, he noticed for the first time that her wispy dress made her look like she had just come from a delicate tea party. The thought made Otto sad. but then he heard the cry again.

A baby's cry.

And it was coming from the swollen belly of the corpse.

Jacob heard it too and hung his head over the hole. The cry came once again. Deeper. Throatier.

Less human.

Jacob jumped into the hole beside Otto. Before Otto could protest, Jacob drew a long knife from his mud-crusted boot and *plunged it into the belly of the corpse.*

"No!" cried Otto, too late.

Jacob turned to him, his eyes wild. "What if the child is alive!"

Otto couldn't argue with his logic and stared down at the gaping hole in the corpse's belly. The two of them stood there in the pouring rain, shoulder deep in the earth, standing on a coffin. Otto still clutched the amulet. Everything grew silent.

They tried to see into the darkness inside the ragged hole in the corpse's stomach. The smell of death was pungent and close, but they were used to that. It was the new smell that they noticed – a sharp sulfur odor. Like rotten eggs.

Jacob frowned at Otto. His voice shook. "This isn't right. This is a sign."

"A sign of what?" asked Otto, trying to maintain his superiority, but the quake in his voice gave away his fear.

"That we shouldn't be grave robbin'."

Annoyed, Otto grabbed Jacob by his filthy wool collar and hissed through his teeth, "We're not grave ro—"

With a deafening roar, something massive and angry exploded out of the open stomach of the corpse. It moved too fast to see. All Otto noticed were teeth – like shark teeth, inside some kind of dark, dripping opening that may have been a mouth. There was little time to ponder that, as the raging teeth and mouth clamped down over his head and bit it off as if it were a carrot. And spit it out in wet, bloody pieces.

Jacob stared open-mouthed, frozen in shock. The black thing turned its blazing eyes on him. *Were there really four sets of eyes?* Before he could scream, the creature thrust its giant head into – and through – the middle of Jacob's body.

The rest was just a blurred killing frenzy, sucking what had been two men into a whirlwind of ripping skin and flying organs, all soaked in a red mist. If Otto could have still entertained a thought, it might have been the realization that there was no more need to fret over his toothache, now that his head was minus a jaw. The screeching creature violently yanked the tattered torsos of the body snatchers into the open grave as if they were ragdolls, and followed them in with a suffocating, suction-like noise.

The attack was over as quickly as it started, and an eerie silence descended on the cemetery. The gentle sound of rain pelting the trees replaced the screams.

A few yards from the open grave, the amulet lay in the mud, soaked in blood.

Still gripped by most of Otto's twitching fingers, at the end of his torn up, disembodied hand.

toward them. "And nobody, I mean *nobody*, is to take pictures of this shithead. I mean it. I will fire your ass immediately."

The group took this as their cue to end the meeting. Angel and Otis fought for the van keys hanging from a peg on the wall. Ersen made sure Jennifer saw how difficult it was for him to get his jacket on over his biceps. And in turn, Jennifer made sure Ersen could see she didn't notice.

Jennifer found herself alone in the office with Clover, while Ersen lingered in the hallway, waiting for the boss. Clover and Ersen had an odd friendship Jennifer couldn't fathom, as they seemed to have nothing in common. Clover regularly berated Ersen's pronounced lack of intelligence, which the muscle-bound Ersen stoically endured. Yet the brooding hulk seemed to never quite know what to do unless Clover directed him.

She watched Clover trace her finger along the glass of the aquarium, apparently trying to get the attention of a recalcitrant clownfish. "What are you doing?" Jennifer asked.

"I'm training Ziti to follow my finger."

Ziti, the clownfish, blissfully ignored Clover's finger as he swam lazy circles around a well-worn plastic scuba diver. "I didn't know you can train fish," Jennifer observed.

"They're smarter than you think."

"I doubt that."

"Don't break my balls," Clover suggested, tapping on the glass.

"You're the second person to say that to me tonight."

"What does that tell you?" Clover asked.

Jennifer shook her head and donned her white lab coat, hoping Clover would leave soon, but knowing she wanted to be here for the arrival of Trevor Pryce. Through the scratched and slightly fogged window in Clover's office facing the hallway, she noticed a gurney with a body bag containing a corpse. Angel and Otis must have just dropped it off before the meeting. "I'll process that guy," Jennifer offered.

"Not yet!" Clover exclaimed. "We haven't done the naming."

Jennifer wanted to protest but knew it would be a waste of time. Now she understood what Ersen was waiting for.

Clover walked out of the office into the hallway. Approaching the gurney, her rubber-soled shoes squeaked on the ancient tile floor. One of the dull fluorescent lights blinked nervously. Ersen smiled, reached for the gurney, and spun it toward Clover, a little like they were playing spin-the-bottle, Jennifer thought.

Unzipping the body bag, revealing the sallow face of a sixty-something-year-old man, Clover grinned at Jennifer. The corpse's crusted eyebrows were pushed high on his forehead, his eyes open wide in surprise, his mouth ajar.

"I'll call him," Clover smiled her cooked smile. " 'Why Me.' "

Ersen guffawed, as he always did at anything Clover uttered that was remotely amusing. Jennifer turned away, disgusted at their treatment of the dead.

TWO

The headlights of the black SUV flashed over the faces of the reporters and fans, giving them all strangely startled expressions. Jennifer and Clover waited by the open door of the morgue building, watching the SUV glide to a halt. A dark-suited chauffeur got out of the driver's side, but before he could round the car, Trevor Pryce bounded out of the back seat.

The crowd roared. Cameras flashed. Trevor gave a high wattage grin to the young women crowding past the police toward him. The English movie star seemed very much at home, Jennifer thought – just the right mix of humble and please-adore-me-more. She was prepared to be disappointed at his in-person appearance. She had heard that many movie stars were seriously short and, without the right lighting and camera angles, rarely seemed as devastatingly handsome as their on-screen persona.

In this case, that assessment was all wrong.

The Desecrated

Trevor was drop-dead gorgeous, there was no doubt about it. Jet-black hair that fell oh-so-sloppily over his forehead, above blazing green eyes that stood out from his taut, chiseled face like high-beam headlights. She guessed his age at around twenty-four or twenty-five, even though the bright camera lights revealed some craggy smile lines around his eyes. She could also see, even from this distance, that he had what she had always thought of as "The Life Force": a certain energy, a power radiating from deep inside those twinkling eyes that demanded attention – a presence that would not be denied. She hadn't ascribed that trait to anyone in a long time. It used to be true of her father, years ago, before the turning, but Trevor was the first person she'd met in years who had it.

Jennifer's train of thought was interrupted when a screaming young woman suddenly raised her blouse to reveal her bare breasts, with her phone number written across them. If Trevor noticed, he didn't bat an eye.

"Thank you guys," Trevor said into a TV camera, his crisp English accent making him sound intelligent and ironic at the same time. "Look, I'm just here to pay my debt. This has been a real wakeup call for me, and I want to thank my awesome fans for all their support!"

With practiced skill, Trevor moved right through the throng of reporters, beaming his smile in a wide circle, ignoring their shouted questions. As he approached the entrance to the morgue, Clover scowled at him.

"You're late."

"Blow me," Trevor answered cheerfully.

***

Trevor studied the exotic fish lazily pulsing through the cloudy water of the aquarium. Jennifer thought he seemed almost wistful.

"Silent motion. Nothing like it. Very soothing."

Ersen glanced at Clover. Employing his usual level of humor, he made a masturbatory gesture with his hand.

"Look," Clover said to Trevor's muscular back. "I don't want any movie star shit from you. You show up on time, do what you're told, and we'll get along great."

"Looking forward to working with you, ma'am," Trevor said, keeping his eyes on the fish.

"You won't be working with *me*. Ersen and I do days."

"Can I apply for a transfer to work days?" Trevor asked innocently.

"No," Clover answered curtly. She pointed at Angel and Otis, who had managed to delay their departure long enough to also witness Trevor's entrance. "That's Angel and Otis. They work in the field doing nighttime body pickups and transfers."

Jennifer pictured Angel and Otis with scythes and plows, crossing a meadow. The nighttime streets of New York did not quite qualify as "the field."

"Can I apply for a transfer to work in the field?" Trevor inquired.

Clover nodded at Jennifer. "You'll be here doing the overnight with Jennifer Shelby."

Trevor turned his full attention to Jennifer for the first time. Doing her best to appear unimpressed, her cheeks burned.

"Do *not* give her any shit," Clover snarled.

Trevor grinned at Jennifer. She almost had to squint from the glare. "No shit. Check," Trevor answered.

"Remember that my reports go to the court every week."

"Every week. Check."

"And just so you know? This celebrity-ass thing means nothing to me. Less than nothing."

Ersen spoke up, chin high: "Same for me." He enunciated a little too clearly, always being sensitive about his thick Turkish accent.

"You both mean less than nothing. Check," Trevor said confidently, looking at Jennifer.

Clover glared at Trevor and gestured with her chin to the clueless Ersen, time for them to go. Clover barked at Jennifer on her way out of the office. "Show him what to do. Start by getting Why Me tucked in." She turned to Angel and Otis. "Hey, what is this, the stage door? Get out of here and get to work." Clover and Ersen left together, Ersen pushing past Trevor a little harder than he had to.

An incredibly awkward silence settled on the office. Jennifer was about to tell Angel and Otis to get lost when Otis spoke. "So . . . like, *Trevor Pryce* in the morgue! That is hella strange, dude."

"Just making the world a better place for the dead," smiled Trevor.

Otis and Angel laughed uproariously, elbowing each other. Jennifer stared at them.

Angel tried to catch his breath. "Dude, you are high-larious."

"I seen all your movies, brah," Otis managed to stutter. *"Kill Or Be Killed, Guts And Glory, Locked and Loaded* – you are awesome, son!"

Jennifer was not in the mood to listen to Otis' fake street jargon. He tried hard to sound like a gangbanger, but in spite of his badass tats and bling, his extreme suburban whiteness rose off of his skin like mist from a cul-de-sac.

Jennifer grabbed each of them by an arm. "Let's discuss *Masterpiece Theater* later. Right now there are dead people lying around all over the city, and they're not gonna zip up their own body bags."

Smiling, Angel and Otis glanced over their shoulders for a last glimpse of Trevor as Jennifer hustled them to the door. When they were finally gone, Jennifer turned to Trevor. It was suddenly very quiet. Trevor gazed at her steadily.

"What?" she asked finally.

"I couldn't help notice that you've been looking at me like I'm some kind of exotic animal."

"Doesn't everybody?" was the only response Jennifer could think of.

Trevor smiled.

Jennifer went to the cabinet in the hallway outside Clover's office and opened it, trying not to dwell on Trevor's slightly crooked, million-dollar grin and the twinkling bright green eyes that promised all kinds of trouble.

"Sorry. I guess I've never been this close to a . . . famous person before."

Trevor turned up the grin another fifty watts. "You could always get closer."

Jennifer turned to him. "This'll do," she said, unsmiling, and threw a lab coat at him.

THREE

His feet were killing him. Maybe it was the tattered boots that were held together by electrical tape. Maybe it was the damp socks, through which his heel and all his toes had long since broken through. Maybe it was the swollen and infected blisters on the feet themselves that made each step a study in agony. The pain had become his new normal.

Ulysses tried to keep his thoughts focused on the task at hand, pulling a rusted and mud-encrusted chain from underneath a tree root. The recent heavy rains had dislodged clumps of trees and crumbling headstones, so Ulysses was always on the lookout for a bit of treasure. If his fifty-seven-year-old eyes were not lying to him, there was real gold in that chain. Then again, those fifty-seven-year-old eyes also mistook the rotted finger bones entwined around the chain for old twigs.

He always had a ready answer if anyone ever asked him what it was like to live in a cemetery. "Quiet. And the rent won't kill you." Ulysses often rehearsed questions and their answers in his head, even though no one ever asked him any. He hadn't always lived in the cemetery, but it was hard to remember living anywhere else. "There was a time . . ." he said to himself often. There was a time when things had been different. There was a time when he'd had good shoes. There was a time when he hadn't been searching for her, because she'd never gone away.

Ulysses was on a quest. And the quest couldn't support a home, or a car, or bills to pay – everything in his life had been stripped down or discarded in service of that quest. To search for her. The few who noticed him, who frowned at him askance, who quickened their step when they came near him, had no idea that he was *on a mission*. They had no idea that *there was a time*. It was just as well that most people looked right through him, he thought. It meant far less explaining. Not that, again, anyone ever asked.

Ulysses made his home in an ancient mausoleum made nearly invisible by the old broken trees that surrounded it and the vines that crawled over it. Ulysses, always one to appreciate irony, had once written an essay about the cemetery for his sixth-grade English class. When it had been a thriving necropolis a hundred years ago, it was a notorious target for grave robbers and body snatchers, due in no small part to the nearby hospital and medical school, long since torn down. He was no grave robber yet felt an odd affinity for those who took their sustenance from the macabre.

Ulysses liked his little mausoleum. True, it had a lot of openings and didn't offer much protection from the elements, but at least those openings were somewhat closed in by rusted wrought-iron bars. All in all it was cozy enough, with his Sterno and his sleeping bag and his dented cans of food. And his candles, lit with matches that Jennifer brought him. And there were the hot dogs and other good, warm things to eat that she gave him.

Jennifer reminded him of her. Not that she resembled her – Jennifer was dark and kind of small, but fierce, even though her brown eyes were bottomless and full of pain. It was her spirit, her energy, her humor, her *fight* that made Ulysses think of her. Jennifer was fierce in the way that she *cared*. And in that way, Jennifer was like her too.

The chain was coming up nicely. He pulled on it gently, careful not to break it. His filthy fingers tugged it from the earth, untangling it from the thick tree root that twisted from the stubborn ground like a femur broken through skin. Finally, his prize emerged. The soft dirt gave up a dull, circular object attached to the chain, encrusted with mud and roots and twigs. Ulysses studied it and reached into his stained, heavy overcoat for the wire dish scrubber he kept for just that kind of thing. Brushing away the dirt, he saw something gleaming.

It was gold. A gold disc, about the size of a tea saucer. He searched his wounded brain for the word – *amulet*, that's what it was. There was a design on it in the center, an Egyptian-style black dog, maybe made out of onyx. Ulysses had no idea what the amulet was, but there was no doubt it possessed *power*. He could sense things like that about people and places and objects. He sensed it about Jennifer. She had levels. Powers. She probably wasn't even aware of it. But he was.

Ulysses stared down at the amulet. It somehow made him feel safe. He wrapped the intricate chain around the gold disc and stuffed them deep within the hidden recesses of his coat.

A hot arrow of pain shot up his shin from his left foot. The throbbing ache had been building up all night, all week, and it would no longer be ignored. Blood oozed out of his broken shoes, staining what was left of the laces. Hating the sight of blood, particularly his own, he turned away quickly. Ulysses didn't like to see anything outside his body that belonged inside.

Looking up and across the cemetery at the building that bordered it – *the morgue* – Ulysses knew what had to be done.

FOUR

"I didn't realize there would be actual work involved," Trevor observed.

"You thought just showing up would be enough?"

Trevor grinned. "It usually is.

Trevor and Jennifer were rolling the gurney containing Why Me down the tiled hallway. They had just come from the Prep Room, where Trevor watched curiously as Jennifer undressed the white-skinned cadaver, folding and slipping all of his clothes into a brown paper bag. After photographing the body, she measured it, and weighed it by pulling the body from its gurney onto a table featuring a built-in scale. Trevor tried to help, but Jennifer had done it many times before. She showed him how to scan the fingerprints by placing four of the deceased's fingers on the glass panel of a small scanner that fed the prints into a laptop.

Jennifer let him do one hand, and a grinning Trevor bent the corpse's index finger to beckon to her. She tore the hand out of his and did the fingerprinting herself.

"I was in a movie once where I had to identify my best mate's body," Trevor said cheerily, while watching Jennifer. "It was in a morgue like this. Except it was on a stage. Obviously. I had to be all emotional and weepy and whatever. It was a real acting challenge as I completely despised the actor playing my mate. Worst. Breath. Ever. And he always sniffed his food before eating it." Trevor shivered with disgust. "But I had to act like I was gutted at the sight of his dead body, when in fact I would've been thrilled."

She glanced at him. "You can cry on cue?"

"Don't have to. They have this menthol stuff they blow in your eyes, and here come the waterworks. Works a treat."

"Sorry I asked," said Jennifer, feeling slightly disillusioned. "Actually, they don't really bring families in for identifications like that anymore. They'll clean up the corpse and take a picture to show to them. A lot of people can't handle seeing a loved one dead, and they'll deny it. They'll say no way, that's not them. That's why they try to do the ID by fingerprints if they can."

"Huh," responded Trevor. "If I were the kind of actor who did research, that would be good to know."

Jennifer stared at him; he returned her gaze innocently. She had the feeling he wasn't kidding. Continuing the intake routine, she showed him how to fill out a Body Control Card, with the basic info available on the corpse: *white, male, 60s, 167 pounds.*

Trevor watched her carefully pour the deceased's wallet, watch, cash, coins, and silver pinky ring into an envelope, on which she wrote the date and case number. She had Trevor fill out and attach the toe tag and, like everything else, he found that endlessly amusing.

They wheeled the body down the hallway to the autopsy room, where the deceased would spend the night awaiting a 9 AM autopsy. The squeaky wheels of the old gurney echoed off of the tile ceiling.

"Doesn't seem to be much adult supervision at night."

"There is occasional supervision. Rarely adult."

"My point is, who's to know if we're actually working or not? It's just the two of us."

"I'm used to it being just me. That's why I took this job."

"Loner?" Trevor asked. "We'll fix that."

"Nothing to fix. Just do your job and stay out of my way."

There was that grin again. She had to admit it was magnetic. Like he was letting her in on a secret.

"Fair enough," he said. They entered the autopsy room, which like most of the morgue, had an eerie hum – in this case from the dented tin rows of fluorescent lights running across the ceiling. Three empty autopsy tables stood in mute readiness, each underneath a suspended flex light. The room and the equipment were old, last updated sometime in the fifties. And of course there was the unmistakable smell. Disinfectant, ammonia, and the hint of decay always right behind it. The truth was that Jennifer didn't think the decay smell was so bad – it was actually kind of sweet – it's knowing *what caused* the smell that made it foul.

Jennifer unlocked the supply-closet door on the other side of the autopsy room, revealing a tiny space with floor to ceiling shelves. It was filled with medical instruments, white sheets, surgical gowns, and other autopsy supplies. Jennifer paused in the doorway; she hated that room, hated any closed-in small space and was careful to keep one foot outside the doorway as she reached for whatever she needed. Not wanting to do that with Trevor there, she delegated instead.

"Get me that body block," she asked, pointing to a

rubber brick on a shelf above his head.

Trevor reached for it, glancing at her. "Not your favorite room, I take it."

She found the fact that he was observant annoying. "Not big on tight spaces."

"You'd hate my Lamborghini."

"I already do."

Jennifer was relieved to step out of the supply closet and she quickly wheeled the gurney so that it was side by side with the center autopsy table. She gestured to Trevor to put the block on the table. The body block was a thick rubber brick, which rested below the corpse's shoulder blades. It caused the shoulders and head to fall back and the chest to protrude forward, ready for the sternum saw the next morning.

Jennifer folded down the side rails of the gurney and pointed to the body's feet as she grabbed the shoulders. She watched as Trevor took the corpse's feet in his gloved hands with no hesitation, and the two of them transferred the body to the autopsy table.

"So what's it like?" asked Jennifer.

"What?"

"Being a movie star."

Trevor thought for a moment. "Disappointing." They covered the corpse with the white sheet. "What's it like being a regular person?" he asked.

Jennifer thought for a moment. "Exhausting," she answered. With the body in place, she took off her rubber gloves. Trevor did the same. "Anyway, we do mostly clerical stuff at night, but when there's an autopsy scheduled the next morning, this is the drill."

"*Je suis fatigue.* I could do with a nap," he said.

"I'm sure you'll sleep well when you get home."

Trevor looked at her and back at the shrouded corpse, whose chest rose proudly past his shoulders. "I heard Clover call this guy 'Why Me.' "

33

"Clover names the bodies."

"Why?"

"For the same reason she likes to answer the phone by saying 'City morgue, you kill 'em, we chill 'em.' That's her idea of hilarious."

"Ah."

"And the bodies are named for whatever she feels they were thinking right before they died."

"Sounds a bit sophomoric, no?" Trevor frowned. Then hastened to add, "Sophomoric means chi—"

"Yeah, I know what sophomoric means," Jennifer interrupted. "As in most of your movies."

"Only most? I take that as a compliment. Which have you seen?"

"None. I don't go to the movies that much."

"No tolerance for fun?"

"No tolerance for stupidity." Jennifer picked up a clipboard and signed her name to an intake form.

Trevor hid a smile as he glanced around the room and saw a double row of glass jars on a cart. "You guys make jam here on the side? Maple syrup?"

"Those are specimen jars," Jennifer answered, not looking up from the clipboard.

"Right. Say no more." Trevor saw something that made him back up fast, causing his sneakers to squeak on the floor.

Trevor's face had gone pale. She followed his gaze: the big toe of the corpse was twitching.

"Sorry . . . but they're not really supposed to move, are they?"

Jennifer suppressed a smile. At last, something that undid Trevor just a little. "Bodies move all the time."

"The dead ones?" asked Trevor, his eyes glued to the now-still big toe.

"Postmortem spasm," Jennifer explained. "Muscles

twitch. Nerve endings still fire. Even our skin cells can live for a few days."

"Charming."

"People think we die all at once. We don't. We die little by little."

A brief flash of her father tore through her mind. His angry face. The vein pulsing in his forehead. Didn't it take him years to die? She pushed the thought away and focused on Trevor. "Is this gonna be a problem for you? Being around the dead?"

Trevor grinned, back in control now. "They can't be deader than some of the audiences I've played to. I was a ghost in a movie once. Had to do the whole thing on green screen. Sucked."

"Wow. Life is tough." Jennifer put down the clipboard and walked back to the supply closet. She felt Trevor's eyes on her ass. Reaching into the closet, she kept one foot outside it, Trevor or no Trevor.

"Right then. Break time?" Trevor asked.

"Restrooms need cleaning," Jennifer said, as she handed him a mop.

***

The church bells again. Jennifer fumbled for her phone – the word *Fish!* flashing on her screen. After one disastrous night when she'd forgotten to feed Clover's fish, and the prized angelfish became . . . well, an angel, Jennifer always set an alarm to remind herself.

Going into Clover's office, she picked up the shaker of gourmet fish food. It was quiet – too quiet. She hadn't heard from Trevor since sending him to clean the restrooms. He was probably sleeping somewhere or tweeting something clever. She didn't care. Having another person around made her realize how much she *loved* being alone. Not having to respond to someone, not having to even consider anyone, was a gift.

Jennifer pinched a bit of the dark, flaky fish food from the shaker and drizzled it into the tank with her fingers. Watching the fish rise toward the sinking morsels, she had to admit they were beautiful. She tapped her finger on the tank, and to her surprise Ziti, the clownfish, swam over to her. Sliding her finger across the glass, the fish obediently followed. She could swear he was looking right at her. Maybe Clover had trained this damn fish after all. His gills sucked rhythmically.

The sound was faint at first; it actually took her a few seconds to realize it didn't belong.

It was the sound of a tortured breath being drawn.

And released.

But not fully human. Machine generated.

It was the sound of a hospital ventilator. The machine that forced breath in and out of a patient who couldn't breathe on their own.

The sucking in *whoosh,* the metallic "knock" at the top of the breath, a slight pause, then the forced expulsion of air.

Jennifer knew this sound all too well.

She glanced around the office, even though the sound couldn't possibly be coming from within the morgue. What conceivable use could there be for a ventilator amongst the dead? Her eyes fell back on Ziti. His little gills were sucking in and out in time with the ventilator breaths.

The bulbous eyes of the fish stared at her.

Her own breathing tried to sync with the ventilator. This must be some kind of weird flashback, she thought.

There was a noise behind her. Spinning around, she jumped when she saw Trevor standing in the doorway. She had no idea how long he had been there. "Shit!" she yelled. "Don't do that!" The ventilator sound stopped.

"Did . . . did you move the body we set up before?"

"Why Me?" She didn't like the expression on Trevor's face. He was scared.

"Yes, that one."

"No."

"Okay. Because it's not there anymore."

Jennifer cocked her head at him.

Trevor swallowed. "I'm serious. The body's gone."

Jennifer pushed past him and walked down the hallway. He caught up to her, and they entered the autopsy room in silence. Jennifer went directly to the center autopsy table where they had left Why Me; it was empty. The white sheet was bunched up over the body block.

"Are you shitting me?" she turned to Trevor. "What did you do?"

"I didn't do anything! I cleaned the restrooms like you said, and when I came back to return the mop he was gone."

Jennifer looked around again.

Trevor was nervous. "C'mon, this is like a hazing thing, right? Scare the new guy?"

Jennifer stared at him.

He turned even paler. "Isn't it?"

Pushing past him again, she strode down to the prep room. From the doorway she turned on the lights, and after a few seconds of flickering and buzzing, the cranky fluorescents reluctantly fluttered on. She took in the room. Everything was exactly as it should be. Trevor came behind her, looking over her shoulder, but she quickly turned and went back down the hall to the body-storage room.

There was the same fluorescent ritual as the tubes pulsed and flickered and spread their dim glow over the room. The eerie buzz added a dissonant note to the steady hum of the refrigerated drawers – two dozen stacked stainless-steel receptacles with thick doors and blunt shiny handles that seemed to dare you to pull them.

There was always an overflow, so the more recent

arrivals were stacked on gurneys in front of the drawers. Jennifer stared at the line of gurneys with bodies silhouetted under their white sheets. Incredibly still, just as it should be. Death's waiting room.

As Jennifer turned, something was out of place in the corner. The body on the far side of the room didn't feel quite right. Walking slowly toward the shadowed corner, squinting to see better, the problem with the body on the gurney gradually became clear: the corpse had an enormous erection.

The sheet, at crotch level, rose above the gurney. When she managed to tear her eyes away from the ghostly hard-on, she noticed a pair of sunglasses has been placed on the sheet where the eyes would be.

Trevor laughed.

"Totally got you," he said, grinning in the doorway.

Jennifer turned on him. "You. Asshole."

"Come on! That's comedy gold right there!"

Jennifer whipped the sheet off the corpse, and saw a cranial drill propped between the cadaver's legs. She turned to Trevor. "What are you, twelve?"

"Don't knock being twelve. I was never happier. Besides, this was a much more creative endeavor than cleaning a toilet."

Jennifer was furious. Poking her finger hard in his chest, she advanced on Trevor, making him back up. "Listen. Unlike you, these bodies are human beings. They are not your props." Keeping her eyes on his, she pointed behind her. "This guy is someone's father. Or brother. Or son. So show some fucking respect."

Trevor, surprised, kept backing up as she jabbed him with her finger, until he slipped and suddenly found himself sitting on his ass in the hallway. He glanced down to see what made him slip. A smear of bright red liquid reflected the lights overhead.

It looked a lot like blood. Jennifer came out into the hallway.

"Is that . . ." Trevor began.

Jennifer didn't answer. Bloody footprints led to the autopsy room. Trevor followed her gaze, for once unable to come up with a glib aside. Jennifer turned her back on him and followed the footprints.

"Really? We're going to follow the trail of blood?" Trevor called after her.

When she left him behind he rushed to catch up with her, trailing behind her shoulder. Once they reached the autopsy room, Trevor hung back. "Shouldn't we call someone,?"

Ignoring him, Jennifer stepped into the autopsy room. Trevor hurried after her so as not to be left alone in the hallway—

And came face to face with a hulking giant glowering at him. Trevor let out a little noise and froze.

Jennifer laughed. Ulysses turned to her and asked, "What's wrong with *him*?"

Trevor looked up at Ulysses and back at the smirking Jennifer, knowing he'd been played.

"You didn't wet yourself, did you?" she asked.

Trevor gathered himself quickly. "He's not nearly as fearsome as his smell."

Ulysses, offended, glared at Trevor, about to say something when Jennifer interrupted. "Which foot this time?"

"Left."

"Let's take a look."

Jennifer carefully cleaned Ulysses' feet with warm water and a sponge, while the homeless man, seated on a gurney, stared balefully at Trevor. They had gone back to the body-storage room, where Jennifer had opened up the first aid kit. Trevor mopped up the blood trail, stealing glances at the two of them.

Trevor leaned toward Jennifer. "So what, are you two a thing? Because, seriously, I've only known you for a few hours," he whispered conspiratorially, "but you can do a lot better."

"Shut up and mop."

Ulysses glanced at Why Me over in the corner, the sunglasses still on his sheet-covered face. "It's dangerous to mess with the dead," he said, glaring again at Trevor.

"I've got news for you, my rather ripe friend," Trevor said while wringing out the pinkish water from the mop. "The dead don't give a shit about their bodies. Or anything else."

"Know a lot about the dead, do you?" asked Ulysses.

"Do you have any idea how many times I've been killed in movies? I've got more experience being dead than any stiff in this building."

Ulysses wasn't amused. "You desecrate a body, you bring bad things down on you." He nodded at Jennifer. "Her too."

"I'll make a note of that," Trevor responded.

Ulysses turned to Jennifer. "Who is this asshole?"

"Arrested for drunk driving. He's doing community service here."

"Community service in a *morgue*?"

Jennifer shrugged. "The genius of the system."

"And they say I'm crazy. How come he's not in jail?" Ulysses demanded.

Jennifer rubbed a clear ointment into the soles of his feet. "Because he's a rich, spoiled movie star. They don't go to jail."

"She's spot-on there, mate," Trevor said with a grin, resting the mop in the bucket.

"How does someone like you become a movie star?" Ulysses asked dubiously.

"Years of training."

Jennifer laughed. "Where? The Steven Seagal School of Performing Arts?"

"I was accepted at RADA. The Royal Academy—"

"Of Dramatic Arts," Jennifer finished for him. "I know what RADA is."

"So do I, by the way," added Ulysses.

Trevor went on. "Where I was just as quickly dismissed once they'd realized their mistake. But I came away from that experience knowing two things: I'm massively good-looking and spectacularly untalented. Very freeing, really."

Jennifer tilted her head at him. Just when she was sure he was an insufferable asshole, he could just as quickly seem self-effacing and funny. It was starting to bug her. "Freeing in what way?"

"It let me fulfill my true potential. I run and jump and fight and shoot and bed women and never do more than two takes if I can help it. And get to the pub by five."

Ulysses pointed at Jennifer. "She went to medical school. That's a lot more important than acting school."

Trevor raised an eyebrow. "Really?"

Jennifer wrapped Ulysses' foot in an ace bandage. She didn't like the direction the conversation was taking and wished Ulysses had kept his mouth shut. "Not medical school," she clarified. "I was pre-med. I dropped out."

Trevor looked at her with new interest. "Huh," he pondered. "Can you get me Vicodin?"

Ignoring Trevor, Jennifer noticed the gold disc Ulysses was clutching in his fist. "What's this?" she asked.

Ulysses opened his hand, revealing the amulet, the chain dripping over his palms.

"Auuggghhhhhhh."

Trevor and Ulysses both jumped at the loud sound. It was a wet, rasping growl that sounded more animal than human.

"Bloody hell!" shouted Trevor as he vaulted to his feet, having no idea where the deep-throated snarl came from.

"Hhhmmmgggg." It came again - like a gravelly, exasperated sigh. Trevor ran his hands over his body, as if trying to scrape the sound off of it. Ulysses, also scared but trying not to show it, stole a glance at Jennifer, who wore a small smile.

"It's just oxygen that's trapped in the lungs escaping," Jennifer said, nodding at one of the corpses. "Happens all the time. No need to panic."

"You mean he's not finished dying?" asked the incredulous Trevor, trying to get his breathing back to normal.

Jennifer shrugged. "Like I said, little by little."

Ulysses frowned and pointed a thick finger at Trevor. "Maybe that's his way of saying he doesn't like you."

Enjoying the look of horror on Trevor's face, Jennifer turned back to Ulysses, nodding at the gold disc in his hand. "So what is that?"

"I don't know. I found it."

Trevor stood over Ulysses' shoulder and saw the gold disc with the carved onyx Egyptian dog head at its center. "That's a protection amulet," he said, his voice still a little shaky. "Egyptian. Fourth century would be my guess."

Jennifer was unable to hide her surprise.

Ulysses squinted at him. "A what?"

"Apropos of your previous brilliant insight about it being dangerous to mess with the dead, it's a charm to protect the living from the dead."

"How do I know you're not making that up?" asked Ulysses.

Trevor shrugged. "Look it up on Homeless Google."

"Wait – how *do* you know that?" Jennifer asked.

"Untalented, yes. Stupid, no. I may have accidentally learned things in between pints at university. Egyptian mythology dealt extensively with death and the afterlife."

Ulysses squinted at him. "You mean this might be from Egyptian times?"

"Costume-jewelry times, more like," Trevor answered.

Ulysses closed his fist tightly around the amulet and turned to Jennifer. "Can I use the restroom, doc?"

"You bet," Trevor answered for Jennifer. He grabbed the mop and handed it to Ulysses. "And while you're in there . . ."

Jennifer snatched the mop away and glared at Trevor as Ulysses limped out of the room.

Trevor looked at her as she packed up the first aid kit. "Interesting choice of friends," he observed.

"He's a good person," Jennifer said defensively. "Just a little lost."

"And you're a collector of lost people?"

"Maybe he reminds me of someone."

"Ah," Trevor smiled. "Daddy issues."

Jennifer slammed the lid of the kit closed. "Why don't you go fuck yourself."

"Don't think I haven't tried."

Ulysses made his way slowly down the hallway and turned to see if he was being watched. Jennifer and the movie asshole were still in the other room. Up ahead was the autopsy room. He shuffled quietly inside.

He never liked being in the morgue – it was only dire situations like the one with his feet that could draw him there to seek help from Jennifer. Tonight he liked it even less. Although grateful that the throbbing had subsided in his tortured foot, the pain was replaced by a feeling of dread. There was bad energy in the morgue – even more than usual. The Englishman was no doubt the source of it. Ulysses hated people like that – so sure of themselves, so judgmental about everybody else. He was certain that Trevor was one of those people who was great at everything he tried the very first time. Had probably never known failure. Never known loss. Never known heartbreak. He'd probably never said to himself *There was a time.*

Ulysses sensed danger. The presence of the arrogant movie asshole was not good for Jennifer. That guy's energy, his attitude, his mocking persona could . . . *unleash* things in a place like this. Things that couldn't be controlled. Ulysses had to protect Jennifer, because it's what she would do for him.

Looking around the gleaming white room, the buzzing sound rose in his ears. Pushing the panic away, he searched for just the right spot. Trying not to think of all the death these walls had seen. Trying not to imagine what it must be like to lay on one of those gurneys and stare up at the hideous white ceiling with the merciless, bright light exposing every inch of your helpless, dead body. He shuddered.

There were no obvious hiding places. The white tiled walls were smooth and even, and for all Ulysses knew, the cabinet drawers were in constant use. However, under the center autopsy table a drain sat in the middle of the sloped floor. Hobbling over to it, he pushed the table aside, and stared down into the rusted, perforated-metal plate that covered the black hole below.

It was old. The drain cover was dented in the center. Ulysses shuddered again to think of what kinds of things got flushed down that drain. The oozing fluids and plasma and viscous tissue that were the detritus of the dead. And of course the blood. Gallons and gallons of blood over the years. Once flowing through someone's body like a mighty red river, bringing life and vitality – now, just so much excess body waste heading for the sewers.

With a mighty effort, Ulysses got down on his knees. He threaded two of his thick fingers through the drain openings and tugged. The plate moved but would not come up.

Undaunted, he reached into the depths of his coat and found a screwdriver. He wedged the screwdriver under the plate and used it as a lever. The drain cover popped off with a metallic clang. Ulysses hurried, concerned that Jennifer or, worse, the movie asshole, would wonder what was taking him so long.

Taking the amulet from his fist, he carefully wedged it into the drain as far as his chunky fingers would allow. Using the screwdriver, he pushed it down far enough so that a casual observer wouldn't see it. He shoved it to the side a bit so solid matter could still get by without clogging the pipe. Placing the drain cover over the opening, he pressed it back into place.

Out of breath, leaning over the drain as close as he dared, Ulysses whispered to the amulet, "Do whatever it is you do. But keep her safe."

He hauled himself back to his feet and got the hell out of there before the buzzing lights and the pulsating white walls drove him mad.

Deep in the drain, a slash of light glinted off a corner of the amulet, but he didn't see it. Nor did he see the sudden, angry pulsing of the onyx Egyptian dog in the center of the amulet.

***

Jennifer had gotten a call to pull another body for autopsy in the morning. Already exhausted from dealing with Trevor, she had no desire to share this task with him. Perhaps that was his technique – to be so annoying that he'd be sent off and left to his own devices. It was working. Jennifer assigned him the unnecessary task of inventorying the prep room. That had been half an hour ago, and she hadn't heard from him since, which made her happy. As she wheeled the cold body toward the autopsy room, a packet of paperwork resting on its stomach, her thoughts turned to Ulysses. She was worried about him; she had nursed him through several infections, bad bug bites, and rashes, but his feet were in terrible shape and really needed serious medical attention. Ulysses didn't trust doctors or hospitals; he believed they intended to trap him and keep him prisoner. Sometimes she thought he might have a point.

Jennifer had met Ulysses nearly a year ago, when she first started work at the morgue. On her second night, she had discovered the shortcut through the cemetery. On the third night, she'd felt someone watching her. Not being a believer in ghosts, she kept walking. On the fourth night, she knew someone was following her. While she may not have believed in ghosts, she definitely believed in muggers and rapists. Hearing the footsteps coming closer and closer behind her and seeing the shadow of a hulking creature spread across the headstones in front of her, she had no problem turning around and kicking her pursuer square in the balls.

The creature bellowed and dropped into the dirt like a stone. He rolled around for a while holding his crotch, allowing Jennifer to take him in: thick, filthy coat; wild, curly hair; bushy beard; his face caked with dirt and what looked like coffee cake crumbs.

Ulysses squinted up at her in agony. "Why did you do that?"

"Why were you following me?"

He held up a pair of ear buds. "Because you dropped these."

Jennifer checked her jacket pocket: no earbuds. She was constantly losing them because she so often stuffed things distractedly in her open pockets. Helping him to his feet, she felt badly. "You shouldn't sneak up on people in cemeteries."

"You shouldn't assume the worst about a person," Ulysses replied, still in pain.

"Says the man who looks like Sasquatch."

He handed her the earbuds.

"Thanks," she said.

"Don't mention it," Ulysses gasped.

Thus began their friendship. She started bringing him food and tried to encourage him to go to one of the many homeless shelters the city prided itself on. He would always bristle at that. "Those shelters are a lot more dangerous than my mausoleum." And he wasn't wrong. Apart from the rampant crime, the shelters had been a breeding ground for infection during the pandemic, and even now, post vaccine, they stayed mostly empty. Besides, as Jennifer would come to learn, he was on "a mission," and needed to be on his own to pursue it. Sometimes he seemed fairly sane, even normal, so it always surprised her when his behavior veered off into the bizarre, revealing how deeply disturbed he was. Ulysses was harmless, she believed, but something had happened to him that had broken his mind. Nevertheless, he was still able to function, think and be a clever observer of the equally disturbed world around him.

Jennifer made the transfer of the body from the gurney to the second autopsy table. The corpse was a woman in her late forties. Heart-attack victim, according to the paperwork. Jennifer glanced at the woman's face as she propped up her back on the body block. She looked like she might have been pretty. Her blue eyes were half closed, looking at Jennifer from under heavy lids, as if wondering what she was up to.

Jennifer covered the body with a sheet, checked her watch, signed the date, time, and her name to the paperwork and turned to leave. Approaching the doorway, she heard a wheel squeak.

She turned around and stared for a moment. At first she

wasn't able to understand what she was looking at. The three autopsy tables and all of the gurneys in the room were now arranged *in a circle* around the center drain, instead of the straight line they had been in a split-second ago.

Jennifer froze in place while her mind tried to make sense of it. Even if they had all somehow rolled into position, it could never have happened in the time it had taken her to turn around.

The hair on her neck rose.

What was that sound? A strange, gurgling noise – like something evil *percolating*. Was it coming from that drain?

Backing up, she dropped the clipboard. Her mouth had gone dry. Had Trevor done this? But how?

"Trevor!" she called out. "Did you—"

One arm from each body slithered from under their sheets, in unison, and dangled over the drain.

Jennifer jumped and gasped.

The arms swung gently.

As the terror rose in her, for some reason the image of an elephant's trunk came to her, lazily skimming the ground. Jennifer lost all of her peripheral vision and was so focused on the bare, veiny, wrinkled arms that she didn't see the sheet-covered body *sit up* on one of the gurneys right next to her.

Sensing the motion, her eyes wide and her mouth open, she turned toward it.

Just in time to come face to face with the corpse.

The sheet slid down . . .

Revealing Trevor, his face in mid-yawn. "Sorry. Just thought I'd rest my eyes and went dead out."

Jennifer stared at him, trying to control her breathing. She had a hard time hearing him because of the sound of her heart pounding in her ears.

Trevor took her in expression. "Wait, did I scare you?"

Jennifer tried to find her voice. It cracked over her dry lips. "Did you do this?"

"What?"

Staring at Trevor, she pointed at the gurneys. "Move these bodies?"

Trevor looked at her cautiously. "That depends on whether or not I was supposed to." He saw that she was really frightened, and for a moment, it frightened him. "What happened?"

Jennifer studied him as her pulse returned to something like normal. She didn't want him to see her scared, especially if he somehow pulled this off. They looked at each other, and Jennifer finally turned away. "Nothing. Help me put these gurneys back. Then we're done."

Trevor slid off the gurney with a sigh. "Finally. I have to tell you, we better figure out some way to have fun on this gig, or I'll never make three days, never mind fifty-three."

Jennifer ignored him and found herself staring at the dangling arms. *What the fuck,* she thought.

***

Detective Marty Bell sucked the last of the Diet Coke from the can that could barely be seen in his giant hand. It was four in the morning, and he was standing under the Brooklyn Bridge with an ever-expanding group of detectives and uniforms. Marty hated coffee, but loved, needed, caffeine, so Diet Coke had always been his friend. Especially while standing over a murder victim at four o'clock on a cold October morning.

Marty was a big guy. In the pre-Covid days, he always found enough time to go to the gym at least a few times a week, so that he hadn't gotten the requisite middle-aged belly that most of his colleagues had grown. He was more vertically large than horizontally. His strength had been legendary when he was a street cop. Just the sight of him emerging from his car, a process that seemed to go on for ages, was enough to make most criminals happy to surrender. His freckled face and red hair and eyebrows might have made him seem more like an altar boy, if it weren't for the ropey, heavily-veined arms and pecs of iron that suggested menace rather than piety. Marty didn't have to rely on his size much anymore, as his life as a detective was more a life of the mind than of rolling around on the ground with perps who wanted to kill him. He was fine with that.

No matter how long Marty had been on the NYPD Nightwatch, he still couldn't shake the surreal sensation he felt when standing at a brightly lit, shadowless crime scene. It felt like what he imagined a movie set must look like, with unnatural giant spotlights flooding the night with artificial daylight, the streets looking even more merciless in their washed-out desolation.

The victim was lying on his back. Young, mid-twenties, like so many of the murder victims Marty saw. He had a wispy mustache, and the shaved head that seemed de rigueur on the streets. A snake tattoo twisted up the side of his neck and curled around his ear. Marty prided himself on his memory for faces, and he recognized this guy from somewhere. Had he locked him up before? A snitch maybe? The snake tattoo would be unforgettable, yet it was more the eyes and the face that rang a bell for Marty somewhere.

Watching the photographer snapping photos, he wondered why he was using the flash in the bright glare of the crime scene lights. Nevertheless, each strobe made the chest wounds stand out in sharp relief. This guy had taken at least three to the heart. His pockets were full: $276 in cash, a snotty bandana, and a cracked glass vial that Marty was sure would turn out to contain meth.

"Random or targeted?" asked Marty's lieutenant. Bill

Bishop was a skinny Irishman in his mid-fifties, whose uniform hung off him like he hadn't had a meal in years. However, anyone who had ever eaten with Lt. Bishop, and Marty had, knew the Loo put away more food in a sitting than a peckish mastodon.

"Give me a hard one," Marty responded. "Money and drugs untouched."

Bishop nodded. "Gang?" he asked, watching as two gloved, crime-scene cops carefully turned the body over, revealing the ragged, enormous exit wounds in the victim's back. Hopefully the shooter or shooters hadn't taken the time to pick up the bullets or the shells.

Marty shrugged. He didn't like these sidewalk chats, preferring to keep his theories to himself and wait for the evidence and lab work to give him a bigger picture. But his gut told him this was not random; this young dude had pissed off the wrong guy and ended up on somebody's shit list.

Bishop turned to Marty. "This is gonna take a while. There's a diner around the corner." Bishop knew where all the good diners and hot dog carts were.

"You go ahead," Marty said. "And try not to make the silverware spark." Marty didn't leave his crime scenes until he was satisfied that every scrap of evidence had been collected. Bishop had already solved the case in his mind – drug deal gone bad, skell vs. skell, case closed. Thus satisfied, the skinny Lieutenant turned and headed for his unmarked car. "I'll bring you back a grilled cheese."

Marty again focused on the plastic evidence bag holding the victim's wallet and contents. He saw the driver's license, expired a year ago, of course. The victim's face stared balefully at him from the license, doing his best hard-guy look, the snake tat clearly visible. His name was Sean Burrows. Marty didn't know the name, but he knew that face.

FIVE

Having just gotten home from work, Jennifer pulled the heavy curtains across her bedroom windows, blocking out the morning sunshine. She was so puzzled over what had happened in the autopsy room – *how it happened* – that she had no recollection of getting off the subway or walking up the stairs of her modest apartment building. She didn't even remember squeezing by the usual tide of worker bees swarming out of the building while she was heading in.

She tried to talk herself into the idea that it was just a weird hallucination. That and the ventilator sound she'd heard earlier. Had to be a rational explanation, like the scientists say. *Nothing to see here.* She could not afford to let herself think, even for a moment, that it was happening again.

***

Jennifer flashed on the therapist's office. She was twelve. The waiting room had been softened by pastel colors and padded sculptures of clouds adorned the walls. There were coloring books and crayons, and golf magazines for the grownups. And there was that odd whooooshing sound – the white noise machine that sat on the beige carpet at the foot of the door to the therapist's office, to make sure no one in the waiting room could hear the secrets being spilled in the sanctum sanctorum of the mysterious therapist. Jennifer imagined the machine was sucking up all of the fear and anxiety in the room, not to dispose of it, but to save it, to build up a powerful reserve of fear, which could be released back into the world unnoticed. Safe to say that Jennifer was not a lighthearted child.

Sitting next to her dad in the waiting room, she could tell he was just as nervous and uncomfortable as she was. He was a carpenter, a builder, a tough man who worked with his hands, who hadn't counted on being a single parent. His world did not include therapists or psychologists, but if it would help his daughter, he'd find the money, and he would get her a therapist. Rick Shelby ached for her, for the sad, unreachable child Jennifer had become since her mother's death. The pain in her eyes when she found the birthday card from her mother in the mailbox, two days after her she died, had made him want to tear his teeth out. He was a fixer of things, her dad, a craftsman, an assembler of disparate parts to make a beautiful whole, and he would not let her lose herself to grief.

She didn't want to be there. Jennifer didn't want to talk about her feelings – she could barely tolerate *feeling them*, let alone trying to describe them. Looking up at her father, she whispered. "Dad, I want to go home."

Looking down at her, his lined face crinkled with a

smile. "Me too. But this won't take long. He's a real nice guy, and you might feel better if you stay."

"I won't," she said, holding his gaze.

"I'll tell you what. Let's give it ten minutes. If you don't like it, we'll go home, I'll make us some pizza bagels, and you don't have to come back. I promise."

Pizza bagels were a Friday night ritual. Her dad would come home early from work, they'd rent a movie, and he'd slather mozzarella cheese and tomato sauce on a couple of bagels from the place on Queens Boulevard, and they would eat them along with root beer floats while they watched the movie. She looked forward to it all week.

None of that mattered to her now. Jennifer felt her face getting hot. She knew her father was not going to relent. She knew she was going to have to go through with it. The fact that he was being so kind about it somehow made it harder. Seeing the distress in her face, he gently put his rough hand on her head. "It's gonna be okay."

At first it sounded like firecrackers – *pop pop pop* – and things starting breaking. A framed print on the wall shattered. A table lamp exploded. Her father sat there in astonishment. The popping sounds had come from the hinges exploding off of the main door, the bolts ricocheting around the waiting room, breaking everything in their path. The hinges from the doctor's door exploded off as well. Both doors slid drunkenly in their frames. Magazines flew violently around the room, a table literally shot into a wall, burrowed into the plaster, and hung there. The other walls splintered and fractured, revealing the cracked plaster underneath, like white bone under ruptured skin. The whole room shook as if an enormous fist was pounding it.

Jennifer's father instantly gathered her up in his arms, protecting her with his body, seeing her eyes squeezed shut, and her face deep red. The white noise machine lifted from its place on the carpet and rocketed across the room, tunneling several inches into the ceiling. Light bulbs popped and exploded, raining down sparks and shards of glass. Later her father would tell her that she slapped her hands over her ears and screamed, but she had no memory of it.

The therapist, a well-fed man in his fifties, stripped of his mystery, stumbled out of his office with a look of sheer terror on his face, his glasses askew, his hands outstretched as if he were going to have to hold up the walls himself. He heard Jennifer scream, and instantly knew it was not a scream of terror, but of rage.

Afterward, she and her dad rode home on the subway together. He held her hand. She didn't want to look at him, but she saw his face in the reflection in the smudged and cracked window across from them. His eyes were shadowed. He looked hollow. He looked scared. Jennifer would later realize that reflected image of her dad was a foreshadow of what was ahead for him.

Jennifer knew, and *he* knew. She had caused the chaos in the therapist's office. Other things like it had happened at home – although milder. Lights flickering, bulbs blowing out, a door slamming shut. It was as if her surroundings were expressing her grief, loss, and anger on her behalf.

She didn't like it; it scared her, but she had no idea how to stop it. She was squeezing her father's hand so tightly, her little knuckles had turned white. He smiled down at her, winked, and gave her hand a little shake.

***

The squealing brakes of a FedEx truck turning the corner under her apartment window broke Jennifer's reverie. Entering her tiny kitchen, she took a bottle of white wine from the refrigerator. She wasn't normally a day drinker, but this was her end of day, and a hell of a day it had been. A drink seemed like the least she could do for herself. Sitting at the small wooden table, she poured an industrial-strength-size glass of pinot. She needed distraction. She needed to think about anything else but the lost years after her mother died. Picking up her phone, she saw there were texts. She read the first one from her friend Chelsea:

Come onnnnnnn... stop making me double text u! Are u like a vampire now?

Jennifer could almost hear the mock whine Chelsea was so good at.

Have brunch with us on Sat. Get over yourself and come out with us.

Her heart skipped a beat when she saw the next text, from her one-time boyfriend, Jim:

Sorry we haven't spoken since the funeral. I know you're going through a lot. You don't have to do it alone. That's all I'm saying.

She hadn't seen or spoken to Jim all year, but he texted her pretty much every couple of weeks. Jennifer never responded, hoping he'd just stop. Jim had become a dim memory to her, but one that came with a pleasant echo promising something familiar, something good, something that she wanted no part of now.

When she started college, she had just begun to feel normal. Whatever that was. The loss of her mother six years earlier had still been an open wound, but the violent, lurching grief had ebbed. As had the household pyrotechnics that she had dubbed "the fireworks." She had met a nice group of friends. She didn't know them all that well, nor did she really want to, always worried about the fireworks recurring and how embarrassing that would be. She was comfortable with them; they accepted her at face value as she did them.

They laughed, drank, and studied, and when she met Jim, he fell right in with all of them. There was no competition, no one fighting for attention; they were a unit, except that at night Jim would come to her dorm room, and they would fuck until the sun rose. She might have fallen in love with him. He was the most genuine person she knew, but she held back. Wanting a career and wanting independence, she was not going to take any chances of denting either one. Maybe attachments were good for you later in life, but when you're young they're just speed bumps, slowing you down. And when the speed bump known as her father came out of nowhere, derailing her, breaking her heart, she decided she never wanted to be attached to any one or any thing ever again.

***

After many years working the streets of New York City, the detective was not easily surprised. Yet when Marty arrived at the address he had found on murder victim Sean Burrows driver's license, he had to admit to a certain level of astonishment. Sean Burrows' address was the long-abandoned Loew's 46th St. movie theater in Borough Park, Brooklyn. Movie palace was more like it – built in 1927, with three thousand seats, it was incredibly majestic. In its heyday, its ceiling had been a blue dome suspended over the vast auditorium, with twinkling stars and projections of clouds moving by, which provided the sense of watching a movie under a night sky. This theater, like so many other cinema palaces, had fallen on hard times in the sixties and seventies, and had begun to crumble. At one point it was renamed the Brooklyn Rock Palace, becoming a venue for live music. The Grateful Dead, The Byrds, Jefferson Airplane, and many other classic acts played there. The theater closed in 1973, and in spite of many attempts over the years to rehabilitate it, it remained a derelict property, with the once grand exterior now shabby and decaying.

Marty knew all that from the graffiti-covered plaque he read on the side of the building, below the rusted fire escape that snaked along the brick wall. How could this work as an actual address for Sean Burrows?

When he found the side door to the theater open Marty got his answer. There was a mail slot in the door, and some junk mail addressed to Burrows was scattered inside. Was this just a mail drop, or had Burrows actually been squatting here?

Marty walked through the massive remains of the once proud theater, his footsteps echoing. It smelled of mold with a hint of sewage. Looking up, he saw the remnants of the blue paint on the crumbling, peeling ceiling. There may have even been some faded stars.

While the main floor was just exposed concrete and pockmarked walls, the balcony still had seats in place, along with sculptures of angels, looking sadly from their decaying arches over the ghosts of audiences past.

Making his way to the projection booth, he found what he was looking for: a cot, a small lamp, and an overturned, cardboard beer case used as a table. The small bed was neatly made, and the drug paraphernalia on the "table" was tidily laid out. Marty found this little slice of self-respect oddly moving. He coughed at the dust mites swirling around the room and spied a shoebox on the other side of the cot.

Bending down with a grunt (*Gotta get back to the gym*) he grabbed the box with his gloved hands and opened it. Inside, there were neatly arranged documents and paperwork. Some correspondence from the Department of Motor Vehicles and a pile of paystubs, organized by date.

The last paystub was dated two weeks ago, from the River View Assisted Living Facility.

***

Trevor, with an American accent and a Special Forces uniform, was in deep trouble. He had already rescued a well-endowed woman hostage and killed at least a dozen bad guys. He was trapped on a bombed-out Iraqi street, surrounded by a lethal looking group of jihadists. Trevor sized up his chances, stealing a glance from behind the battle-scarred wall that was shielding him.

He looked at the frightened woman who held him close – into her terrified but well mascaraed eyes. "Right. I'm not dying today. And neither are you. Come on!"

Jennifer poured the last of her wine without taking her eyes off of her computer screen. Trevor and the woman ran across the road while bullets ripped up the streets and buildings around them. Jennifer wondered how it could be that movie villains were always such terrible shots. Why did anybody even bother running from them? She knew she was watching crap, yet she was riveted. Having never experienced a Trevor Pryce movie, she had to admit that he had incredible screen presence. The camera loved him, along with his incredible green eyes, and she couldn't look away.

Jennifer had climbed into bed an hour earlier, but even with her heavy blackout curtains blocking every trace of light, sleep would not come. The image of those dead arms swinging above the drain in the autopsy room kept nudging its way into her brain. To stop dwelling on it, she had opened her laptop and logged onto Netflix, deciding to see for herself what all the Trevor fuss was about.

Trying again to focus on the movie, she couldn't help but think how much more enjoyable it would be if even one minute of it were believable. More wine was called for. Pausing the movie, she swung her legs over the edge of the bed to get up, when her foot stomped down on something unfamiliar.

Looking at the floor, she saw her foot was resting on a

tube. A thick, blue, coiled tube. It came from under the bed, and she followed its path with her eyes. The ribbed hose snaked across the floor and out of the bedroom. Her mind raced. Was it some project her superintendent had forgotten to tell her about? Or worse, had he told her, and she had forgotten? Had it been here all night and she hadn't noticed? Bullshit, she thought, just as—

Whoosh! The tube suddenly expanded and swelled with air being pumped through it powerfully enough to knock her foot off of it. A sense of dread raced through her body – she knew what was coming, and she was right.

The sound of a hospital ventilator echoed through her bedroom.

The horrible, all too familiar mechanical sucking in and out of air. Rhythmic. Relentless. Inhuman. The sound got louder. Jennifer took a step toward the bedroom doorway. The thick blue tube curled around the threshold. Her mouth went dry. Her heart hammered in her ears.

The mechanical breathing got louder. *Innnnnnnnnn. Click. Ouuuuuuttttttt. Innnnnnnnnn. Click. Ouuuuuuttttttt.* She followed the tube out of the bedroom. It coiled across the hallway floor leading to the bathroom. It was wrapped low around the bathroom door, which was half closed.

There was a dim glow coming from the bathroom; Jennifer could only see its reflection on the wall through the barely open bathroom door. The glow pulsed in time with the strained machine-driven breathing. She kept moving, following the tube. Reaching the bathroom door, she raised a shaking hand and pushed it open. She stared in shock at what was inside.

In the middle of the dark bathroom was a *hospital ventilator*, a square monitor on a wheeled cart. There were numbers and graphs on a screen, which glowed blue. The tubes snaked to it and connected to several parts of the machine. An outgoing tube stretched from the right of the ventilator, across the bathroom, and behind the shower curtain, which was drawn closed.

Jennifer was all too familiar with ventilators. And she knew what she'd find – *who* she'd find – on the other end of the breathing tube. Taking another breath, she stepped into the bathroom—

And jumped at the sight of someone in front of her.

She breathed a shaky sigh of relief, realizing it was her own reflection in the medicine cabinet mirror. Glancing at her face, she saw how pale she looked, her eyes wide with fear.

Reaching over to the shower curtain, her own breathing now in sync with the monstrous-sounding machine, she grabbed the shower curtain, yanking it open as fast as she could—

Something was moving fast in the bathtub. Flopping around like a desperate fish at the end of a fishing line. It flipped and spun out of control, bouncing off of the shower walls. It was a *tracheal tube* at the end of the ventilator hose, being propelled like a miniature rocket by the air pumping through it, slamming around in the shower. The sound of the mechanical breathing got louder, faster. It became so deafening that Jennifer had to hold her ears. Backing herself into a corner of the bathroom, she slid down the wall, her eyes squeezed shut.

The breathing stopped. The room was quiet; she could tell through her closed eyelids that the blue glow was gone too. Taking her hands off of her ears, she opened her eyes.

The bathroom was empty. Just a dim streak of sunlight coming from the frosted window above the shower. The silence was almost as loud as the breathing had been.

She suddenly knew. It was irrational; it made no sense, but she knew.

The Desecrated

***

The woman behind the reception desk at River View Assisted Living squinted suspiciously through her thick glasses at Detective Marty Bell. "Visiting hours don't start until ten AM."

He resisted the urge to speak louder. "I'm not here to see a patient. I'm here to see the person in—"

"They're guests."

"Sorry?"

"They're not patients. They are referred to as guests," the woman croaked, glaring at him as if he were ready to be wheeled back to the memory ward. Marty was not in the mood for this. Not being a morning person, and since the assisted-living facility would have frowned on a visit at four AM, he had stuck around after his shift had ended at 8 AM. It was 9:30, and he was tired and hungry.

"I understand." Marty showed her his badge. Again. "I need to see the person who is *in charge* of the guests."

"What is this in reference to?" she asked as she tipped his badge holder toward her with dark-blue fingernails.

"That's a secret," Marty said with a smile that he was quickly growing tired of. The woman glared at him, and reluctantly punched some numbers into her phone.

While Burrows' paystubs had revealed New York City's latest murder victim had been gainfully employed here at River View Assisted Living (although as far as Marty could tell, there was no river and no view), Marty wasn't able to find out much more about the mysterious Mr. Burrows. He had an arrest jacket: some armed robbery and assault and battery, a couple of months-long jail stints, but all strictly small time. No drug arrests, which surprised Marty. And there was no information to be found about his family or even where he was born. Marty guessed Burrows had several other identities that would provide those answers.

"There's someone here who says he's a detective," the

receptionist said crankily into the phone.

Marty felt the heat rise. The woman listened. She glanced up at Marty again and spoke into the phone. "No, he's definitely not a patient. At least I don't recognize him."

Marty got up. "You mean *guest*." The woman's eyes grew wide as she watched him reach his full height, putting his badge away. "Tell me where your boss is. Right now."

After she told him where to go (she was probably thinking of a different place than the one she told him, Marty thought), he walked down a carpeted hallway. There was quiet music playing through hidden speakers. A soft-rock instrumental version of *All Along The Watchtower*. *Oh-kay*, Marty thought. He passed several "guests" while making his way to the administrator's office. They looked at him hopefully; maybe he was there to visit them. Or to liberate them. One old man, with thick white hair and black bushy eyebrows saw Marty coming, smiled, and said, "Dennis! Did you bring the folding chairs?"

Marty smiled back at him. "Next time," was all he could think of to say.

He hadn't been in a place like this since the last time he'd visited his mother, just before her death. There was some comfort in realizing that the place he had arranged for her was much nicer. Cheerier. All that bright light and those long bingo games and smiling attendants hadn't seemed to make her any happier though. Marty's heart still pinged with guilt at having to put his mother in a facility. Like a child who demanded independence, she didn't understand that she wasn't capable of taking care of herself.

Her crippling claustrophobia hadn't helped. Often feeling that the walls were closing in on her, she couldn't take an elevator or a subway, nor had she ever been on a plane. Whenever he drove her into the city, they had to take the Brooklyn Bridge, never the tunnel. It had caused her life to become smaller and smaller, and it broke Marty's heart. He hated feeling helpless. She never really came to terms with it, just as she had never come to terms with his becoming a cop.

Marty had surprised everyone, himself included, when he joined the NYPD. Of all the guys he hung out with in his native Bay Ridge Brooklyn, Marty had always seemed the smartest. He liked books, was interested in history, and had learned to speak Spanish. His eyeglasses and, at that time, tall but thin frame did not suggest someone who might be comfortable rolling around the streets with various and sundry perps. His father, Lloyd, was the owner of the neighborhood laundromat, a hotbed of more gossip and drama amongst its clientele of housewives, divorced men, starving students, and elderly observers than most soap operas could provide. Lloyd used to look at his son, and say, not so much with pride, but with bewilderment: "That boy is real college material." In Marty's Brooklyn neighborhood, that was code for, *This kid doesn't have what it takes to make it in the real world.*

In high school, Marty had discovered the weight room, and over the course of four years, his thin build had given way to a thick pad of muscle, and his eyeglasses were swapped for contacts. Nevertheless, it was still a bolt out of the blue when he announced he was becoming a New York City police officer. He had taken the test secretly and passed in the top five percent. When asked why by his perplexed but delighted friends, he could only shrug and say, "It's the only thing I can imagine myself doing and not being bored shitless."

Marty was the best kind of cop: brainy and built like a tank. He brought a lot to the table; he was streetwise, tough, fair, and was clear eyed about who the givers and takers were in life. He learned to negotiate the serpentine politics of the NYPD and learned how to stay away from the haters and the assholes in the department. He rose steadily. What made him different was that he actually liked most of the street people he encountered, he was interested in them, got to know them, and they learned they could trust him.

However, in his younger years, he'd somehow always had the feeling that his career as a cop would be temporary. Marty had believed that someday something would present itself to him, an opportunity he didn't see coming, but that would turn his world upside down, and would transform him into a different person, with a different life. As he approached fifty, looking at the horizon line of his existence, he could only see more of the same.

"Why are the police interested in Sean?" the assisted living administrator asked, looking at the murder victim's driver's license. The administrator, Jeff Jaworsky, was a craggy-faced man in his early fifties, with thinning, silver hair pulled tight across his head, ending in a ponytail. His fingers were adorned with turquoise and opal Native American jewelry.

Marty took the license back. "We're just trying to get some background information on Mr. Burrows."

Jeff smiled. "Well, for one thing, he lives in a famous old movie theater!"

"Yes, I was there last night. Did you ever visit him there?" asked Marty.

Jeff suddenly looked like he smelled something bad. "Sean's not the kind of guy you 'visit.' "

"Okay. So what does he do here?"

Jeff shrugged. "As little as possible."

Marty smiled and said nothing.

Jeff fidgeted with a pen. "Is he in trouble or something?"

"What is he *supposed* to do here?"

"His main job is to oversee transfers. Sometimes a guest deteriorates to a level where we can no longer care for them properly, so they need to be transferred to another facility. Also, when guests pass away, Sean's job is to facilitate removal of the body to a funeral home or the morgue, depending on the family's wishes."

"How long has Mr. Burrows been employed here?"

Jeff sucked on the end of the pen. " 'Bout a year." Leaning forward, he lowered his voice. "No one likes him, if I'm being honest."

"Why not?"

"He just gives everybody the creeps. The tattoo around his ear and everything. We try to keep him in the back." Lowering his voice to a whisper, he added, "Sean always seemed to be kind of . . . up to something, if you know what I mean."

"I *don't* know," Marty whispered back.

Jeff shifted in his chair, warming to the subject. "This morning, for example, one of our security people found him going through the guest files right here in my office. Outrageous! But it's so hard to find anybody reliable, it's just—"

"Wait," Marty interrupted. "*This* morning?"

Jeff nodded.

It was Marty's turn to lean forward. "Mr. Jaworsky," he said, "Sean Burrows was murdered last night."

Jeff's eyes widened. "What? How?"

"So he couldn't have been—"

"Not possible," Jeff sat back in shock and shook his head adamantly. "He was here this morning."

"Is he still here?"

"No. He wasn't supposed to be in today at all. I don't know why he even—"

"Did you see him yourself?"

"No, I hadn't gotten in yet. The security guard did."

"I need to talk to him."

"Marvin Aquillar. He's on the night shift; he already

clocked out."

"Of course he has. When does his next shift start?"

"Midnight."

A perfect time to talk about a ghost, Marty thought.

***

The lights flickered as the subway car roared through the tunnel. The 2 train still had a lot of old cars, which could be plunged into darkness on turns when the connection with the third rail broke. Jennifer sat on the train, the "six feet apart" social distancing decals now faded and peeling. A few people still wore masks, but for the most part these commuters leaned a little too sloppily toward each other, in Jennifer's opinion, vaccine or no vaccine. She couldn't help the feeling that sickness was all around her, especially after the experience in her bathroom. Finally managing to fall asleep, she had been awakened two hours later by the ravenous crunching of a garbage truck, greedily inhaling bag after bulging bag of trash. Giving up on slumber, she braved the bathroom (no tubes, no machines), took a long shower, and waited for the sun to go down before she left for work, like any good vampire would. She even forgot to check if the hot dogs she bought were plain – Julio had to just come out and tell her they were. He seemed disappointed that there was no argument to be had.

When night falls in New York City, it gets dark from the bottom up, especially as it edges toward winter. The shadows envelope the streets first, and the sky is the last thing to give up its light. For this reason Jennifer usually enjoyed her walks to the subway, but she was so distracted that she hadn't even noticed the streets or even the subway platform. On the train, clutching the grease-stained paper bag containing the hot dogs, she glanced around at her fellow travelers. Wished that she, like most of them, were headed home on this late-night ride, instead of only starting her workday. Jennifer jammed in her ear buds and cranked up Dua Lipa's "Levitating." Staring at the stained, sticky floor, she practiced the time-honored New York subway technique of making no eye contact whatsoever. Trying to reason with herself, she wondered if she *really* saw that awful vision in the bathroom? And did she *really* see what she thought she'd seen in the morgue last night? Somehow the passage of just a few hours, and a little restless sleep, made those events seem far away and not as menacing. She began to relax a bit. Her mind was playing with her; maybe this is no big deal.

A chill ran up her spine when the lights in the subway car went out again; but instead of them flickering right back on as usual, it stayed dark.

She heard the man next to her breathing. Wheezy, rhythmic breathing, through his mouth.

The old woman across from her also started breathing audibly. Strained, forced breaths.

Everyone on the entire row of seats on either side of her was breathing loudly. The shadow of a young man loomed over her, holding onto the handrail above, long, noisy breaths pulling and pushing in and out of him.

The lights flickered back on, and everyone in the subway car took long, laboring breaths in unison.

As if they were all on the same ventilator.

They turned to Jennifer.

Their faces blank.

Each chest rose and fell together. The collective breathing got louder and louder, their torsos expanding and contracting more violently. Everyone was looking directly at Jennifer, their faces without expression, their mouths opening ever wider to accommodate the deep breaths they were somehow being forced to take.

Jennifer sat frozen, fighting her own breathing reflex,

for some reason she felt it was very important not to let her breathing sync with everybody else's. She was gripping the seat underneath her as everyone stared blankly at her. As their chests expanded farther and farther.

Some of their coats started tearing open. Buttons popped off of shirts and blouses. It seemed like their very lungs were about to burst from their chests. Jennifer held her ears against the roaring breaths, squeezed her eyes shut, once again hoping the horrible vision would be gone when she opened them. She could tell through her eyelids that the lights had gone out again. The breathing stopped. All the noise stopped; she couldn't even hear the sound of the train anymore.

She opened her eyes. There were two feet standing in front of her.

Bare feet. Bare legs. Even in the dark she saw they were veiny and blue.

A morgue tag was attached to the big toe of the left foot. The lights blinked back on. The feet were still there. Jennifer felt the presence of the corpse looming over her before she actually saw the rest of it. She bolted up in her seat as she found herself staring into the face of—

Her father. Not the kind, crinkly-eyed face of the man who brought her up, but the sallow, ravaged face of the man who had lost his mind before he died. Glaring balefully at her in the darkness. His mouth opened, revealing blackened gums. She smelled his fetid breath. He was trying to say something. His cracked and swollen lips twisted with effort, his tongue thudded against his teeth, but the words wouldn't come.

Instead he opened his mouth wider than humanly possible and screamed. The unearthly scream melded with the squealing subway wheels as Jennifer felt something squeezing around her heart as the lights died again.

When the lights blinked back on, and the normal

sounds of the subway roared back at her, her father was gone. She just saw the bored, numb faces of the commuters around her. A few eyes turned her way – they had noticed her jerk in her seat. They must have seen the alarm on her face, but they turned away just as quickly, for fear that they might be asked to help.

The train roared into a station. Jennifer got up quickly; her legs were numb, and she stumbled. Not even noticing what station it was, she just got off as soon as the doors opened wide enough for her to squeeze through. Racing to the stairs, she took them two at a time, and kept going, out of the station and onto the street. She turned up the volume on Dua Lipa and began to run.

SIX

The desperate young woman stuffed a photo into Jennifer's hand. "Please give this to him! He's my soul mate!"

Jennifer hadn't realize she'd already made it to work. She was in front of the morgue on Winthrop Street, in the crush of media and Trevor's fans. A large van with a satellite dish blocked the entrance, and a police car sat at the curb across the street.

Jennifer looked down at the photo she was now holding. It was of a totally naked woman, hands on hips, with a winning smile. A reporter shoved a microphone into her face. "What's it like to work with Trevor Pryce?"

Instead of answering, she shoved the photo into the reporter's hand and kept going.

An older woman "journalist" pushed against Jennifer. "Have you slept with him yet?"

The Desecrated

A young man shoved a digital recorder in her face. "On a scale of one to ten, how would you—"

Jennifer managed to get around the media van and into the morgue, slamming the door behind her. *Holy shit,* she thought. Was that what it was going to be like for the next fifty-plus days? Her legs were still buzzing from the run, and her heart had not yet quieted. She thought she might have a fever.

***

Jennifer had just gotten her coat off and hung on the coat tree in Clover's office when she heard a muffled voice. Her heart raced again. A thin line of sweat beaded on her forehead in spite of the always-chilly morgue temperature. The voice was coming from the autopsy room. She doubted it was Trevor – that would mean he had come in on time. Making her way quietly down the hallway, the voice slowly become clearer:

"I don't know who you are. I don't know what you want. If you are looking for ransom, I can tell you I don't have any money."

Jennifer quickened her pace and turned into the autopsy room, where she was met by a bizarre tableau.

Trevor was pacing the floor, in front of a row of corpses on gurneys. Three drop-dead gorgeous women were sitting behind him; their eyes glued to his every move. Trevor, not yet seeing Jennifer, continued speaking to the corpses. "But what I do have are a very particular set of skills. Skills I have acquired over a very long career. Skills that make me a nightmare for people like you. If you let my daughter go—"

"What the *fuck* is this?" Jennifer demanded. All eyes, except those of the dead bodies, turned toward her, the women jumping in fear at Jennifer's sudden appearance. Trevor turned to her and gave her his best grin as the women laughed nervously. Jennifer thought she recognized at least two of them from the crowd of fans outside last night.

"Impromptu master class."

Jennifer was right – one of the women was from the night before – the one with her phone number written across her breasts.

"Leave, now!"

The breast-barer pouted at Jennifer. "You're not the boss of me!"

Trevor stepped in. "Alas, she *is* the boss of me. So, until next time . . ." He took the ladies gently by the arms and led them to the hallway.

"There's not gonna be a next time!" Jennifer yelled after them.

Jennifer cocked her head at the drain in the center of the room. Had she just heard that gurgling sound again when Trevor and his groupies stepped over it? She was immediately distracted when she noticed the door to the supply closet was open.

Giving the drain a wide berth, she walked over to the closet and saw that the tiny room had been ransacked. When she leaned into the closet, the low ceiling and close walls felt like they were suffocating her. Looking down, she found the rubber doorstop, and kicked it in place under the door, holding it open. She took a tentative step inside.

She looked around at the carnage. Autopsy saws, rib shears, forceps; all the tools of the trade had been torn from the boxes and thrown all over the room. The now-empty boxes were scattered on top of them.

Jennifer was dumbfounded. She was thinking of how badly she wanted to strangle Trevor when she tripped over an open box, and its contents spilled out. White plastic pipe. PVC pipe, she thought it was called. There was a logo on the box: *National Pipe and Plastic.* She'd never seen anything like it before – not anywhere in the morgue. She reached down to pick up one of the pipes—

And the closet door *slammed shut* with a harrowing thud, plunging her into complete and total darkness.

Jennifer gasped. She wasn't sure, but she thought she heard her own scream. The dark was so total that she lost all sense of space and perspective. Not even knowing what direction she was facing, Jennifer reached her hands out, surprised when they hit the wall, which was much closer to her than she imagined.

Those walls closed in. The ceiling pressed down on her. Fighting the rising panic, she felt her way around, trying to get to the door. It was so fucking dark.

"Trevor!" she screamed. "Open the door *right fucking now!*"

The image came to her out of the darkness. *A closet door slamming in her face.* But it wasn't the supply closet door. It was the closet in her room at her father's house. Jennifer couldn't stop the words: "Dad! *No!*"

She saw herself pounding on the door. Kicking it. She wasn't sure which door it was. Dad's closet or the morgue supply room? "Let me out!" Who was she yelling to?

She jumped when she saw the ghostly white old man, her father, shirtless, not in the closet, but on the street outside his house. The images came fast and furious now; she was unable to stop them and barely able to register them.

There was a dusty bedroom. A hospital bed in the middle.

An IV bottle swaying back and forth.

A ventilator standing guard over the hospital bed.

She saw herself weeping over a coffin.

Her father's face filled her vision. The age spots in sharp relief against his preternaturally white face. His accusing voice rang in her ears, even though his mouth did not open: "I know what you're trying to do to me."

Jennifer heard the banging sounds. Heavy hammer blows that made her ribs vibrate. She raised her unseen hands to her face just to make sure it was still there. She felt her own sweat. And tears.

She saw the hammer. And the withered but still strong hand wielding it. The hammer pounded nails into the closet door. Sealing her in.

Jennifer tried to scream, but only a hoarse scratching sound came out. She heard her blood rushing through her veins, her heart pounding.

Light flooded the closet as the door opened, hurting her eyes, and when she squinted she saw Trevor standing in the supply closet doorway, staring at her.

He was frightened. His eyes wide. "What happened?" he asked, his voice shaky.

Although she was still in shock, the anger came, white-hot and full. Slamming into him, she knocked him out of the way, finally getting free of the stifling closet. "You son of bitch!"

"What? I didn't do anything!"

Noticing his seemingly genuine shock, she disregarded it and strode to the hallway. "You are *done*."

Trevor went after her. "I came running as soon as I heard you scream."

He barely got out of the way of the cranial drill that Jennifer picked up and flung at him with adrenaline-fueled strength. It whizzed by his head and slammed into the wall, tearing open a large hole with a puff of plaster and dust.

When Trevor turned back to the doorway she was gone.

SEVEN

Idris Elba gazed at Clover. It was the same look he always gave her at moments like this – exasperation mixed with lust. "You clever minx. You thought you could get away from me," he purred at her. "When will you learn?"

Clover felt her cheeks burn as Idris pushed past her and entered her humble apartment. She thought he might have been miffed at her after their encounter at the gym. Her attempt to body check him into the steam room and lock the door behind them was a bit forward, after all, and when Idris had screamed in fear Clover retreated. But perhaps it was just a scream of surprise, not fear – because here he was, in the flesh, his skin all wet and glowing from the shower at the gym, his white t-shirt clinging to him.

Swallowing, Clover picked up the pizza box and beer cans from the sticky cocktail table in her living room. "I'm sorry the place is such a mess, I—"

Idris knocked the pizza box out of her hands. She could hear the remaining crumbs slide off the wax paper and onto the wood floor. Idris drilled into her with his eyes.

"If I was interested in being somewhere nice I would've taken you to my place. I'm in the mood for something a little . . . dirtier." He slowly pulled off his t-shirt, never losing eye contact with her.

Just as Clover was worrying that if she held her stomach in any longer she might pass out, her cell phone rang. She groped around the room for it, not because she wanted to answer it, but because she wanted to throw it out the window before letting it interrupt what she was sure was about to happen. The ring kept getting louder and louder as she rummaged through the couch cushions, but she couldn't find that damn phone. Idris, bare chested, folded his arms and looked at her impatiently.

The ringing finally got so loud that it woke her up. Blinking the sleep from her eyes, Clover peered around the dark bedroom, disoriented. Groping along the floor, she found the source of that *fucking* annoying ring and answered it.

"Hello!" she demanded, checking the rest of the room, just to make sure Idris wasn't really there.

"Clover, it's me."

"Me who?"

"Jennifer!"

"Wait – what time is it?" she asked, trying to shake off the dream.

"One o'clock."

"Which one o'clock?"

"The morning one," Jennifer answered dryly.

"Why the hell are you calling me? That place better be on fire, Jennifer!"

"Could happen. You need to get here. Right now."

"Why?"

"Because I can't guarantee Trevor will still be alive if you're not here in ten minutes."

***

"Girls? What girls?" Clover asked as she followed the furious Jennifer down the hallway. Blinking at her, she tried to get Jennifer in focus. Clover was still wearing her pajama top and sweatpants, her hair spiking in different directions.

"I don't know," Jennifer answered. "Groupies I guess. *In* the autopsy room."

"That son of a bitch," growled Clover. She found herself stealing a glance at Jennifer while trying to keep up with her down the hallway.

"What!?" Jennifer demanded.

"I've just never seen you this pissed before. I have no training for this."

"I'm calm compared to fifteen minutes ago."

"I don't know whether to be amused or intimidated."

Jennifer glared at her. "Do I look like I want to amuse you?"

"No."

"You gotta get rid of him, Clover. He doesn't give a shit about anything. *He knew.*"

"Knew what?"

"That I'm not good in small places. So he locked me in the supply closet. *After* he trashed it."

"What do you mean, trashed it?"

"It was like he ransacked it. There were instruments everywhere. He was probably looking for drugs, that idiot. And what's with all that plastic pipe?"

"Plastic pipe?"

"PVC pipe. There was a case of it, ripped open on the floor of the closet."

Clover looked at her, puzzled. "What are you talking about?"

"I'll show you."

However, when Clover and Jennifer stood in the doorway of the supply closet, Jennifer stared inside, shocked. "No, no," she said, "This was totally trashed."

They stared at the neat rows of shelves, and the supplies that were all tucked in exactly where they belonged. Jennifer pointed to the floor.

"The pipes were right there."

There was nothing on the floor.

"Jennifer," Clover began.

"I know what I saw," she replied defiantly.

Clover looked at her and saw something in her eyes she didn't like. Not quite panic, but a nervous, unsettled vibe that made her seem on the brink. She took Jennifer by the shoulders. "Look, I'm sorry this asshole put you through the ringer. Why don't you call it a night and go home early."

"I want him gone, Clover."

"Where is he now?"

"I sent him to the prep room."

"Okay. You get some rest, I'll take care of this dipshit."

Jennifer suddenly seemed vulnerable. Clover had the impulse to hug her, but then remembered she wasn't a hugger.

"I'm not crazy," Jennifer said, wanting, needing her to believe it.

"I know that." She held her gaze. Squeezed her shoulders. "I know that."

"I don't want to go home," she said softly.

"Why not?" she asked, surprised. Clover always wanted to go home.

"I just came from there," was all Jennifer could manage.

Clover looked at her. She had no idea what she meant

by that, but she nodded wisely anyway. "Okay. I understand."

Jennifer glared at her, exasperated, and left. Clover was seething with anger. She was very protective of Jennifer; she knew she was in pain and at a turning point in her young life. Clover had made a lot of mistakes along the way; there was much to be regretted. When she looked at Jennifer, she saw someone with promise, someone who was bright and beautiful and smart as hell. She also knew all that could mean nothing in the face of one bad choice. One wrong turn, one road not taken. Clover had taken more wrong turns that she cared to remember. She wished for something better for Jennifer.

It was time to set Trevor Pryce straight.

***

It was nearly two in the morning before Marty was able to get back out to River View Assisted Living. Marvin Aquillar, the security guard who claimed to have spied Sean Burrows at work after Burrows was shot dead, turned out to be a bookish, chunky man in his mid-twenties. He wore eyeglasses that magnified his eyes to at least three times their size, giving the effect of someone who was perpetually surprised. They sat in two plush chairs in the TV area, empty given the hour. Marty thought of all of the "guests" sleeping their uneasy sleeps, some hating where they were, some not knowing where they were, some wondering how much longer they had to feel anything. He remembered how his mother had hated her assisted-living home at first, like a rebellious teen who's been forced to move to a new neighborhood. Marty had been sure she would never admit to liking it, even if she did eventually come around.

Which she had. Although she did her best to keep their visits chilly, her arms wrapped around her thick sweater, not making eye contact with him, eventually she started asking him to reschedule his visits so as not to interfere with the activities. "Thursdays, there's bingo." Then there were movie nights and special lunches where jazz bands came and played. He knew his mother was starting to feel at home there, not because she'd ever admit it, but because she stopped complaining about it.

Not that it was all fun. Because of her claustrophobia, she couldn't use elevators, so the administrators had to find her a unit on the first floor, which happened to be the Alzheimer's unit. She also didn't want her door closed at night, again because of the claustrophobia. So, his mother had to get used to a parade of Alzheimer's patients mistakenly entering her unit and making themselves at home, often in the middle of the night. Thus, when she had a bathroom call, the attendants would often have to respond to two elderly people screaming in fear at each other.

"This is some place," she would say to Marty, while shaking her head. Marty smiled at the memory, and at the same time his heart clenched. He missed his mother.

"Do you?"

Marty came out of the memory, realizing Marvin had asked him a question he hadn't heard. "Sorry, do I what?"

"Like working nights?" repeated Marvin.

Marty shrugged. "I'm used to it. How 'bout you?"

"I love it. I didn't think I would, but I love that there are so few people around. Anywhere. The streets are empty, the subways are empty, this place is quiet. Sometimes I feel like I'm the only person left in the world."

That wasn't Marty's experience of working nights. *His* night world was full of people – night people, street people; some good, some bad, some who needed his help, some who wanted to hurt him, but all fascinating. Whenever Marty had to move around the world in the daytime on his days off, or when he had to run mundane errands to the bank or the post office or the grocery store, it struck him as way too safe, and way too dull. Like a charcoal drawing, instead of a full-color painting.

"I wanted to be a cop," Marvin confided. "I took the test and everything."

Here we go, Marty thought.

"My eyes weren't good enough though. Do you think they'll ever change the vision requirements?"

"Do you really think they should?" asked Marty, reasonably.

Marvin's giant eyes swam in the glasses. He nodded sagely. "Good point."

"So, Marvin. Your boss said you saw Sean Burrows here yesterday morning."

"That's right."

"When was this?"

"Just as I was ending my shift. So around eight, maybe 8:15 AM."

"Where was he?"

Marvin leaned forward. He lowered his voice. "He was in Mr. Jaworsky's office. By himself."

"And that was unusual?" Marty asked, trying to get the image of a cartoon character out of his head every time Marvin looked at him.

"Very. Nobody's supposed to be in there. He was going through Mr. Jaworsky's file cabinet."

"And what did you do?"

Marvin leaned back. "I told him to get the hell out of there, or I would kick his ass for him."

Marty doubted that. "Uh huh. And what did he say?"

Marvin seemed less sure of himself. "He didn't even turn around. But he said something weird: 'I'll be out of your way in a minute.' "

"Why was that weird?"

Marvin smiled ruefully. "Usually he'd say something like 'fuck off, asshole,' or 'blow me,' something along those lines."

"You guys didn't get along?"

"Nobody gets along with Sean. He's mean. That's why they keep him in the back, away from people. He's very . . ." Marvin trailed off.

"Very *what*, Marvin?"

"Very secretive. Like he's always got something going on." Marvin leaned forward. "He lives in this crazy dilapidated movie theater."

"Have you ever been in it?"

"Yeah, right," Marvin snorted. "I'd have to get my Hazmat suit back from the cleaner's first."

From his jacket pocket Marty took out a plastic bag containing Burrows' driver's license. He held it up for Marvin to see. "Just to make sure. This is the guy you saw, correct?"

Marvin startled Marty by bringing his face to within an inch of the bag, his magnified eyes greedily taking in the photo on the license. "Yep. That's Sean."

Marty thanked him and left. As he walked out onto the deserted street, the far-off sound of a car alarm made it seem even more desolate. He wasn't sure he should take Marvin's word for it, given that his eyesight seemed a bit . . . suspect. Marty would have to find out where Burrows' body had been taken and go there to have another look. Just to satisfy himself.

It was probably the city morgue on Winthrop Street, he figured, since that was the closest one to the crime scene.

***

"What the fuck is wrong with you!" Clover began. Trevor sat beside the giant aquarium, watching the fish glide through the murky water. Clover thought Ziti cast the odd glance Trevor's way, but she couldn't be sure. "You let civilians in here? I mean what kind of skeevy people come to a morgue for fun?"

"Not the time or place, I know," Trevor answered, "But that's not actually the proper use of "skeevy.""

"Let's discuss the proper use of 'you're fired.' "

Trevor finally looked at her. Clover saw the movie star realize this might be worse than he thought.

"Look—"

"Shut up and listen, Daniel Day-Lewis. Number one: Jennifer's had enough trouble in her life. She doesn't need any shit from you. If I were a few years younger I'd punch your pretty-boy face in for real, not like in one of your sissy movie scenes."

"*Sissy* movie scene?" Trevor bristled. "Name one!"

"Number two: I'm reporting all this shit to the court as soon as they open in the morning. And just so you know? When they revoke your community service, you go to *jail*." Clover leaned in close to Trevor's face. "Where you'll learn the proper use of the term 'toss my salad.' "

"Now hang on," Trevor pleaded, his nervousness suddenly showing. "Let's talk about this."

"We just did." Clover turned away and stomped over to her desk. She plopped down on her worn leather chair and immediately regretted the embarrassing noise the leather made as she sat. She kept moving around on the seat hoping to repeat the sound.

"Look, I'm sorry," Trevor came around the desk. "Really, I am. I like to push the boundaries a bit. It was stupid to bring those girls in here, I admit it. But I did not lock Jennifer in that closet. I wasn't even in the room when it happened."

"So . . . ghosts?" Clover stared at him.

"A breeze maybe, I don't know. But I wouldn't do something like that to her."

84

Clover wondered if that was actual sincerity she detected in Trevor's voice. Then she remembered she was dealing with an actor. "She wants you gone. Case closed."

"Please. Give me another chance. Let me apologize to Jennifer. And let me do something for you."

Although she pretended to be looking at the paperwork on her desk, this got Clover's attention. "Like what?" she asked with what she hoped sounded like indifference.

Trevor's eyebrows raised. "Anything at all."

She looked up at him. "Honey, don't flatter yourself, I am more woman than you could *possibly* handle."

Trevor went pale. "That's not what I mean. At all."

"So, what then?" Clover shuffled the paperwork. "What could you possibly do for me? Tickets to Shakespeare?"

"I wouldn't dream of it." Trevor shrugged innocently. "I was thinking more along the lines of . . . drugs? Maybe hard to find sex toys?" He leaned closer to Clover. Whispered seductively in her ear. "What's the best thing I can do for you?"

Clover looked up at Trevor. "Do you know Idris Elba?"

Trevor blinked. "What's the next best thing?"

Clover studied at him for a long moment, thinking. She shifted her gaze to the old, dented fish tank with the scratched glass. Trevor followed her gaze.

Ziti looked at them both quizzically.

***

Ulysses swallowed the last of his hot dog, gazing out of the opening in the wall of his mausoleum. From here he could see the front of the morgue. He shivered; the autumn nights were getting colder. It must be down in the forties now. At one point he had a plan to stretch some Saran Wrap across the openings, to create makeshift windows. He'd have to make a mental note to revisit that idea. It would be a matter of buying the Saran Wrap, no small feat without money, and also finding a way to attach the wrap to the smooth marble walls. Hmm. No wonder he had put that notion on the back burner.

Watching Jennifer leave the hot dogs for him earlier, he had decided to stay in the shadows. He didn't want to talk to anyone, and there was also the fact that sometimes Jennifer was so beautiful it hurt him to look at her. It was also obvious she was upset – maybe even crying – and much to his shame, he had no idea how to console her. So he waited for her to leave the cemetery and enter the morgue building, fighting her way through the throng of reporters and fans, before retrieving his feast.

He was sorry he hadn't spoken to her, especially after witnessing Clover, the morgue supervisor, arriving around 1:30 that morning. By that time the crowd was gone, and even the most diehard fan had given up catching a glimpse of the Movie Asshole. Clover had struggled to get out of her car, her hair messy and wild, although Ulysses supposed he was a fine one to judge. It also looked to Ulysses like Clover was wearing pajamas, which you didn't have to be James Bond to figure out was a sign something was up. Clover worked strictly days, and never went to the morgue during the night. Ulysses counted on that, which was why he only made nocturnal visits to the morgue for things he needed. Jennifer had a soft heart; Clover looked like a tough customer.

But Clover showing up unexpectedly paled in comparison to what happened shortly after, when *Jennifer* left unexpectedly. Ulysses couldn't remember that ever happening before, not that he kept watch or anything – but he kind of did. It was 2 AM, which was six hours before her shift ended. Ulysses thought she looked tired and pissed. He put off going to sleep to see if she came back. Maybe she had to run an errand – although even someone with his addled mind knew that wasn't likely at 2 AM.

Ulysses decided he needed a closer inspection.

He limped across the cemetery toward the side wall of the morgue building. His feet were better, thanks to Jennifer, but the torn heels of the leather boots still chafed along the edges of the blisters. Baby powder would help that. That would be another addition to his mental shopping list, along with the Saran Wrap.

Ulysses wasn't quite sure what could be learned by getting closer to the morgue. There didn't seem to be any windows on the side of the building, but sometimes he could *feel* things by just getting close enough. That was one of the main advantages of stripping down his life, of reducing the noise in his brain: he could feel more, *intuit* more. Like a blind person who suddenly develops a heightened sense of smell. It was a gift.

His nerves tingled with a feeling he definitely *didn't* want to feel. Some kind of presence. Some kind of evil. He stopped. The feeling got stronger. Taking a breath, he turned around slowly.

At first there was nothing, just the bent and twisted trees casting moving shadows along the old brick of the morgue building. But as he stared into the darkness, something slowly materialized out of it.

It had the shape of a man, but Ulysses couldn't quite make out any details in the darkness. It was dressed in dark clothes and had a weird-shaped head. Maybe it was a hood?

Ulysses' heart skipped a beat. The man looked like Death. *The* Death, not just someone sick.

The apparition moved slowly closer to Ulysses. It seemed to be looking at him, or at least toward him. Ulysses stared up into the darkness where a face should be. All he could see was the outline of the hood as the thing towered over him.

The Desecrated

It spoke. "Stay away. Or you will die." The voice was clear and without rancor. Just stating a fact. There was an accent, but Ulysses couldn't tell from where.

Ulysses backed away. His entire mind and body were filled with a sense of darkness. Of something so evil that it was impenetrable. He thought he might be suffocating. Running back to his mausoleum, suddenly not noticing any pain in his feet, he had the thought that perhaps the ability to feel, *to sense*, was a curse, not a gift.

***

Assistant Morgue Supervisor Ersen Tekin yawned. He had been up for nearly twenty-four hours. This double duty, day and night, was taking a toll. Thinking of the money, however, made him smile. It was worth it. Even having to deal with the homeless freak he had to scare off last night was no big deal. No doubt he'd stay on his side of the cemetery from now on, and away from the morgue.

Ersen had decided to stay at the morgue over lunch, and skip going out with Clover. Not that he wasn't always happy to have a chance to get out of the morgue, and not that Clover wasn't good company. She could be funny, and he was always amused by her endless complaints about everything, from the tightness of her shoes, to her nonexistent sex life. No, it was the fact that Clover ate so much fat and carbs. You couldn't even get a basic salad at most of the places Clover ate at. It was like having lunch with a high school student. Besides, Ersen was into intermittent fasting, and today was a fast day – six hundred calories only. Clover would consume six hundred calories with her first order of garlic knots. Ersen did not want to witness it, or, worse, be tempted by it. In any case, when the phone call from the cop came into the morgue, Ersen would be damn glad he was there to take it, and not Clover.

Ersen admired how confident Clover was, how comfortable she seemed to be in her own skin. He liked being around her because there was always the chance some of that confidence and – what was the word in English? Poise, that was it – would rub off on him. Ersen repeated the word "poise" to himself, then decided it would be better to never say that word out loud. He had the vague feeling it would make him sound gay. At the same time, Ersen also resented Clover, for the same reasons he admired her. If Ersen had Clover's confidence and her . . . well, the "P" word, *and* her resources, he'd be unstoppable. The more he worked with Clover, the more he saw her as soft; she talked a tough game, but underneath Clover was sentimental and stupidly generous. Her ambitions, in Ersen's view, were limited. Ersen's ambitions suffered no such boundaries. Yes, he did kiss Clover's ass every chance he got, but only to hide his real feelings, namely, that he, Ersen, should be running this operation, and the body-building behemoth was waiting for his moment to unseat the good natured but clueless morgue manager.

Because of his Nordic-looking blond hair and blue eyes and his first name, most people thought Ersen was from Norway or Sweden ("most people" being those few who felt Ersen merited any thought at all). However, he had been born in Turkey, and had grown up on the streets of Istanbul. Ersen was a devoted weightlifter, a habit picked up in the Pondville Correctional Center in Massachusetts. He had served nearly two years for robbing an Uber driver in Boston not long after coming to the U.S.

It was hardly his first brush with the law. He had been a long-time offender, mostly petty crimes in the U.S. and Turkey and all poorly thought out. Case in point – the crime that sent him to Pondville was a simple robbery of an Uber driver. Unfortunately, Ersen didn't understand that Uber drivers carry no cash. His second mistake was choosing to rob that *particular* Uber driver, who, before he came to the U.S., was the former kickboxing champion of Bangladesh.

Ersen ended up with a broken nose, bruised ribs, and to add insult to injury, the enraged Uber driver threw Ersen's sneakers down a drainage pipe. This could be seen as an apt metaphor for Ersen's life - poor choices meet even worse luck. The barefoot, bleeding criminal mastermind was taken into custody and sentenced to twenty-four months and deportation back to Turkey.

In prison, Ersen kept to himself. Having spent some time in Turkish jails, he felt the American penal system was actually quite pleasant in comparison. Always allergic to learning, Ersen turned down every opportunity to take a class, or even to read a book. He decided it was a much better idea to spend all of his time lifting weights. Even on the typical high-carb prison diet, his body had become a formidable machine.

Released after eighteen months, his body newly muscled and his brain untouched by knowledge of any kind, he was resigned to being deported back to Turkey. However, when brought to his INS hearing, it was discovered he had been given the appointment of another Turk with a similar name. To his astonishment, they gave him a new appointment and told him to come back two weeks later. He left the building a free man, stole a woman's purse on Newbury Street and bought a bus ticket to New York. As Boston receded in the rear window of the bus, Ersen remembered smiling, feeling happy to be living the American dream.

The ringing phone brought him back to reality. "Kings County Morgue," he said, in his thick accent.

"Hey, this is Detective Martin Bell with the NYPD. You guys are holding my murder victim, Burrows, Sean."

"Okay, if you say so," Ersen replied. However, he knew exactly to whom Bell was referring.

"Has he been autopsied yet?"

"Um," Ersen stalled. "Do you have the case number for this?" His mind raced. Why was this cop asking about Sean Burrows' body?

"25126."

Ersen waited, as if he were looking something up. "Uh, no, no autopsy yet."

"OK good. Listen, I need to take another look at this guy. I'm gonna come in tomorrow afternoon before my shift. Can you pull the body for me?"

"Oh ya, will do," replied Ersen.

Hanging up, he knew this was going to take some special handling. He would leave detailed instructions for Jennifer to pull the body and leave it in the autopsy room. Everything had to look like it was done by the book. Who knows, if he was lucky, maybe they would blame Jennifer when they realized what happened.

***

Jennifer came to work that night after another day of fitful sleep. Bad dreams and nightmare images of waking up in a sealed morgue drawer had erased any chance of getting rest. The crisp fall air did a lot to revive her. She wished she could stay outside a little longer, instead of having to run the usual fan/reporter/police gauntlet in front of the morgue. At this point, the throng was used to the fact that she wouldn't answer their questions, so few bothered to even say anything to her as she pushed her way through. Having not heard from Clover at all during the day, she wondered if she had actually had the balls to fire Trevor.

The answer came to her as a resounding "no" when she walked into Clover's office and saw Trevor behind the desk with his feet up. Jumping up when he saw her, the reason he was not fired became crystal clear to Jennifer as she stared past him.

The Desecrated

Clover's old, beaten-up fish tank was gone. In its place was a huge, sleek, black, hi-tech state of the art aquarium. A hundred and seventy-five gallons, with LED lighting, a *reef system*, and beautiful, amber-hued gravel. Ziti and Clover's other fish were gliding around happily, now joined by a rainbow of at least a dozen new, exotic, extravagant tropical fish. Jennifer had once shopped for fish like these when she was looking for a gift for Clover's birthday. After she had seen the prices, Clover had to settle for a generous Starbucks gift card. She guessed there was at least $25,000 worth of sea life in that tank. Shaking her head in amazement, she glowered at him. "Must be nice to be able to make any problem go away with money."

Trevor looked at the aquarium proudly. "I don't know if I'd say nice . . . more like bloody fantastic." Jennifer noticed that the humble plastic scuba diver that had been in the old tank had now been replaced by a solid brass, tricked-out, deep-sea diver. A motorized mini-replica of the Deep Sea Challenger submarine hummed past from behind one of the reefs.

"Although Clover did make me promise to never cross you again. I have to say the way she looks out for you is kind of—"

"Flexible?" Jennifer interrupted.

"Touching is the word I was thinking of." Trevor bent toward the aquarium and watched the fish glide around their new home. He sighed wistfully. "Welcome to the fishbowl, guys."

He straightened up and looked at Jennifer. "Look, I know what you went through was traumatic. And I'm sorry you think I did it. Would you at least consider letting me do something like this for you?" he asked, nodding at the fish tank.

Jennifer didn't want to give Trevor the satisfaction of her being amazed at the aquarium any longer. She busied herself at the desk, searching through stacks of paperwork.

"Not a fish person," Jennifer answered.

"Something nice, is what I meant."

"I know what you meant."

"It's just that Clover told me—"

Jennifer eyes flashed. "Told you what?"

Looking at her, he decided to not go there. "Never mind."

Jennifer sat angrily at the computer and hit the space bar much harder than necessary to wake it. What the hell had Clover told him? She hadn't told her boss everything about her recent past, but what she did tell her, she assumed would be in confidence.

Opening a file of intake documents, she started entering information from the paperwork on Clover's desk. She knew she had done some of these already but was glad to have activity. She supposed it was better to punch the shit out of the keyboard than Trevor's perfect face. Or Clover's imperfect face for that matter.

Trevor paced the office, stealing glances at her. "I don't understand people who keep pets anyway," he said, trying to shift the conversation. "Responsibility. The care and feeding of. Who needs it?"

"Attachments form," Jennifer said, keeping her eyes on the screen.

Trevor looked at her. "To fish?"

"It requires caring about something outside yourself. I understand that's a non-starter for you." Jennifer couldn't sit there anymore. She got up, left the office without looking at him, and strode down the hallway toward the body storage room. One of the overhead fluorescents flickered as she passed under it.

Trevor caught up with her. "Okay. I feel bad about what happened."

"Really? How can you tell?"

"I guess I deserve that. Look, I have no problem admitting the bad things I do. I'm usually proud of them.

But I promise you I did *not* lock you in that closet."

She glared at him. "So you're saying I'm crazy?"

"I'm not saying it, but maybe *you're* thinking it?"

Jennifer looked away; that stung. *How does he know that*, she wondered? How did he know that's exactly what she was thinking?

She flashed on her father's face again. His younger, kinder face. She was thirteen, and she had just overheard him talking to yet another doctor about the increasingly tense situation in their house. About the bizarre things that happened around Jennifer when she was angry, or confused, or scared. The slamming doors, exploding light bulbs, the toppling furniture.

"It might be time to consider taking the next step. Are you familiar with the Rockland Children's Psychiatric Center?" The doctor had three greasy strands of hair plastered across his otherwise bald head.

"You're telling me to put my kid in a nut house?" Hearing the faint note of panic in her father's voice made her tremble.

"Not at all," the doctor replied with practiced calm. "It would be an opportunity to monitor her closely and determine what treatment is best."

Her father and the doctor moved to another room to continue the discussion, so Jennifer didn't hear the rest.

Later, they sat together on the subway. Another of their many subterranean journeys to and from specialists. She could feel his worry in the tense grip he held on her hand. She looked up at him and spoke quietly.

"You're not gonna do it, Dad, are you?"

Looking down at her, he was surprised at first, but the crooked grin she loved broke across his face. "Are you kiddin'?" he asked, in that rough New York accent that was like music to her ears. "What would I do without my best pal? Who would I make pizza bagels for? You ain't going nowhere, kid."

He squeezed her hand even harder, Jennifer was flooded with such intense love for him she couldn't speak.

The memory clutched at her heart as Trevor bent over to try and find her eyes as they walked down the hallway.

"Hello?" he sang. More overhead fluorescents flickered as they passed under them.

"Come on, why can't you loosen up, just a little?" Trevor cajoled. "When I was your age I was tearing up the world!"

Jennifer laughed out loud and finally stared at him incredulously. "When you were my age? What, five minutes ago?"

"I'm thirty-three," Trevor said matter-of-factly.

Jennifer stopped and stared at him in shock. She had guessed his age at twenty-four, twenty-five tops. Even standing close to him he looked nowhere near thirty.

"I know," he went on, "I play early twenties because of my amazing genes or whatever. How much longer do you think I can get away with that? And you think you have problems."

She continued walking. "Okay, I think I see it now. Underneath those first couple of superficial layers, the true shallowness begins."

Trevor again rushed to keep up with her. "Tell me something about yourself, and I'll show you how attentive I can be."

"You're an actor."

"Yes – but remember, I'm not that good. Let me prove I'm interested in you, tell me how you go from pre-med to a morgue."

"None of your business." She entered the prep room with Trevor close on her heels.

"Something you're ashamed of perhaps?" he asked innocently.

"My father got sick," she said, glaring at Trevor. "There was no one else to take care of him."

"So you had to leave school."

"Man, you are smart," she said, while wheeling the gurneys with corpses on them next to each other, lining them up in neat rows. There was no reason for her to do that; it was busywork at best. Why wouldn't he just leave her alone? She could, of course, tell him to get lost, but . . . but that English accent could be so soothing. And there was the smile.

Disgusted with herself, she turned away. "I wasn't gonna put him in some kind of institution or something."

"You mean he was a nutter?" Trevor observed wisely.

"You are nothing if not sensitive."

Jennifer flashed on her father's sick, twisted face, struggling to speak on the 2 train earlier. Did that really happen? *Was* she crazy? Sick in the head, like he became? She didn't want to think about any of that. And the last person she wanted to talk to about it was Trevor Pryce. Yet she felt the need to make him see that not everyone had a charmed life.

"He had a brain tumor. It took away his sanity."

Trevor looked at her. No wisecrack. Instead he cocked his head, taking her in. "He was lucky to have you."

"He didn't even recognize me. Toward the end he thought I was trying to kill him."

"I have to admit I was hoping for a happier story," he said, scratching his neck, hoping she'd smile.

"Me too," she answered.

Trevor started helping her line up the corpses. "After he died, why not go back to school?"

"Because the tuition died with him. I found out he had taken a second mortgage on the house to pay for my medical school. There was no way he could've made the payments, even if he didn't die. They foreclosed a month after he was gone."

Trevor looked away. He was out of his depth for sure,

unable to imagine money, of all things, being an obstacle. They were both silent. Trevor said, quietly, "I'm sorry."

"Just as well," Jennifer glanced at him. "Turns out I'm not much of a healer. Couldn't even stop my dad from . . ." she trailed off, thinking she had said enough.

Trevor was genuinely interested. "From what?"

He was being very disarming, letting her glimpse a different side of him, and she was getting too comfortable. Too comfortable talking about things that should be kept in the dark.

"Doesn't matter. Not anymore." She spied a pile of death certificates on a counter in the corner.

"So how did you end up here?" he asked.

"End up?" She looked at him.

"Excuse me. How did you come to work here?"

"One of my professors knew Clover from her gym and got me this job."

"Clover goes to the gym?"

"So she says. Anyway, she called me and offered me the night shift. It would just be temporary, she said."

"Will it be?"

Jennifer had thought about that a lot. She still didn't know the answer. She looked around the green-tiled room. "This work – it feels somehow like penance. The right penance."

"Penance for what?"

"My father kept me safe growing up. It was just the two of us, and he took care of me. I couldn't do the same for him." She scooped up the death certificates.

"So we're both doing some kind of penance." He looked at her, tried the grin. "I suggest we discuss further over dinner tomorrow night. As a way for me to say—"

"You're sorry?"

"You're special."

"Ah!" Jennifer laughed. "I'm so special I rate dinner

with the nearly geriatric Trevor Pryce. Sorry, I already have a dinner date tomorrow."

"At 4 AM? With whom, Why Me?"

Handing him the stack of death certificates, she said, "I need you to match these with the deceased's paperwork." She walked out of the room, leaving him staring at the pile of forms in his hands. "Because you're special too," she said over her shoulder.

***

Jennifer snapped on a pair of rubber gloves. Ersen had texted her about the body she had to pull – a detective was going to come and check it out tomorrow. Ersen spoke slightly better than he wrote, so she had to read the text several times to get the gist of what he was trying to express with his fractured English. He gave her the creeps, even though he had stopped hitting on her after she "accidentally" kneed him in the balls one night when his hand "accidentally" found its way to her thigh. All the weightlifting and protein drinks in the world can't stand up to a knee in the balls. It gave her a much-needed smile when she remembered the shock on his face and the way his entire huge body doubled over on itself as he clutched his crotch. It had somehow made him look like an umbrella folding.

Rolling a gurney up to one of the morgue drawers in the body-storage room, she pulled the drawer open, dropped the front panel, and slid out the oblong tray that held the corpse of Burrows, Sean, a twenty-three-year-old male. A gunshot victim. She had done the intake. She remembered the shaved head and snake tattoo that curled up his neck and around his ear.

Sean Burrows' chest had been torn apart by three bullets. As she prepared the body to be moved to the gurney, Jennifer saw the star-shaped entrance wounds; they were no bigger than dimes, black around the edges, and stark against the pale white skin. They were so small, almost harmless looking; a person could be forgiven for wondering how such little holes can kill you. Jennifer knew, though, that if she turned his body over, she would see the three much larger exit wounds, which would be ragged with torn skin, tissue, and extruded bone and muscle. Bullets wreaked havoc on the human body.

It was unusual for a detective to want to look at a body before the autopsy. Maybe it was connected to another case. The guy was probably a gangbanger. Jennifer could never understand the tendency for these guys to get these outrageous tattoos that made them instantly identifiable.

Expertly sliding the body off of the tray and onto the gurney, she flipped up the side rails of the gurney, and rolled the morgue drawer closed. She remembered someone else she once knew who'd had a snake tattoo. Although hers was much smaller and wrapped around her ankle.

***

Miss Nadja was a psychic, very well known in the neighborhood when Jennifer was growing up. She told fortunes out of a room in her apartment, which was above a dry cleaners and so always smelled of cleaning solvent. She had achieved a small bit of fame when she helped a family find their missing child – unfortunately not in time to save the little girl's life. Her family was grateful nevertheless as Miss Nadja had been more successful than the police had been. After that it was rumored that she was asked to help the police from time to time, although the cops always denied it. She claimed to be a widow, but never said a word about her mysterious, late husband. The sense of mystique around her was helped enormously by the fact that while her right eye was a deep, mysterious brown, her left eye was a cloudy white. No one knew if she could see out of it, but it certainly gave her a spooky air.

The Desecrated

Miss Nadja claimed to be able to "channel" dead loved ones, so that you might be able to speak with them, to ask them that one last question, to tell them that one thing you never got to say – to get closure, and comfort – for forty-five dollars an hour.

When Jennifer was fourteen, she was still grieving her mom, and worried sick about the strange events that were becoming a part of her and her dad's life. *Manifestations* – she'd found that word in the same book that described "poltergeist activity," which sounded a hell of lot like what had been happening to her since her mother died. Saving up enough money to have a session with Miss Nadja, she didn't know if she believed in her or not, but if there was any chance Jennifer could see or talk to her mom again, she was going to take it. She wanted to ask her mother why lights sometimes blew out near her. Why doors slammed and drawers opened around her. Jennifer wanted to ask why she felt so angry at times that she thought she'd actually detonate.

She wanted to ask her mother why she had to go and die.

Miss Nadja sat comfortably in the front room of her tidy apartment, her legs crossed casually. Around her bare ankle was a tattoo of a snake biting its tail. Miss Nadja was thin, almost fragile looking, with an angular face that was pretty but a bit hard. She gave off an aura of confidence and strength and deep mystery. Especially because of that murky eye. She wore faded jeans and a thin, sleeveless blouse, which was unbuttoned at the top, revealing a surprising amount of cleavage. It was hard to judge her age. Maybe forties, Jennifer thought, although she had never been good at guessing how old someone was. Her father, for instance, seemed ancient to her, although he was only thirty-nine at the time. Her mother had always seemed young. And now she would be, forever.

The large, bowed windows overlooked the street, and filled the room with light. Miss Nadja gave Jennifer an appraising glance. She finally spoke with a deep, Russian accent. "Forty-five dollars please."

Dollars came out like "Doolaarz."

"You haven't done anything yet," Jennifer pointed out. Granted, she had not done many transactions like these, but she knew as a general rule, a service was performed first, then paid for.

"That's because you haven't given me forty-five dollars yet," Miss Nadja purred.

"I'd rather you do your thing first."

"Don't work that way, darling. What if I tell you what you want to know, then you decide you don't like, and you don't pay?"

"I wouldn't do that."

"Good for you! Let's not test it, though. You pay forty-five dollars first, then we see about your mother."

Jennifer was slightly startled. She hadn't told Miss Nadja why she was there. Hadn't mentioned a word about her mother. She handed over the two folded twenties and a five. Miss Nadja tucked the cash into her jeans pocket. Jennifer looked around and wondered if the lights were going to go off, curtains were going to close – this bright and somewhat stark room seemed like an unlikely place for a séance.

Miss Nadja closed her eyes. She took deep breaths. The breaths became more and more shallow.

She stopped breathing.

Jennifer leaned forward. Had she made "contact?" She waited. Miss Nadja's eyes remained closed. She still didn't breathe.

What seemed like minutes went by. Miss Nadja had still not taken a breath. Jennifer, ever suspicious, stared at Miss Nadja's ample chest, looking for any telltale movement. There was none.

Another minute or two or three ticked by. Miss Nadja's chin sagged onto her chest. Jennifer sat back. Holy shit. Had this lady just up and died right in front of her? Had she had a heart attack or . . . what was the other thing her uncle had? A stroke?

Jennifer was about to get up when Miss Nadja's head whipped up, her whole body pulsed, and she sucked in air through her open mouth with a rather unattractive, wheezy rasp. She looked around the room in surprise, as if she had just arrived. Seeing Jennifer, she jumped, then focused on her.

Her breathing slowed. She seemed to remember where she was and what she was doing.

"Are you okay?" Jennifer asked. "What happened?"

Miss Nadja smiled weakly. She had lost some of the color in her face. Even her lips had gone pale. "I am fine. This is the way it happens."

"The way what happens?"

"The way I go to the other place."

Jennifer swallowed. "Well, did you see my mother?"

Miss Nadja reached for a bottle of water. She drank greedily. Replacing the cap on the bottle, she gazed squarely at Jennifer. "Your mother gone."

"Yeah, I know, that's why I'm here. What do you—"

"She is gone from this veil," Miss Nadja clarified. "She is not earthbound. Your mother has crossed over to the other side, which is a good thing."

Jennifer felt the rage rising. *What kind of bullshit was this?*

Miss Nadja's eyes flicked to the water bottle, which was suddenly wobbling on the table. She looked back at Jennifer and leaned forward in the huge chair. "This is a *good thing*. It's the way it's meant to be. Only tortured souls linger with us."

"You're telling me you can't see her on the 'other side'?"

102

"I only see the earthbound spirits."

The water bottle suddenly crushed in on itself with a loud crackling sound.

"I want my forty-five dollars back," Jennifer said evenly.

"Doesn't work that way, darling."

The water bottle shot across the room and smashed into the opposite wall, causing a mini-explosion of water and shredded plastic. The lights flickered. The lamps swayed. Miss Nadja leaned back and took it all in. Curious, but unafraid.

Jennifer stood up. Her anger was getting out of control.

All of the windows suddenly flew open. The two end tables in the room flipped over. The framed photographs, the ceramic sculptures, and neatly lined-up magazines and books churned up and swirled around the room.

It made Jennifer feel good to be in the center of this hurricane. She waited for Miss Nadja's reaction, expecting (hoping for?) fear.

But Miss Nadja abruptly jumped to her feet and yelled, "*Enough!*"

Jennifer swayed; she felt dizzy and had to sit back down in her chair. Without warning, everything in the apartment dropped to the floor. Silence and stillness filled the room.

Miss Nadja calmly sat down again. "You will pick everything up, please."

"No. It wasn't my fault."

"Do you believe that?" Miss Nadja tilted her head toward Jennifer.

Jennifer looked away.

"Clean this up, and I will give you back twenty dollars. Since it's true I could not see your mother."

Not knowing what else to do, Jennifer got down on the floor and started collecting the debris.

Miss Nadja watched her coolly. "This kind of thing happening many times?"

Jennifer just nodded, now embarrassed.

"Did you know that you are a 'sensitive'?"

Jennifer looked at her. "What does that mean?"

"There is pathway between you and spirit world. You could learn to walk this path, but for now it is blocked."

"Blocked by what?" Jennifer asked dubiously.

Miss Nadja leaned closer to her. "Your anger and your rage are barriers. A clog in the pipe. Nothing can get through."

Silence fell on the room while Jennifer thought about that. She continued picking up the room. When she spoke, her voice sounded weak. Frightened. "Why does this happen?"

A flicker of sympathy flashed in Miss Nadja's one good eye. She leaned even closer. Touched her face. "Be careful in the world. Your feelings are more powerful than you know." She handed Jennifer back one of the folded twenties.

***

The sound of the clattering metal wheels echoing off the tiled walls brought Jennifer back. She wondered what had become of Miss Nadja; Jennifer had never seen her again. If she could, she would have a lot of questions.

She rolled the gurney down the hallway toward the autopsy room. Her thoughts turned back to Trevor and his claim that he hadn't locked her in the supply closet. She couldn't deny that the expression on his face when he opened the closet door and freed her seemed to be one of genuine surprise – even fear. And he was right; he was not that good an actor. But if it wasn't him who locked her in, then who?

At first it was just a whisper, she almost didn't hear it until it got just a little louder. A sibilant, desperate murmur of words she couldn't make out.

It was coming from below her.

It was coming from the corpse on the gurney.

Jennifer stopped dead as she looked down at the sheet-covered face of the body. The faint outline of its facial features could be made out through the cloth.

And she saw that the lips *were moving*.

Jennifer whipped the sheet off the corpse's face. Sean Burrows' expression was still. His cloudy eyes were half open and staring off to the side. The snake tattoo was jet-black against his bloodless white skin.

She stared at the face for a long time, almost daring it to move. The lips were cracked and parted, revealing a chipped front tooth. Total stillness.

Coming around the gurney, she willed herself to stay calm. To not give in to fear. She leaned down close to the body. Inches above his face. There was the familiar odor of death – something like rotting fruit. Turning her head, she brought her ear right over his mouth and nose. Was there any chance this guy was breathing? Was still alive?

Nothing. She straightened up and looked back down at the face. The eyebrows were slightly raised, as if he too were waiting for something else to happen. Jennifer pulled the sheet back over his head and continued down the hall.

When she turned into the autopsy room, she accidentally banged the edge of the gurney into the doorway. She jumped when the corpse's head rolled to the right, the face sliding under the sheet. Jennifer backed the gurney up, straightened it, and rolled it into the room,

For the second time that night she stopped dead. It had nothing to do with the gurney.

And everything to do with the *old woman* who was standing in the middle of the autopsy room. She was dressed in dark business clothes, which stood out in stark contrast to the bright walls of the room. She had thick black eyebrows, and a shock of gray through her dark hair. The old woman was looking down at the floor, confused.

Jennifer stood there frozen. The woman finally noticed her. She opened her mouth – it was clearly an effort for her to speak, and her voice came out dry and cracked. "What happened to me here?" she demanded. "Do you know?"

Unable to move or speak, Jennifer stared at the woman, so incongruously *present* in this room of death and dissection.

The woman jerked and walked toward Jennifer in a fit of disjointed stops and starts, like her limbs were not quite speaking to each other. Her voice was still hoarse but suddenly loud and strong: *"Do you know what they did to me here?"*

Jennifer finally moved, or more accurately, stumbled out into the hallway, barely feeling the wall that stopped her. She could still see inside the autopsy room, where the woman was now on her hands and knees, in the center of the room.

Her arm was almost elbow deep in the center drain, as she rooted around in it, seemingly trying to grab something out of it. The woman looked up, and Jennifer saw the bloodshot yellow of her eyes. Her mouth opened unnaturally wide, and an animal-like bellow issued from it: "Give it to me! *Give it to me!*"

Jennifer flashed on the image of an angry wild boar. She tried to move farther away but was already plastered against the wall. In numb horror, she watched as the woman struggled to get to her feet, with her hand still in the drain, ripping her arm off at the shoulder in the process. A heavy glop of dead blood fell from the opening in her shoulder as she hobbled toward Jennifer.

The arm stayed lodged in the drain.

Jennifer heard a high-pitched laugh. As if it were coming from a speaker. She turned and peered down the hall. Trevor walked across the adjoining hallway at the other end, Facetiming the beautiful blond who'd been one of his guests the night before. She could barely process what was happening, not sure at all what was real and what wasn't.

When she looked back into the autopsy room, it was empty.

No woman; no arm in the drain; no black, decayed blood. Just the gurney in the doorway, at a crooked angle, the body's head under the sheet turned to Jennifer, as if waiting for her next move.

Jennifer felt the cold sweat on her back as her body came away from the wall. She took a shaky breath; the first since she'd seen the woman.

She needed help.

***

Otis drove the black van along the Gowanus Expressway, supremely pissed off. He hated when Ersen gave him an after-hours errand to do. The wannabe gangbanger had just spent his usual night shift driving around the city alongside Angel, trying to avoid working as much as possible. Not only could Otis not go home after a long night of doing little, he was expected to do some actual work.

Work that he was afraid of.

Otis didn't like handling bodies, which was not a helpful trait in someone whose job it was to transfer corpses in and out of the morgue. He tried to let Angel do most of the work, and when handling a corpse couldn't be avoided, he put on two pairs of rubber gloves and kept his eyes off of the body. Otis was also quite frightened of being in the morgue; it really creeped him out, and he did his best to avoid having to go there.

Nevertheless, his instructions were to go there as soon as Jennifer left, and before Clover got there, and deal with the corpse in question.

By himself.

Off the official clock no less!

Shit! But when Ersen told him to do something, he did it, because he was afraid of Ersen, too.

The number of things that Otis was afraid of would astound most people who judged him only by his appearance. He was very intimidating to look at, even though physically slight. There was a teardrop tattoo below his left eye, and tats with various number combinations on his neck (the hope was people would think these numbers were gang codes, and he also hoped they would take attention away from the acne scars on his pale-white cheeks). Otis liked to talk about growing up on the mean streets of the South Bronx, even though, in fact, he'd grown up on the well-mannered streets of genteel Tarrytown, in tony Westchester County.

Otis felt that he had been born into the wrong family. His father owned a florist shop on the quaint Main Street of Tarrytown, and his mother ran a craft store that Otis used to have to work in after school. As much as he hated arts and crafts, at least he didn't have to work in the flower shop. An only child, Otis was often lonely, especially because his bad temper and spoiled nature did not exactly land him on the A-list for neighborhood birthday parties and Easter egg hunts.

Otis longed to rebel. Wanting to be like the tough guys on TV and in the movies, he idolized the gangstas who ruled the streets. Not that he knew any of them or had ever even seen an actual gang member in person, but that didn't stop him from bemoaning the fact that he had grown up pretty much conflict-free in the comfortable, two-story Victorian that his parents obsessed over. Why couldn't he have been born in a place like Compton in the nineties, or the South Bronx in the eighties? Why had he been cursed with such stability and comfort?

He became an oddball figure in the neighborhood, adopting the gang patois that he read in graphic novels. While that sounded hilarious coming from a middle-class white kid, it still easily intimidated his teachers. And while acting tough and being feared by the privileged kids he grew up with thrilled him, Otis never fully grasped how lucky he was to never have to mix with genuine tough kids, amongst whom he would wilt like one of his father's hydrangea.

As a young teen he had quickly become known to the police for his vandalism and shoplifting. Proud that the local cops dubbed him "homeboy," he didn't realize it was purely ironic. Beaming with pride the day he was kicked out of high school in his sophomore year, he wore the expulsion like the ultimate suburban street cred it was. Turning eighteen, Otis yearned for more independence. Wanting to stand on his own two feet, to forge a life of his own. He insisted that his parents make the downstairs playroom into a living space for him. They balked at first. *The expense! Wouldn't he rather get out there and get his own apartment, blah blah blah?* As usual, Otis got his way. Unfortunately, though, not his own private entrance, so he still had to enter the house on the main floor, try to ignore his parents watching television, and take the stairs down to his lair.

He didn't want the morgue job at first, which his father had arranged for him because a city councilwoman owed him a favor. When Otis balked, his parents, in a rare show of solidarity, insisted he contribute financially to the household or go get himself an apartment for real in the big bad world. Otis relented.

And he grew to love it. Working nights felt good, especially because he loved sleeping during the day. Working with the dead gave him even more bad-boy bona fides. Driving around deserted areas of the city at night, safe in the van, made him happy, even though he never really warmed up to Angel. The pudgy dude was flaky and not that bright, a dreamer, always talking about his next get-rich-quick scheme while they hid out at the Burger King on Fulton Street, eating Croissan'wiches and Cheesy Tots. Otis would usually tune out Angel's bullshit and think about how much he'd rather be working with a cool guy like Ersen.

Otis revered Ersen's strength and criminal ambitions. He didn't know much about Istanbul, but guessed it was a scarier place to grow up than Tarrytown. And, like Otis, Ersen had absolutely no moral compass whatsoever, so their behavior and goals were limited only by what they believed they could get away with. Hence, Otis made a natural recruit to the various after-hours enterprises that Ersen was involved with.

Even though Ersen worked days and Otis worked nights, they recognized something in each other that they found familiar and comforting. Perhaps it was the fact that they were both basically idiots who thought they were geniuses. When the commute between Brooklyn and Tarrytown became hellish, Ersen offered to let Otis stay on his couch, especially when Otis started working after hours with the Turkish weightlifter. However, one of Ersen's neighbors was an ex-con with a Rottweiler named Thor, who scared the shit out of Otis.

Once, when Thor was roaming the hallways unleashed, he had chased Otis back into the elevator. Thor was waiting on every floor when the elevator door opened. Otis spent that night in the basement of the building, where the staircase the dog was using didn't reach. He eventually decided to make the trip back to the suburbs rather than risk any further encounters with Thor.

In Otis' mind, Ersen was the real deal, maybe even a killer, so he treaded lightly around him. Otis hoped to prove himself one day to Ersen, maybe even by being a killer himself, if he could ever summon up the courage.

It had taken Otis longer to get there than usual because

of the rising morning rush-hour traffic. He had parked a few yards from the morgue. It was just a matter of waiting until Jennifer left. Although he usually tried to steer clear of her, he had to admit to being a little put out by the fact that she never really paid any attention to him and was in no way intimidated by his whole street thug persona. Just as well; having heard her razor-sharp mouth, he never wanted to be on the receiving end of her wrath.

Finally, Jennifer exited the building. When she had turned the corner toward the subway, Otis got out of the van and headed to the morgue, dreading what he was about to do.

EIGHT

*H*allucinations + Visions.

Jennifer stared at the words she had just typed onto her laptop screen. Her apartment was dark in spite of the edges of sunlight trying to break through the corners of the heavy curtains. The gentle glow of the string lights around the walls gave her the comforting illusion of continued night. She had finished the last of the wine, cursing herself for not remembering to buy more.

Her finger hovered over the enter button on her keyboard, but before pushing it she decided to add something:

+ *Brain Tumor.*

Her eyes scanned the pages and pages of text that scrolled past. She knew this was a mistake; Googling anything of a medical nature was never a good idea. However, she was not about to Google *ghosts and demons*.

She clicked on a WebMD article about how brain tumors cause hallucinations. She was so intent on reading that she didn't hear the faint noise behind her.

The closet door slowly started to open.

Jennifer was oblivious as she scrolled through page after page of medical horrors. But when the door opened all the way and bumped gently against the wall, she jumped at the noise and whirled around in her chair.

She saw the open closet door, and the pitch-dark space inside.

Before Jennifer could process that, the sudden sound of loud hammering almost knocked her out of her chair. The entire apartment was filled with the pounding noise, books fell from their shelves, her wooden dining table slid along the floor. Lamps swayed.

Jennifer let out a surprised yelp as her chair jerked away from the table and slid across the floor to the closet. She tried to get up, but some unseen force kept her pinned to the chair.

It lurched even faster, whipping her toward and into the closet.

The door slammed shut behind her.

Total, complete blackness. She heard her own breathing. At least she was able to get out of the chair, but when she stood, her head crashed into the bar above her, causing a clang of hangers and unseen clothing to drop all around her. The material creepily brushed her face and arms, like furry creatures rubbing against her.

The hammering got even louder. It pounded in her ears, in her pulse. Panic rising, Jennifer reached out to try to feel for the door, and a ray of light appeared from a keyhole. There was no keyhole in her closet door, she thought, but nevertheless she dropped to her knees and pressed her eye against it.

She saw not her own living room, but her old bedroom

in her father's house. She jumped when her father's face suddenly filled her view. His hair was wild, he was unshaven, and had several nails pressed between his lips. Muttering something she couldn't understand, his voice was choked and muffled. Again, the image of a wild boar flashed into her mind.

He was swinging a hammer. He was nailing her closet door closed.

It was less of a realization, and more of a memory.

"Dad!" she shouted. "What are you doing?"

The hammering stopped. Hearing him move away, she craned her neck to try to see a different angle through the keyhole and could just about make out her father on the other side of the room. She tried to open the door, but it was nailed shut.

Her father yanked an extension cord out of the wall, yelling, bellowing angry unintelligible words. She watched in helpless horror as he stood on a chair. He tied one end of the extension cord around the overhead light fixture.

He tied the other end around his neck.

Jennifer felt the tears, hot as they flowed down her cheeks. "Dad, no."

Knotting the cord, he pulled it tight. The skin of his throat wrinkled around the bright orange cord.

"Dad!"

As the chair wobbled under his weight, he raised one leg, put his foot against the back of the chair, and pushed it over. The chair banged hard to the floor, and his feet dangled a few feet over the wooden floorboards as his body twitched and danced in obscene circles under the light fixture.

Jennifer sobbed. She called his name, but even she couldn't understand what she was saying. She banged on the closet door, trying to break it down.

The light fixture pulled partly out of the ceiling, plaster, dust, and sparks cascading over the twitching body below. Jennifer watched through her tears, having the perverse memory of her father taking her to watch fireworks by the Brooklyn Bridge on the Fourth of July when she was ten. The sparks and flashes glinting over his swelling head mocked that memory.

She didn't know how the police got there – had she called them? Did they let her out of the closet? The EMT worked on her dad. One of them was talking about a movie he saw last night, which had an EMT scene that was all wrong.

Her father was still alive. They packed him onto a stretcher, IV bottles swaying above him. Raising his head, he looked for her. She came closer. The veins strained against the red and purple bruising on his neck as he attempted to speak. Jennifer tried to get closer as they maneuvered him through the bedroom doorway.

"Find it. We need it," he said.

Wait. That wasn't right. That didn't happen. He'd left the room unconscious, she was sure of it. One of the EMTs looked over his shoulder at her and told her they didn't have room for her in the ambulance. She could come to the hospital when the police were finished taking her statement.

She remembered looking at the floor, littered with the detritus of an attempt to save a life. Discarded tubes, syringes, a bloody sponge. She'd have to clean it up when the police left. When she was alone.

The church bells pealed.

Opening her eyes, she lifted her head, and saw that she was sitting at her table in front of the laptop, the screen of which swam with a screensaver of squiggly lines. Her back ached and her neck was stiff. The church bells got louder.

She had fallen asleep at her computer. The realization slowly settled in that it had been a dream. She had a rush of relief at first – that reprieve people feel when they realize that a terrible experience was just a dream. That relief turned to despair as she remembered the dream may not have been real, but the incident was. Although her father had survived his suicide attempt, that marked the beginning of the betrayal of her promise to him.

Grabbing for her phone, which was next to the laptop, she turned off the alarm. She couldn't remember why she'd chosen church bells as her alarm sound, but they were way too loud and obnoxious. She would have to change that. Her eyes went wide when she saw the time – she had been asleep for hours and had to get ready to go back to the morgue. She was filled with dread.

She hadn't wanted him to die. She wanted to live with him and take care of him. She had promised him she would. At first his symptoms were mild – confusion, forgetfulness; but then the anger came. The paranoia. He showed up at her school more than once, accusing her of having him followed. Once he tried to punch Jim, her boyfriend, believing he was sneaking around with Jennifer's mother behind his back. Often, he'd forget her mother was dead and worry about where she was and go looking for her.

When he was diagnosed with the brain tumor, the doctors warned her that there was no getting better; it would only get worse. He would need to be institutionalized at some point. Jennifer rebelled. No way. She wouldn't do that to him.

You ain't going nowhere, kid.

They told her his behavior would be impossible to control. He might hurt himself. Or others. Or her.

Still, she refused to "put him away."

She quit school and moved back into the house. Tried her best. But the doctors were right. Despite ever briefer moments of clarity, even affection, and gratitude, sometimes wrenching contrition, his behavior had been getting more and more unpredictable, more and more violent. That night, as he was loaded into the ambulance in front of their world-weary house, neighbors gawking, Jennifer knew he wouldn't come back. Couldn't come back.

And she hated herself for what she had felt amidst the grief and the guilt.

Relief.

Stumbling into her bathroom, the after-effects of too much wine pounding in her temples, she looked at herself in the mirror, tears still wet on her cheeks. She considered calling in sick. How could she face another day in that morgue after last night? What would happen tonight? She wondered if she should call Clover and tell her what had been going on. She wondered if she should check herself into a hospital and have a brain scan. She wondered if she should go back to sleep.

Instead, she turned on the shower and stripped off her clothes. She made the water as hot as she could stand it.

***

"How the fuck do you lose a body?"

Detective Marty Bell was pissed. He stood in the body-storage room of the morgue, next to the supervisor, Clover Hare. Marty had come to take another look at Sean Burrows, just to make double sure the ID was correct, as he tried to figure out how young Sean could be shot full of bullets one night and be at his job at the assisted living home the next morning. But as soon as Marty had walked into the chilly morgue that afternoon he knew something was wrong – in spite of her intimidating size, this lady Clover was skittish and sweating.

"We have a little problem," Clover began, with a weak smile.

"What might that be?" asked Marty, always willing to be entertained.

117

"Sean Burrows' body seems to have been misplaced."

Marty hated that kind of incompetence. He saw it all around him, especially when dealing with any kind of city bureaucracy. But really, for fuck's sake, how do you misplace a corpse?

He made Clover search the entire morgue. They opened every drawer. In one hour Marty saw more dead bodies than he had in his entire career. No Sean Burrows. None of the other morgue attendants knew anything. The assistant supervisor, some guy named Ersen, who apparently was the genius Marty had spoken to about coming to see the body, had taken a sick day.

Clover told Marty that the night attendant would have pulled the body for Marty to see, but there was no way she could have screwed up. "She's the only one working here who has an actual brain," she asserted.

Marty was dubious and had to wait until this attendant came in for her shift. He was now tired and pissed, having spent another day working when he should have been sleeping, and had only his own night shift ahead to look forward to, so he was off to a less than polite start when Jennifer Shelby finally arrived.

"How the fuck do you lose a body?"

Jennifer stared at him. "I don't know how *you* lose bodies, but I don't."

Marty had to admit he liked that comeback. Maybe Clover was right, and this Jennifer was the only one who worked there who had a brain.

Jennifer turned to Clover for an explanation.

"When Detective Bell here came to see the body, it wasn't where it was supposed to be," Clover ventured.

"It wasn't *anywhere*." Marty stared at Jennifer. "Can I assume that bodies don't usually take field trips?"

"Not without a note from one of us," Jennifer answered calmly.

Shit, thought Marty, *she did have brains*. And the deepest, saddest eyes he had ever seen. He was trying to hide his smile when the main door opened, and Marty did a double take. Wait – was that – what's his name, Trevor somebody? Big movie star?

Trevor joined them in the body-storage room and took them all in with a grin. "This looks like a meeting of the sad person's club. Why the long faces?"

Clover scowled at Trevor. "Where were you when Jennifer pulled the body?"

Ah, Marty thought – he had read something about this. Some movie star got sentenced to community service in a morgue. This morgue. Marty smiled, admiring that judge's sense of humor. And he now recognized the actor – Marty had seen a bunch of his movies. Trevor Pryce. Could this day get any more bizarre?

"I've never seen Jennifer pull a body, and I'll fight any man who says she has."

"He was goofing off as usual," Jennifer said, answering Clover's question and turning to Marty. "Look, I left the body in the autopsy room last night, with the paperwork. Same as I would do if he was scheduled for autopsy."

"Is there a chance he was autopsied by mistake?" Marty asked.

"Even if he was, we don't normally throw the body out afterward," Jennifer responded.

Trevor looked at Marty. "She's got you there, mate."

"Has this ever happened before?" Marty asked.

Clover thought for a moment.

"The fact that you have to think about it is not a good sign," Marty observed.

Clover looked at Jennifer. "Is there a chance Angel or Otis took him somewhere by mistake? A funeral home or something?"

"Maybe they needed an extra body for the carpool

lane?" Trevor suggested helpfully.

Clover ignored Trevor. "Angel and Otis are on their way in. I gave them a funeral home transfer they have to come and pick up. Jennifer, check it out with them," she said, letting Marty know that she herself had no intention of still being here.

Marty was ready to leave as well. Having spent hours here, on his own time, he needed to get to the precinct house. After making sure Clover knew he was counting on her to find Burrows, Marty gave Jennifer his card. "Call me immediately if you find out anything." She nodded at him; Marty took a last look at the movie star and left.

Walking down the damp hallway, grateful to be leaving, happy that being in that place was only a small part of his job, he heard the night attendant behind him.

"Can I ask you something?" she said.

He turned and looked at her. Her dark eyes locked on his. Marty did not normally pay much attention to beauty, he didn't trust it, but she was so stunning that he struggled to find a reply. It was clear that she was tired too, her eyes were even a little bloodshot – the tension in her jaw screamed stress. Yet still, the underlying beauty could not be denied. Twenty years ago, Marty would have avidly pursued a woman like that, trying to make her laugh, trying to win her over. He'd be sure that he could somehow cure whatever that sadness was in her eyes. Twenty years ago Marty had been an asshole and had since learned that you can't really cure people of anything they don't want to be cured of.

"Sure," he managed to get out.

"Why did you want to see that body again?"

"Why do you ask?" Marty was curious – why would she want to know that?

She—seemed unsure of what to say. "I was just wondering."

Marty wanted to know the question behind the question, but he didn't think she was going to go there. "Just wanted to clear up some ID confusion."

Nodding, she stayed put. Marty watched her. Did she want to tell him something?

"Well, sorry about all this," she said. "I'll try to figure out what happened."

She moved away and walked back down the hallway. It was with some effort that Marty finally turned and left.

***

Angel slammed the van door closed and walked toward the parking lot entrance of the morgue. Parking on the street in front of the morgue would have actually saved him a few steps, but he hated walking near that fucking cemetery. Especially after midnight. Besides, using the small lot allowed him to avoid the circus in front of the building that Trevor Pryce had caused.

Meeting that dude was unbelievable. Angel was a big movie fan and had seen every notable action and horror movie ever made. He was pretty sure he had, anyway. He was still so blown away by his proximity to a major movie star that he felt kind of paralyzed. His only frustration was not yet coming up with a way to monetize it, but he was working on it. Maybe if Trevor could be persuaded to pose with a body. A picture like that would sell for a fortune.

Angel entered the morgue, his head on a swivel as he tried to spot Trevor. Instead, there was Jennifer, looking like shit, he thought, which was rare. That she was looking like shit was rare, he meant. Although some might argue any actual thinking on his part was also rare.

Clover had called him earlier to tell him that a body needed to be transported to a funeral home. Angel had left his partner Otis at the all-night Burger King where he was playing a wicked game of Doom Eternal on his iPad. They were still hurting about the Mustard Whopper being taken off the menu. Another example of how life was just so fucking unfair.

"Where's Otis?" Jennifer asked, distracted.

"He had to go to the all-night dentist. Toothache."

"Right," she said, with that tone that let him know she knew he was full of shit. "When was the last time you guys transferred a body?" Jennifer looked at him expectantly.

Angel's antenna went up. Why was she asking that? Had he fucked something up? His mind raced over the last few nights. His mind, in fact, didn't really race, so he thought the best thing to do was point her to his partner. "I think Otis took the last few. Why?"

"We lost somebody."

"Holy shit," Angel laughed. "You mean like a body? A dead body?"

"Any chance you or Otis might have mixed up some paperwork?"

"Well, Otis, I don't know. But I always check everything real good."

"Like the time you brought a body to someone's house instead of a funeral home?"

"Hey," Angel protested, "They gave us the wrong address."

"Yet you still knocked on the door and asked the owner of the house to sign for the body."

"How do I know it's not the dude's uncle or something? Some kind of home funeral thing, like during Covid." He followed her into the body-storage room, where she quickly found the correct morgue drawer. Always loving a chance to watch Jennifer move, he hoped she didn't notice him observing her leaning forward and grasping the drawer handle. Her hair was tucked behind one ear, and one strand danced over her forehead. As attracted as he was to her, Angel nevertheless had never come on to her. Not because he was gallant in any way, but because even he recognized something fragile in Jennifer. In spite of her tough talk and take-no-shit bluster, there was a depth there that was so far out of his league he was better off not taking a chance. Besides, there were other outlets for him.

Jennifer slid the drawer open, revealing a slender, zipped-up black body bag with paperwork resting on its abdomen.

"How's the movie star?" Angel asked.

"Still an asshole," she answered.

He helped her slide the body bag onto a gurney. Not that she needed help; Angel knew that she was more adept at handling bodies than him or Otis.

"Where is he?" Angel was still hoping to see him again. Maybe Trevor would like Angel to score something for him. Coke or meth maybe. *Drug Dealer to the Stars,* he thought with a smile.

Jennifer shrugged. "I told him to stay out of my way tonight. He's probably Facetiming any female with a pulse."

As she slid the side rails of the gurney up, Angel noticed her hands were shaking. He looked at her. "You okay?"

She stayed focused on the gurney. "I have no fucking idea." She signed the top page of the paperwork, spun the gurney toward him and walked away.

Angel watched her go, not sure what to think. There were two options to be weighed: go after her and find out what was wrong, taking the chance that he'd maybe have to listen to her talk about her feelings, or get back to the Burger King as soon as possible. Burger King won.

Wheeling the gurney down the hallway, he saw the paperwork on the belly of the corpse slide a little bit over the rubber body bag. Angel slowed down. He looked behind him. No sign of Jennifer.

Stopping the gurney, he picked up the paperwork, and examined the Body Control Card. *Sex: Female. Age: 25.*

The Desecrated

Angel looked around again. *This place is dead.* He chuckled; damn he was funny. How come he wasn't a movie star? Did it have something to do with the Beretta 92 tattooed on his face? Or the expanding spare tire around his middle? Nah, they have makeup and, like, girdles for that shit. He just never got the kind of breaks guys like Trevor Pryce got, that was his problem.

Angel wheeled the gurney into the autopsy room. Without realizing it, he positioned it right over the center drain. After taking one final survey of the room to make sure no one was nearby, he reached toward the body bag and unzipped it down to the feet.

Gently separating the two parts of the bag, he gazed at the naked corpse of a beautiful young woman. To Angel's considerable relief, her eyes were closed. He hated it when their eyes were open; sometimes zipping the bag right back up if they were staring at him. How had she died, he briefly wondered? There didn't seem to be any injuries, or marks on her flawless body. Maybe it was one of those internal things that girls get. He shrugged, having exhausted that line of thinking.

Slipping his iPhone from his back pocket, he swiped opened the camera. Holding the phone vertically, he started snapping pictures. Remembering how someone had made fun of his vertical hold – real photographers held the camera *horizontally,* so it became more like a movie screen, he turned the camera.

As Angel concentrated on photographing the naked corpse, he was completely unaware of the spark of activity on the floor underneath the gurney. In the depths of the drain, where the amulet Ulysses had deposited there dwelled, something started to hum and vibrate.

The strong smell of sulfur filled the room. Angel assumed the rotten-egg smell was from the corpse.

Inside the drain, the onyx Egyptian dog set in the

John Gray

middle of the gold amulet began to pulse. And it seemed to melt, becoming a pool of jet-black, thick liquid.

The oozing fluid flowed off of the amulet, and, defying gravity, traveled up through the grate of the drain cover and across the floor to one of the wheels of the gurney.

The black ooze continued up the gurney and into the body bag near the dead woman's head. Angel was busy photographing down south and didn't see it.

Sliding under the corpse's neck, the black liquid entered her body with a low sucking sound just under her right shoulder blade. The fluid burrowed under her skin and disappeared – another assault on her body that left no mark.

Angel was finished, putting the phone back in his pocket and smiling apologetically at the corpse. Young gorgeous women didn't die all that often, and when one crossed his path he had to memorialize her. The photos would be added to his very private collection. He was not being disrespectful of the dead; quite the opposite, from his point of view.

Zipping the bag closed, he went on his way.

***

Ulysses opened the brown bag. "Plain I hope?"

Jennifer watched him unwrap the foil from the two hot dogs. "I fought the good fight." She watched his eyes light up when he saw that, indeed, his hot dogs were condiment free. Jennifer and Ulysses were sitting in the mausoleum, which, in spite of the warm, wavering candlelight, still looked pretty spooky. The candle threw their flickering shadows against the walls like a film noir movie.

"Why is plain so important?" she asked.

"I don't like disguises," he said while chewing. "I want the essence of the thing."

"Makes sense," Jennifer said. She looked around the

125

mausoleum. They sat on two stone benches, which were opposite each other, extending out from the walls. When he didn't have company, Ulysses slept on the bench Jennifer now occupied. She saw his sleeping bag and blanket roll neatly tucked into a corner. His Sterno stove and jugs of water lined the far wall. Ulysses was nothing if not tidy.

The sound of crickets and frogs filled the night air, which they could hear because the surrounding city streets were quiet tonight. Happy to be here and not at work, she smiled at the thought that her only refuge from a morgue was a cemetery. "How are your feet?" she asked.

"Better," he answered, mouth full. Ulysses did not like to speak while eating. It interfered with his savoring of the food.

While he ate, Jennifer turned and looked at the large, yellowed poster board that covered the opposite wall of the mausoleum. The board was crammed with an odd assortment of mixed media that was taped, pinned, and fastened to the board with twist ties. There were children's key rings, some with whistles, others with little penlights; discarded, cracked iPhone cases, some with beads; and cartoon character stickers, including Sponge Bob and Dora The Explorer.

"You added some things," Jennifer observed.

"She loved stickers. She used to put them everywhere. Even on my things. Found a bunch of them on the subway."

Jennifer saw a batch of newspaper articles tacked to the bottom of the board. She'd never noticed them before, but when she leaned over to read one, Ulysses spoke, his mouth full. "Those are private."

"Sorry," she said, immediately moving away.

Ulysses nodded, finishing the first hot dog.

He had been searching for his missing daughter for years. Jennifer didn't know all the details; sometimes Ulysses hinted at certain things, but she tried not to push.

Her guess was that the poor girl was never coming back. Ulysses had faith, though, and in spite of a nervous breakdown after her disappearance, or perhaps because of it, he wasn't going to rest until he found her. It seemed to Jennifer that he had limited his search to the immediate area, however, for she had not known him to wander beyond it.

"I saw Death the other night," he said.

She watched him as he chewed thoughtfully. "*The* Death?"

He nodded.

Ulysses could seem so lucid, she thought, then veer so seamlessly into bizarro world.

"Where?" she asked.

"Near here. He was big. And scary. I think he wants to stop me from looking for her."

She decided to just go with it. "How come?"

Ulysses shrugged. "Maybe he wants me to think he has her. But I know he doesn't. I can feel her. She's alive."

Jennifer didn't know how to respond. They sat in silence for a moment.

Ulysses turned to her with a smile. "I know you think I'm nuts," he said, reading her mind.

"No! No, I don't. It's just—"

"I've been called crazy enough times by some very smart people to know it's probably true."

She leaned toward him. "If you're really trying to find your daughter, there's got to be a better way."

"She's near here. I know it. I can feel it. Just a matter of time."

"She's not a little girl anymore, you know that, right?"

He nodded. "She was twelve the last time I saw her. She's about your age now. She may not even recognize me."

Jennifer smiled sadly, looking at his full beard and shaggy hair under a ratty Tilly rain hat pulled low over his ears. He must have harvested it from some garbage can. Not even his mother would recognize him. "But you'll know her, right?"

Ulysses nodded again as he bit into hot dog number two.

She thought she might just push a bit and see what happened. "There are places that can help you, you know. Help you get better."

Ulysses smiled. Waited to swallow. "Yeah. My wife put me in one." He looked away. "How do you do that to someone you're supposed to love?"

It was Jennifer's turn to look away. She listened to the wind in the trees. The bent branches scraped against the stone of the mausoleum.

"You don't," she answered quietly.

Ulysses studied her. "Why did you leave early the other night?"

She looked at him, startled. She hadn't thought about the fact that Ulysses could easily monitor the comings and goings at the morgue. "I wasn't feeling well," she answered truthfully.

"And now?"

"Better. I guess.

He didn't take his eyes from her. She found it difficult to meet his gaze. "You're not," he said simply. "What's wrong?"

Looking at him, his open face, his kind eyes, she felt her own eyes fill. She found the idea that someone was concerned for her suddenly heartbreaking. Smiling to ward off the tears, she asked "What's your stance on ghosts?"

He didn't blink. "What kind of ghosts?"

"What are my options?" she asked, laughing nervously.

"The kind that scare you, or the kind that haunt you?"

"Maybe both."

Ulysses suddenly grinned, flashing his yellowed teeth.

"Now who's crazy?"

She smiled.

He got to his feet with surprising ease. "Being crazy has its charms, I'm not gonna lie." Picking up the paper plates and the tin foil, he put them in a burlap bag near one of the benches. Jennifer assumed that was his version of recycling.

"You seeing things?" he asked. "Things you shouldn't be?"

Looking at him, she wasn't sure what to say. She thought back to Miss Nadja. *"You're a sensitive."* Maybe so, but the fact was that the manifestations that had tortured her and her father had gradually lessened as her teen years went by. She'd gotten involved with school, started a love affair with science, and loved hanging with boys. There were still little reminders every now and then. She'd have an argument with her dad or a boyfriend, and nearby streetlights would blow out, or windows rattled. But by the time she had started her short-lived stint in college, she'd stopped experiencing these incidents altogether. Was she now dipping a toe into supernatural waters so that she could avoid the likely real reason for what she'd been seeing? Her inner debate became moot when Ulysses leaned toward her.

"Doc," he said. "It's the Movie Asshole."

"What?"

Ulysses was serious. "He's pissing off the dead."

Jennifer laughed out loud. "Well, he's definitely pissing off the living, that's for sure."

He came even closer. There were hot dog bun crumbs in his beard. "Don't worry about it," he whispered. "*I got you protected.*"

"I don't feel protected," she said, searching his eyes. "I feel insane."

They looked at each other; Ulysses searching for something to say and Jennifer feeling she said too much. Getting up quickly, she checked her watch. "Gotta go. Who knows what Trevor's up to in there."

Ulysses turned away, frustrated that he couldn't help. "Thanks for the dogs."

Jennifer smiled and pointed down to the bench she was just sitting on. "That's for you."

Ulysses followed her gaze to the large yellow box on the bench that her body had been blocking. Before he could ask her anything, she was gone.

Sitting on the bench, he opened the box, and feasted his eyes on a pair of brand new Helly-Hansen winter boots. *Fleece lined.* Yellow and black laces. Beautiful brown leather.

The tears that he felt were so close all night finally came.

NINE

The black coroner's van sped along Third Avenue in Brooklyn, barreling toward Bay Ridge. Angel was at the wheel, gunning the engine to blow past another yellow light. Most of the transporting Angel and Otis did for the morgue was in and around Brooklyn, so his knowledge of the streets was thorough. He always liked going to Bay Ridge; it was a mostly-white neighborhood, but still, there were lots of hot ladies always going in and out of the bars, especially now with the vaccine in place. That's why Angel liked science.

Thinking about Otis, he wondered why that crazy dude didn't seem to like him. Angel never made fun of him for the stupid way he imitated gangbangers, although it was really kind of hilarious. Otis' fake gang persona would probably fool the people in Bay Ridge, but Angel knew that Otis would never have any real street cred. Angel, on the other hand, was a black belt in Aikido, and he never put that shit in Otis' face. He didn't have to. Actually, Angel rarely brought up his martial arts studies, mostly because he'd never even achieved a yellow belt, never mind a black one. Receiving a discount coupon in the mail, Angel signed up for a few classes, imagining himself as a warrior, able to dispatch muggers and thieves with a dizzying flurry of moves. Saving and protecting girls who had previously never even noticed him, only to discover that mastering Aikido took an enormous amount of work. It would probably take years, and Angel only liked things that promised instant results. Why not just *say* he was a black belt; the likelihood of anyone challenging him was small. Angel smiled at the thought, pleased with his ability to pivot.

Driving through the little Brooklyn neighborhood, Angel appreciated the really big houses he passed down on Shore Road. These stately homes overlooked The Narrows and the sparkling Verrazano Bridge. People with money lived there. When the riches he dreamed of finally arrived, he would definitely live there too, or at least get a house there. Angel had just turned thirty and felt a bit more urgency for the getting-rich part to begin. Once again, his thoughts turned to Trevor Pryce. That guy was filthy fucking rich and was probably only twenty-five or six. A guy like that probably didn't even know what to do with his money. Angel would know how to spend it. He would know how to treat people right.

He'd get a house that had all those Roman things around it – what do you call them? Round things? Pillars! That's right. There'd be nice shiny pillars all around his house. Inside too. Let Trevor Pryce see some of that shit and get all envious. It was just a question of how. *How* was he going to get rich? There were lots of ways – check out all the rich people in the world, and most of them were assholes.

He would really need to start putting some thought into that.

But then his Spotify started playing "Mi Gente" by J Balvin, and Angel's brain immediately emptied as he cranked up the volume and screamed the song at the top of his lungs.

He had listened to that song a million times, but had never before heard that high-pitched sound before – what was that? He stopped singing to listen. It was like . . . crying. Like a baby crying. Listening harder, he realized the sound wasn't coming from the song at all.

It was coming from behind him.

Angel lowered the volume. It was quiet for a moment; then the crying started again. Definitely like a baby crying, but even higher pitched. The hair on his neck rose as he remembered the only thing back there was that hot-girl corpse he was transporting.

There was that horrible, rotten-egg smell again.

And the screaming started.

He whipped his head around and stared into the back of the van.

The screaming got even louder, and he understood why – because he was screaming too. Eyes wide, mouth gaping, his screams came loud and sudden, uncontrollable, like a panting animal.

He screamed because the beautiful young cadaver was sitting up in the back of the van. The body bag was unzipped down to her waist. Angel was not focused on her breasts this time, but rather her obscenely distended, naked belly. Her naval protruded, as if she had somehow gotten pregnant in the fifteen minutes they had been driving.

The tortured, evil, baby scream came from that ballooning belly.

The dead woman's hair was standing on end, and her red-rimmed eyes were open and locked onto his face. Her mouth opened wide; then even wider, and finally so wide that Angel heard a bone crack – he thought her jaw might just break off.

Instead, she started screaming as well. A hoarse, guttural wail.

The inside of the van had become a scene from Dante. Two people and one unknown entity screaming in dissonant unison. Angel tore at his seatbelt, desperate to get out of the hell wagon.

With all this going on, it had been some time since Angel had assessed the traffic situation outside his windshield. When he glanced out it was obvious the van had strayed into the wrong lane, and a city bus was heading directly for him. Desperately twisting the steering wheel to the left, he barely missed the honking bus.

That was the least of his problems, though, for when he squinted into the rear-view mirror, he saw the true horror unfolding:

The corpse's blue-veined belly was pulsing and throbbing. Getting bigger. The muffled cries from within it, separate from the corpse's wailing, became deeper and angrier. *Something inside wanted out.*

Angel's eyes stayed glued to the mirror as he watched the dead body's arm reach shakily for the back-seat seatbelt. She lifted the male end of the buckle—

And *plunged it into her belly.*

The sound was horrific – like a watermelon being gouged. Angel's vocal cords had failed him, and, with his mouth still open but nothing coming out, he watched in mute horror. The corpse ripped the inserted buckle across her stomach, in a ghastly, improvised C-section.

Cars and taxicabs were spinning out of control trying to avoid the black van careening down Third Avenue. Angel's eyes remained glued to the rear-view mirror, as he stared at the gaping hole that the seatbelt buckle had opened across the dead woman's abdomen. What he saw next almost made his heart stop.

Shiny black tendrils, at least four of them, emerged, twitching and shaking from the body.

They raised themselves above the open wound, and for some reason Angel had a crystal-clear thought. They were sniffing. They were smelling *him*.

What happened next was too fast for Angel to understand. A solid, wet mass violently tore out of the body cavity. There was a flash of sharp yellow teeth, and at least four legs of some kind. Were there two pairs of eyes? Angel would never know because he finally found the strength to clamp his own eyes shut.

The creature slammed into him from behind with astonishing force, and Angel violently expelled his last breath as his chest was crushed against the steering wheel. Although dying rapidly, he was still conscious as the creature, its fur soaked with blood and bodily fluids, coiled itself around him.

In his last seconds, Angel's eyes popped open again involuntarily. In the rear-view mirror he saw flashes of himself being consumed. He was torn apart in a flurry of blood, cracking bones, and those fucking fangs tearing his throat out.

His foot involuntarily slammed down on the gas pedal.

The van roared through a red light. In and out of lanes. A motorcyclist wiped out over parked cars trying to get out of the way. The van mounted a curb. A mailbox and garbage can flew in opposite directions like toys as the out-of-control vehicle tore through them.

At the end of the block, the black van slammed into a streetlight. It folded around it like a piece of cardboard and corkscrewed back into the street, bounced off of a parked car, and flipped completely over onto its roof.

The wrecked van slid across the intersection, upside

down, the sound of groaning metal almost deafening as sparks ignited between the blacktop and the roof of the van. The whole surreal, spinning, upside-down mess finally came to rest against the opposite curb.

An eerie hush settled over the street, and even though all that could be heard outside the van were the lazily spinning tires, the attack continued inside. An explosion of blood suddenly bloomed across the spider-web-cracked van windows, and flying body parts ricocheted around the cabin.

A loud, hollow "pop" sounded as the front windshield detonated, and something blasted through it and shot across the street.

Angel's ankle and most of his left foot came to rest against a restaurant door. The remaining toes, including his pinky toe adorned with a toe ring, were still twitching.

***

After her dinner with Ulysses, Jennifer got back to the morgue to find it quiet. She had barely seen Trevor that night, which was fine with her. The more he made himself scarce, the happier it made her. Turning the corner to go into the office, she stopped dead and took in a sharp breath.

Standing in the office was strange man she had never seen before. He was dressed in some kind of brown uniform, his hand resting on a silver hand-truck. When the stranger turned and saw her, he screamed with fright, which made Jennifer jump again.

"You scared *the shit* out of me!" he yelled.

"What are you doing here!" she demanded.

"Delivery," he answered, trying to catch his breath, pointing to the two large cardboard boxes on the hand truck. "Nobody was here. I'm guessing none of the stiffs can sign for it." Tall and skinny, he had a full head of red hair. His UPS uniform hung on his thin frame. He held out a piece of paper to her. In spite of his wisecrack about stiffs, she saw his hand was shaking as she signed the receipt.

Wheeling his hand-truck out, he glanced at her over his shoulder. "You couldn't pay me to do your job."

"Wow, you mean someone would pay me to be here? I only do this because I love it so much," she retorted, but wasn't sure if he even heard her as he hurried down the hall and out the door. *Another genius heard from,* she thought, as she bent down and looked at the two cartons. The was no label or any identifying marks on the boxes themselves, but when she looked at the shipping bill taped to the top, she saw the contents listed as *Cast-Iron Eyehooks.*

Eyehooks? She lifted a corner of one of the boxes; it was heavy. What the hell does the morgue need with big hooks? Were they going to start hanging bodies meat-locker style?

The familiar church bells stole her attention, and she pulled out her phone, which was flashing the word "fish." Retrieving the container of fish food from Clover's desk, she approached the tank. It took her a couple of minutes to locate the cleverly hidden door at the top of the hi-tech tank through which she could tap the food.

As she watched the small army of overpriced tropical fish swim happily toward the little flakes that were snowing down on them, she thought about her discussion with Ulysses. What did he mean by *"I got you protected"*? It had escaped her then, but she had the feeling he knew something she didn't. Ulysses was the only person in the world she would broach the subject of the supernatural with. His response only made her more certain that her problem, like his, lay within her brain, not in the world of the paranormal. Warming at the thought of Ulysses wearing his new boots, she hoped they would make his days a little more bearable.

Thoughts of Ulysses vanished when her eyes fell upon Ziti. Instead of going after the morsels of food, the little Clownfish was suspended in the middle of the tank, his face right at the glass. He seemed to be staring intently at something.

Jennifer watched him. Was he dead? No. His tiny tail gently swayed back and forth, his gills billowed, and his little "o" mouth sucked intently. An image of her father came to her, his mouth closed around the ventilator tube, his eyes wide and red.

She pushed that thought away as Ziti started to move back and forth, his eyes never turning away from whatever it was he was looking at. Jennifer felt a chill when she saw that Ziti was doing exactly the same kind of movement from when Clover was trying to train him to follow her finger. Except that now it seemed to be following a finger only it saw.

Jennifer watched in silence as the fish gracefully moved to and fro, its bulbous eyes fixed on something behind her. She turned and tried to follow its gaze but saw nothing except the dimly lit hallway through the office window. When she turned back to the aquarium, Ziti was swimming with his fellow fish, competing for the last few specks of dinner, as if he had never been at the glass. She asked herself the question she had been asking a lot lately: *Did I really see that?* Shaking it off, her bladder pinched. She needed to pee.

On her way to the ladies room, she checked the prep room. No Trevor. Continuing down the hall, she took a look into the body-storage room. No Trevor. He had to be in the autopsy room, doing what, she had no idea, but the ladies room came before the autopsy room, so she'd have to wait to find out.

In the badly lit bathroom, she examined herself in the cracked mirror. Like everything else in this aging building, the rest rooms were outdated: cold, yellowed tile, old sinks with fractured enamel and rusty faucets. She studied her face, which wasn't even helped by the kindness of the fogged glass of the mirror. Her eyes were bloodshot. She thought there were thin lines appearing around her eyes, and her cheeks seemed a little sunken. Was she losing weight? She knew her diet was awful, but was she at least eating enough crap to maintain her weight?

Entering the tight stall, she had to turn all the way around in order to close the door, which she only closed halfway because her of claustrophobia. She yanked down her jeans and panties and sat, cellphone in hand.

Her screen announced new Instagram photos from people she followed. Opening the app, she saw pictures of a great-looking bunch of people at an outdoor café in a park. Jennifer knew the park and knew that café. Her friends sat around a festive table, mimosas in hand. That was the place with the famous blueberry pancakes. Looking at their faces, their plates, and the happy people at all the other tables around them, it felt like a snapshot from another lifetime. Or someone else's lifetime – could Jennifer remember being that free? That unencumbered?

She saw her ex-boyfriend Jim sitting next to Chelsea and Hope. Was he seeing one of them? She knew that Chelsea had always seemed to try to get near him. *Who cares,* she thought. Although she did feel a pang of nostalgia for the days when she worried about things like another girl moving in on her guy.

The ladies room door creaked open. Her head snapped up from her phone. She was the only "lady" in the building – who the fuck was coming in?

"Who's there?" she yelled, the sound of her own frightened voice surprising her.

There was no response. Instead, there was just the sound of footsteps.

Slow, *wet* footsteps. With something being trailed along. She heard wheels rattling on the cracked tiled floor.

Jennifer craned her neck to look out past the half-open stall door. She could only see the mirror above the sinks.

And in the fogged reflection was the blurry image of someone walking toward the stalls.

Then the breathing started.

The mechanical, forced breathing that filled her with dread. It grew louder and louder until it was echoing off of the damp walls. She slammed the stall door closed. Claustrophobia was not her problem now. She leaned over as far as she could to try to see under the stall door.

Clapping her hand over her mouth, she saw the two bare feet walking to the stall.

Trailing behind the feet was some kind of a machine on wheels.

She knew what the machine was.

The feet were veiny. The nails cracked. There were black lividity marks in stark contrast to the pale white skin.

They were the feet and legs of a dead man.

They were the legs of her father. He was coming to her stall with jerky mismatched movements, the feet sometimes pointing in different directions.

Jennifer stood and yanked her jeans up with shaking hands. The soggy footsteps were getting closer. Slow, limping, but unrelenting.

She pressed her hands against the stall door, determined to keep it closed. The footsteps stopped. She tried to listen over the sound of her wildly beating heart. Had he just stopped right in front of her stall?

She moved so she could see past her extended arms and with a grunt lowered her head as far as she could to see under the door. She couldn't see much, but what she saw made her scalp ripple with static electricity.

The swollen, dead toes of the feet were lined up with the stall door. Facing it. Waiting.

Jennifer stood in the cramped space, frozen. Her arms hurt from the pressure she was exerting on the stall door. The silence grew deafening; she stared at the floor until the stained tile swam.

Bang bang bang! Jennifer jumped a full foot when the pounding started, as if someone were banging on the stall door with a bowling ball. She fought hard to keep the door in place, but it was bending, knocking her back with every blow.

She pressed her entire body against the door, her feet pressed against the toilet to wedge herself against the savage pounding.

A dent was forming in the door.

Her face was near the narrow crack where the door met the stall. She saw something through the crack. She closed one eye and focused.

In the worn glass of the mirror across from her was the reflection of her father's back, in front of her stall, in a hospital gown, the ventilator beside him, tubes sprouting from it and into his mouth.

Jennifer jumped when his face suddenly filled the crack of the open stall door. His head was inches from her on the other side. There was a blur of movement as he pounded with a heavy fist.

The sound of the air being forced in and out of his lungs had become deafening. His wild eyes stared at her, shot through with red veins, desperate. The blue tube snaked into his mouth; the lips trying to form words around it; spittle flying.

Just when she thought her heart couldn't beat any faster, the pounding stopped, and her father moved his eye closer to the narrow crack. His gaze locked onto hers. He was trying to say something, his voice husky and cracked, as if he were learning to speak all over again.

She started to cry. She was exhausted. Her body ached from the tension. She rested her forehead on the stall door. "Please, Dad. Please. Please stop this."

Silence. Minutes passed. Jennifer let her hands fall away from the stall door. Somewhere, water was dripping.

The footsteps moved away. She began to breathe again when she heard the restroom door open and close.

Waiting for what seemed like a very long time, she remained frozen. After several minutes had passed and there were no more sounds, she opened the stall door a crack. Peeking through the opening, she saw no one was there, although she also saw her own indistinct reflection in the mirror. Even in the clouded glass she looked terrified.

She left the stall, raced to the door, and got the hell out of there.

Jennifer ran through the streets of downtown Brooklyn. The crisp autumn air felt good against her skin and her tears dried. The leaves crunched under her feet, and the breeze shook the trees above her. She thought she smelled wood burning – someone was using their fireplace. Someone was having a normal evening. Maybe a romantic evening. Jennifer kept running. She didn't give a shit about the morgue. Let Trevor handle things.

***

She still heard the ventilator breathing its alien, synthesized breaths. That sound had become the center of her life in the last months of her father's. After his suicide attempt, the EMTs had taken him to Elmhurst Hospital in Queens. Barely conscious, he couldn't speak because of the damage to his throat. Jennifer had to sort out his insurance, which was a mess – no one knew yet how long he'd have to stay.

Because the universe had such an amazing sense of humor, her dad was infected with Covid-19 while hospitalized. Refusing to take the vaccine when it was first introduced, he claimed it was a plot by the government to track him. As his mind failed, he'd stopped believing in science, in the rational. Jennifer had not yet understood that his paranoia was fueled by a brain tumor, not politics.

His lungs deteriorated fast, and he had to be put on a ventilator, which was the beginning of the end. Jennifer still felt those long days and nights by his bedside; she still smelled the antiseptic and sanitizers and would never forget the suffocating sound of the artificial breathing. She'd sit there with her head in her hands, fighting the urge to just get up and run. She had found her own breathing would sync up with the mechanical breaths, and it made her feel like she was smothering. Even later, whenever she heard that sinister-sounding machine, she had to take a deep breath in to steady herself. It had given her father air, but it felt like it was stealing hers.

Within days his kidneys had failed, and the doctors told her to be prepared. "Time is very short now," one of them said to her, in what struck her as a novelistic turn of phrase. She watched her dad wrestle with his tortured sleep, his tortured breathing, and she wished his suffering would go away.

One horrifying night, he opened his eyes and raised his hands to his mouth. Jennifer looked up from her book, and before she could register what was happening, he was pulling the respirator tube from his throat. Jumping to her feet, she shouted, tried to grab his arms, but her dad was still surprisingly strong. She found herself momentarily mesmerized by the sheer *length* of the tube as he tugged it out of his throat. How the hell could something that long go down anybody's esophagus?

When the tube was all the way out, he glared at her, a bridge of thick saliva still connecting the hissing respirator to his red, wet lips.

"You did this to me," he croaked at her, his voice oddly distant and abrasive. "I didn't want to come here. You promised I'd never be here."

She had nothing to offer in response.

The Desecrated

Rick Shelby, carpenter, single father, maker of pizza bagels, died later that night. He had the dubious distinction of being the last patient at Elmhurst Hospital to die of Covid-19.

Jennifer knelt by the body of her father. Stroking his slack face, she thought he looked relaxed, and for the first time in a long time, at peace. His eyes were open, gazing upward, somewhere over her head.

Gently reaching for his face, she closed his eyes with her thumbs. Time to sleep. Time to rest.

***

Jennifer couldn't run anymore; her lungs were about to burst. Slowing to a trot and then to a fast walk, she looked around. The streets were familiar. Had she really run that far? Looking up at the street sign, she saw the dry cleaners on the corner. She had no recollection of making a decision to come here. It was completely unconscious. Or was it?

She checked her watch (a thin Mondaine given to her by her father for her eighteenth birthday, bought on an installment plan). It was 3:30 AM. The windows above the dry cleaner were dark, but she was not going to turn back. Approaching the dented door, she rang the bell. And kept ringing. Finally, she saw the familiar face at the window above the store. It had been six years, and she had hardly changed.

"Who are you and what the *fuck* do you want at this hour?" Miss Nadja inquired.

***

Miss Nadja wrapped her red robe tightly around her as she moved around the cluttered kitchen making tea. She looked surprisingly young without makeup, Jennifer thought. The sweet, hot smell of cinnamon tea filled the room.

Miss Nadja's mysterious Russian accent seemed to have gotten thicker.

"Yes, I remember you. Hard to forget hurricane you make in my living room."

"Sorry about that. And sorry I woke you."

"Me too. I have to open store in two hours."

"What store?"

"Dry cleaners downstairs."

"You work at the dry cleaners?"

"I own dry cleaners." She waved her hand at her modest surroundings. "You think I live in this splendor from telling fortunes alone?"

"I'll pay."

"No kidding. And it's extra for dead of night."

"Whatever."

"You want a coupon?"

"For a psychic reading?"

"For blouses and pantsuits."

"I'm good."

As Miss Nadja poured the tea, she looked at Jennifer. "You grow up nice."

"That's debatable."

Miss Nadja put the teakettle back on the stove and sat at the small table across from Jennifer. "So, what, you're making more hurricanes?"

Jennifer gave her a brief synopsis of her life since they last saw each other, and what she was now experiencing in her home and at work.

"Wow. Trevor Pryce. Hot guy. I wouldn't mind folding his underwear."

"Be that as it may. Can you tell me if . . ." Jennifer hesitated to say it. She wasn't somebody who asked questions like this. She lowered her voice. "Do you see my father around me? Do you know if he's . . . here somewhere?"

145

Miss Nadja gazed at her over the edge of her teacup. "You feel him near?"

"I think so." Jennifer gestured toward the living room. "Should we go inside and do the—"

Miss Nadja waived her off. "Please. Trance is just show business. What people expect. I don't need it."

Jennifer regretted coming. *What the hell had she been thinking?*

Miss Nadja crossed her legs, sat back and spoke. "Your father cannot rest. There is pain. He's stuck in that place."

"What place?"

"The cold place. There are many others with him. He doesn't want to be there."

The morgue? Her mind raced. The thought of her father suffering made her heart drop. "Why would he be stuck there? My dad had nothing to do with the morgue. When he died, he was picked up and taken to a funeral home."

Miss Nadja looked blankly at Jennifer.

Was she waiting for an answer, or making one up? Jennifer stood. "Look, I'm sorry, I just don't know if I believe any of this. No offense, but everything you've said is kind of general. Any smart person could piece it together from what I've told you."

"No offense taken, darling. You came to me. And you pay whether you believe me or not. And since it's four in the morning, I'll tell you something. Sometimes I know what my client want to hear, and I go for it – put sprinkles on top and make it nice, you know? Everybody happy. You're not asking for happy, you're asking for truth, so I'm giving it to you. But if you believe I am making all this up, maybe that means you are making up these things that happen to you? Maybe you are just . . . crazy?"

Jennifer looked at her. Sat back down. "Am I? Crazy?"

Miss Nadja laughed. "Now you want me to be doctor too? We are all crazy, darling. It's matter of degree."

Jennifer thought of Ulysses.

Miss Nadja leaned toward her. "These things, what's happening to you – they don't come from brain. They come from the dead."

"So what do I do?"

She shrugged. "I told you all those years ago, you're more powerful than you know. The dead are trying to tell you something. Stop fighting it and listen."

They looked at each other. The tea had gone cold. Jennifer smiled. "Still pretty general stuff."

Miss Nadja got up and took the cups to the sink. "And yet, you're going to pay me sixty dollars." Doolaarz.

Pulling the cash from her pocket, Jennifer counted out three twenties, leaving them on the table. She glanced at Miss Nadja and walked to the door.

Miss Nadja watched her go. "One more thing," she called out just as Jennifer got to the door.

Jennifer turned back to her.

"He wants you to know he's sorry for what he said at the hospital. He understands you had no choice."

***

Her face wet with tears, Jennifer hurried back to the morgue, worried about what Trevor might be up to unsupervised. She felt somehow lighter as she walked. Maybe Miss Nadja wasn't a total fraud. If her parting shot was true, it would be a huge weight off of Jennifer's shoulders. Maybe there was an even more important takeaway:

"Stop fighting it and listen."

Making it back to the morgue, she was relieved that the fans and the press were nowhere to be seen at that hour. She wondered if Ulysses saw her, and she glanced toward the cemetery, but it was dark and quiet.

Inside the morgue, she was struck by the silence. Just the steady hum of refrigeration, and the buzz of the fluorescents. She passed Clover's office; empty except for the lazily moving fish. She looked up and down the hallway.

"Trevor?"

Nothing. Maybe he had just up and left. She actually hoped for that; she didn't feel like dealing with him and would love to pass the last few hours of her shift by herself. The landline rang in Clover's office as she entered.

"Kings County Morgue," she answered.

"Yo, where Angel at?"

Jennifer recognized the unmistakably phony street jargon of Otis. "Isn't he with you?"

"Nah. I'm waitin' here at Burger King, and he never came back."

"Don't you mean you're waiting at the all-night dentist?" Jennifer asked, rolling her eyes.

Otis hesitated. "Oh yeah, whatever. Anyway, where he at?"

"I don't know where he at, Otis. I sent him to a funeral home in Bay Ridge with a body transfer a few hours ago. Did you try his cell?"

Otis snorted. "I'm not stupid, yo."

"Uh huh," Jennifer responded.

"Well he left me here with no ride. What am I supposed to do?"

"Call your parents?"

"Yo, why you gotta be dissin' me like that?"

Jennifer heard a wispy sound and caught a blur of movement out of the corner of her eye. She turned in time to see what appeared to be the rail-thin figure of a woman turning a corner down the hallway. Some kind of white fluttery material trailed behind her as she ran. Jennifer was too exhausted to be afraid – instead her vision turned red with rage. She would not be fucked with like that. Hanging up on Otis, she raced out into the hallway after the apparition.

The corridor was empty. When Jennifer got closer to the prep room, she slowed, hearing sounds, Faint whispered voices. A cry of pain. Picking up her pace again, she turned into the autopsy room – and froze in place.

There had been a cry, but it was not pain-related. Trevor was lying on a slab, while a mostly naked young woman rode him. She was wearing Trevor's white lab coat and nothing else. Jennifer recognized her as the same woman who'd written her number on her breasts, and who was there the other night for Trevor's "Master Class."

Jennifer was rooted in the doorway, having no idea what to do. Anger quickly replaced surprise; that was a new low, even for Trevor. She wanted to turn and get the hell out of there. But she didn't.

Instead, her eyes slid over Trevor's ripped chest as the woman's long, blond hair swept back and forth across it. She watched the muscles move under his taut skin as he reached for her.

His head turned to Jennifer. Seeing her, his eyes went wide, and he jumped up, cracking his forehead against the blond woman's cheek. "Owww," she complained in a sing-songy whine, holding her face. Trevor looked at Jennifer, stricken, clearly experiencing a feeling he wasn't used to – embarrassment.

Disgusted with him, Jennifer finally turned and got the hell out of there.

On her way out, she passed the large hole in the wall she'd made when flinging the cranial drill at Trevor. If she hadn't been so furious, she might have heard the faint sounds coming from the airshaft that hole revealed.

She might have heard the muffled voices coming from somewhere far below.

The Desecrated

"Clover gave you a second chance. I gave you a second chance. You just don't give a shit about anyone, do you?"

"Death turns her on. Who am I to deny her?" Trevor protested.

They were in the autopsy room an hour later. Jennifer had spied the woman leaving, still wearing Trevor's lab coat. She'd thrown him a sponge and a spray bottle of disinfectant and made him swab the slab as she paced angrily.

"I really don't understand what the big deal is," Trevor continued.

"It's disrespectful to the dead, obviously. And I could be fired! I know that means nothing to you, but my job actually matters to me."

Trevor gave her the grin. "Jealous much?"

She'd never wanted to punch a human being as badly as she wanted to punch Trevor's arrogant face in that moment. "Are you serious? Of what?"

"Of young Miss Meadow, of course." Trevor sprayed some more disinfectant on the table.

"Yeah," Jennifer snorted, "Doing it on a morgue slab. Now that's what I call romance. Although I am impressed you know her name."

"You really think I'm some oversexed cretin don't you?"

"What's her last name?"

Trevor blinked. "Smith."

Jennifer rolled her eyes. "You do realize that these bimbos are only interested in you because they think you're the same guy on the movie screen, right?"

"Realize it? I count on it!"

"That's disgusting."

"Hey, if you've got it, flaunt it."

"Yeah. Well, not everyone can sail through life just on their looks."

"Oh come on! Look who's talking! You're stunning! Are you going to tell me you're not aware of the effect you have on men?"

Jennifer's face got hot. "I'm aware that people judge me for how I look. Who I am doesn't really matter."

"Exactly! That's been a lifesaver for me!"

"Well it's been one fucking big obstacle for me. You don't know what it's like to be treated like a piece of meat who can't possibly have a brain."

"Don't I?"

"At least you get paid millions of dollars for it."

"Good point."

Noticing something behind him, on the other side of the room, Jennifer frowned. "Where are the specimen jars?"

"What?" Trevor asked.

Jennifer walked over to a rolling cart in the corner of the room that had previously been home to rows of empty specimen jars. The cart had had three trays and a white cloth covering the top, where the jars rested.

It was completely empty.

"You were supposed to inventory them and stock them in the supply closet."

"Ah. Yes. Hadn't quite gotten to that yet."

She turned and glared at him. "Where are they?"

"No idea."

"Do not fuck with me right now, Trevor."

"Okay. I stole them. Very handy for cocktail hour."

Staring at him, the anger rushed back. She turned and walked away. "You're done. This time I mean it."

"That was a joke!" Trevor ran in front of her and stopped her before she could get to the doorway. "Look, look, look. If you kick me out, I go to jail." There was real fear in his eyes. She would not let herself be manipulated by it.

"And you've known that since day one. Hasn't stopped

you from being an asshole." She pushed past him.

"You're not completely without sin yourself, you know."

"True. But I accept the consequences. Sorry to use a word you're not familiar with," she said over her shoulder.

"You sound like my mother. And I was talking about your homeless mate."

She turned.

Looking sheepish, he came closer. "After all, you've let a derelict into this facility and given him free medical treatment. Let him use the bathroom and wander around. If someone found out about that . . ." he shrugged.

"You are such a shit," was all she could summon.

"Now you really sound like my mother," Trevor grinned.

Her fists clenched, she quickly tried to process how Clover would react to her hosting Ulysses. She had done it many times over the past months without her knowing. She might be able to make her okay with it but didn't know if it was worth taking a chance on.

"Shall we call it a draw?" asked Trevor.

"Don't call him a derelict. He has a name. Ulysses."

"Was Ulysses your dinner date the other night? A little dumpster diving at the local bistro? Now that's what I call romance!"

"Ulysses has a purpose, which is more than I can say for you."

"Really? What is it? Seeing how long socks can go unwashed?"

"He's searching for his daughter."

"Ah. Real or imagined?"

Jennifer hesitated. "Undetermined," she answered, knowing she sometimes wondered about that herself.

"I know where I'd put my money."

"Look, you should've been doing the paperwork I told you to do instead of fucking someone who probably has algebra homework."

Trevor turned and yanked a clipboard off of a hook on the wall behind Jennifer, pressing it into her arms. "You mean this paperwork?"

Jennifer took hold of the clipboard. Looked at the intake forms she had told him to reconcile with the death certificates. His handwriting was neat, and every space appeared to be filled in.

"Amazing what one can accomplish during a reverse cowgirl," Trevor observed cheerfully.

Grimacing, Jennifer gingerly took the paperwork off of the clipboard with two fingers. "I'll be checking these," she promised.

"I should hope so, because they're riddled with errors."

She looked at him. He pointed to the forms. "The death certificates don't match the intake forms."

She paged through the paperwork. "No. You must have read them wrong."

"Did I?" he asked, with the grin she was growing to despise.

***

In the body-storage room, Jennifer slid out the morgue tray holding Why Me. She spread the paperwork over the corpse's belly.

Trevor watched over her shoulder. The buzzing of the overhead lights seemed louder than ever. "Right there." He pointed. "This guy's obviously in his sixties; the death certificate lists him as forty-five. Cause of death on the *intake* form is 'coronary artery disease.' The death *certificate* says, 'injuries sustained from an accidental fall.' "

Jennifer studied the forms. "I don't understand this. We did that intake together."

"And I'm still tingling. But here's another." He handed her more paperwork. "Cause of death on this intake form is 'lymphoma,' the certificate says, 'automobile accident.' And the age is changed from seventy-two to fifty-one. There are four others who were made younger on the death certificate than they were on the intake form. And their causes of death were changed from illnesses to accidents."

Jennifer read through the other forms. This was a serious error. The intake form was just for use in-house, but the death certificate was official and would travel with the body from here on out.

"Whose handwriting is it on the death certificates?" Trevor asked.

Jennifer studied it again. She recognized the scrawl.

"Ersen."

TEN

The old woman stood in the middle of a burning building. Even at her age, her hair was still dark, with a wide silver streak running through it. Her eyebrows were black. She was calm, seemingly oblivious to the raging fire just inches from her face.

She started to weep softly.

Tears rolled down her face. Sobbing, shoulders shaking, her eyes beseeching, wanting to understand. He heard her voice, close, in his ear, even though her lips weren't moving. "Do you know what they do to us here?"

A buzzing sound creeped in over the noise of burning wood and collapsing walls. The buzzing became louder, soon overwhelming the sounds of the fire and the old woman's sobs.

Marty rolled over and turned a light on. Squinting, he searched for the buzzing cell phone. Dreams of his mother didn't come too often, but when they did, they always involved flame. He Googled it once – apparently fire can represent transformation. Something no longer in its original form. Another useless fact filed away in his brain.

Finally finding the phone, he squinted at the caller ID. It was Lt. Bishop. *Shit.* He looked at the time – 5:10 AM. Swiping open the call, he glanced quickly at the open urn on his dresser, the lid lying beside it, as if to make sure his mother was still there. He kept the urn open as per his mother's final instructions.

"What is it, Bill?"

"That's Lieutenant Bill to you. Rise and shine. You're needed."

"It's my night off."

"Suspicious death. Very dramatic. You're gonna love this one."

"Let me love it from afar."

"Think of the OT."

"OK, I just did. I'd still rather sleep."

"This is the price of being the go-to guy, Marty. Third Avenue and 68th St. See you in ten."

***

Marty walked tiredly from his car to the crime scene ahead, cracking open another can of Diet Coke. Maybe catching a new case was just what was needed, he thought. He was getting nowhere fast with the Sean Burrows murder. The guy was a shadow. Burrows seemed to have been a lazy but reliable worker at the assisted-living home; so much so that he'd shown up there the morning after being shot to death. But not to actually work, apparently – he was seen rifling through the boss's filing cabinet. Then his body, or whoever's body it was, disappeared. Nobody knew how or why or where. On top of it all, Marty still had the nagging feeling that he knew Burrows. That face resonated with him, and it seemed like he was not going to get a chance to see it again.

Standing on a corner, Marty watched three geniuses from the NYPD tow command standing around their heavy-duty tow truck, trying to figure out how to right the upside-down black van that lay against the curb like a giant dead insect. At first Marty thought he had been called to the scene of a traffic accident. What the fuck? Had he been demoted, and that was the way Bishop chose to tell him? He soon realized it was more complicated than a car crash.

The crime-scene unit was scouring the streets to see if there were any other body parts besides the partial ankle and foot that some hapless dog walker had found while all the official attention was on the crash site. Marty had seen his fair share of body parts during his twenty-five years as a cop, ten of them on the streets in uniform, and the last fifteen as a detective. He could only imagine what awaited him inside the van.

Marty had already gleaned from the license plate that the black, unmarked panel van was an official city vehicle, from the coroner's office, no less. There were the usual side of the mouth wisecracks from the uniforms at the scene:

"I guess the M.E.'s office figured they'd save a step if they just killed somebody already in the van."

"Yeah, they love it when the stiffs come pre-dissected."

Marty used to laugh at that kind of stuff, but for some reason nothing really seemed funny to him anymore. Or tragic, for that matter. Or even surprising.

One of the EMTs beckoned to him to approach the van. Marty drained the Diet Coke, crushed the can with his bearish hand, and, with no garbage can in sight, stuffed it into his pocket. Hopefully he would remember to recycle it later, but most likely he'd feel it when taking his jacket off at home. Whenever that would be.

He felt the eyes of the uniforms and the EMTs on him as his tall frame ambled across the street to the stricken van. Getting closer, it was obvious that the inside was covered with blood.

The EMT, a surprisingly fat guy whose scrubs strained over his belly, turned to Marty. "Two bodies. The weird thing is one looks like it's been dead a lot longer than the other."

Marty frowned at the EMT. Another dimwit. "Well it's a coroner's van, right? Let's puzzle this out together. Can you think of a reason why there might be a body who was already dead in a coroner's van?"

"That's not why it's weird," the EMT answered nervously. Nobody liked it when Marty frowned at them. "The thing is the corpse's body bag was open."

"You mean it was torn open in the crash?"

"It was unzipped."

Great, thought Marty. This can't just be a simple traffic accident with a drunk or high driver carrying an unusual load. No, this has to be body parts and corpses climbing out of their body bags. Or, worse yet, the driver was a perv who was diddling the corpse and not exactly keeping his eyes on the road. In truth, Marty had seen all of those things before, just never in one package.

Snapping on a pair of extra-large rubber gloves, he took out his Maglite, which was comically small in his oversized mitt. Grunting, he got on his hands and knees and knelt by the passenger side, shining his light into the van. Yep, pretty gruesome alright. Blood and tissue dripping from every surface in the overturned van. There was the vague shape of a torso resting on the roof, now the floor of the van, under the upside-down driver's seat.

There was scattered paperwork that had spilled out of the open glove box. Glancing at it without touching it, he saw a registration certificate with an address: 599 Winthrop St. Brooklyn, NY.

That was the morgue that lost Sean Burrows. *Holy shit,* he thought.

Craning his neck to the left, he aimed his light into the rear of the van. The top part of what he assumed was a corpse – it was a woman – was face down, with just her shoulders and the top of her head visible under the equipment and other debris covering her.

Something caught his eye near the corpse's shoulder. Something liquid, but it didn't appear to be blood. It was pooled onto the inner roof of the van, which the body rested on. It was black and it was thick, almost like motor oil or something.

Leaning too far into the van, the Maglite slipped from his fingers. Being careful not to touch anything, he retrieved it, and again shone it on the small pool of liquid.

The pool had moved.

Marty stared hard at it, sure that the half-dollar sized puddle of ooze was an inch closer to the body than it was before he dropped his light. Leaning back out of the van, he called out to the chubby EMT. "Hey, check this out, tell me what you think this is."

The EMT reluctantly got down on his knees with a mighty effort and followed the beam of Marty's flashlight.

The black pool of liquid was gone. Marty swept the area around the body, and there was no sign of any liquid at all except the smeared blood that was everywhere.

"That's blood," said the EMT, looking at Marty like he was the dimwit.

Marty shone the light in the EMT's face. "You're a comedian?"

"Absolutely not," he replied immediately.

Marty shone his light back into the van. *What the fuck,* he thought.

The Desecrated

***

Ulysses watched the sun rise over the only other mausoleum in what was left of this once-sprawling cemetery. He loved seeing the sunrise; it provided him something like hope, at least for an hour or so. It also gave him great pleasure to imagine his daughter watching the same sunrise. With that came the hope that somehow, maybe she knew they were watching it together. That's why he had trained himself to wake just before the dawn.

A couple of hours after sunrise, he expected to see Jennifer leaving the morgue. Her shift was over at 8 AM, and she was generally out of there by 8:05.

Not today though. He watched the black SUV roll up at five to eight as usual, and double park in front of the morgue, waiting, its lights flashing. A couple of minutes later, the Movie Asshole bounded out of the morgue, waved to the very few morons who had come out this early to see him, and jumped into the SUV, which quickly screeched away.

But no Jennifer. Ulysses' heart skipped a beat. The bad feelings he'd been having since the Movie Asshole had come on the scene welled up in his throat. There was something off. Something not right going on in that morgue. Maybe he should have told Jennifer more about his encounter with Death the other night. Seeing that she was already worried, though, he hadn't wanted to make it worse. But maybe she needed all the warning she could get.

Soon after, Clover, the supervisor, arrived, with her sidekick, Ersen. Ulysses was unimpressed by Clover. The woman seemed unconcerned about her appearance for one thing; a trait Ulysses despised. If he had access to hot water and soap and shampoo and razors, he would never walk around as unkempt as Clover. Clover's clothes looked like a laundry hamper had exploded, and she had just gone out with whatever landed on her.

And Ersen seemed like a cave man who was still getting used to walking upright. He was one of those muscle guys who always bought his shirts a size too small. His short sleeves gripped his keg-like biceps so tightly that you could just about eyeball his blood pressure. He wore a beard with no mustache, which gave him an old-fashioned look that Ulysses found vaguely unsettling. And yet here were two people who were engaged with the world, who had jobs, money in their pockets, and a place to go at night, and so they were considered better than Ulysses.

There was a time, Ulysses remembered, when he'd worn suits. A time when his hair was cut at salons. When there was money in his pocket. He was engaged in life too, once, but engaged in all the wrong things. Meaningless things. Every day that time got further and further away, but he knew it was there, lurking in his rear-view mirror. Serving as a warning to him. There was a time.

Ulysses snapped out of his reverie. Looking over at the morgue, he saw it was quiet. Even the last few hangers-on had left knowing that Trevor had gone home. Ulysses wondered how much longer he should wait. How much more time should go by before he had to intercede and save Jennifer from whatever terrible thing that morgue was going to do to her?

***

Clover was deep in thought, tapping her index finger against her thin, pursed lips, her brow knitted tightly above her eyes.

Across from her in the prep room, Ersen stared at Clover pensively, pulling distractedly at his mustache-less beard. Clover heard Ersen's stomach rumbling. *This idiot must be on one his "fasting" days.* Clover had long ago given up any idea of weight control and was endlessly amused by Ersen's efforts to tinker with his bulky body. His "fast days" often ended up with Ersen punching the vending machine, trying to liberate a bag of potato chips to quell his unbearable hunger.

Clover and Ersen stood on either side of a gurney containing a new arrival to the morgue. It was a forty-ish man with braided hair, thin, manicured sideburns that stretched to his chin, and a clean bullet hole in his forehead just above his left eye, about the size of a dime. His eyes were open and staring up at the fire sprinklers lining the stained ceiling above him, giving him a slightly confused look.

Clover was totally still as she contemplated. Ersen did his best to imitate her. The tension built. Clover slapped her hand down hard on the Formica counter, making Ersen jump. Pointing at the corpse, she looked at Ersen: "Is that thing loaded?' "

Ersen exploded with laughter. Clover bent over and bellowed. They traded high-fives.

"Great name!" Ersen exclaimed, in his thick Turkish accent, laughing so hard his eyes squinted shut and his capped teeth squeezed together. He wondered how long he had to keep up this hysterical laughter, opening one eye wider to see if Clover was satisfied with his display of mirth.

Clover turned in mid-guffaw and was surprised to see Jennifer in the doorway. She wasn't wearing her lab coat and seemed upset.

Clover reflexively checked the time on her phone. "What are you still doing here?"

"I have to talk to you."

***

A few minutes later, in her office, Clover went over the paperwork Jennifer was showing her, very unhappy at what she saw. "Holy shit. How many?"

"Five that we know of."

"That fucking numbnuts," Clover commented as she watched Ersen through her office window. The over-muscled goliath was trying to put his lab coat on, which was never easy given his out-of-proportion shoulders, but he seemed particularly vexed by it now. After getting his arms and hands tangled hopelessly in the sleeves of the lab coat, he threw the whole thing on the floor in frustration.

Clover closed her eyes. "Half the dead people in here have more brain power than that idiot. I'm gonna have to go over everything myself now," she said to Jennifer. She blamed herself - she knew damn well Ersen was too dim to be trusted with anything more complicated than lifting something heavy.

"This is more than just a mistake," Jennifer insisted. "Don't you think it's weird that he's making them younger on paper? And changing the cause of death?"

Clover picked up the shaker of fish food and approached the tank. "That moron is probably getting different bodies confused. Or he's just making shit up so he can get it done faster."

"Oh. That makes it all right then."

"I'll talk to him, trust me."

"He needs to be fired."

Clover glanced at Jennifer. "You ever try to fire a city worker?"

"Not recently, no," Jennifer replied dryly.

Clover gently tapped the fish food into the tank. "Tons of red tape. It's very hard."

"And we wouldn't want to try to do something that's hard."

Clover looked at her sharply. "Tell you what. You let me worry about Ersen, and you worry about Master Thespian. How's it going with him anyway?"

Jennifer shrugged and headed to the door, frustrated. "Still an asshole. Although he is the one who caught this."

"So he may actually be good for something?"

"Not really," she answered. "Hey, what happened to those hooks that were delivered?" Jennifer asked.

Clover turned and saw Jennifer looking at a spot on the floor near her desk. "Hooks?"

"There were two cases of eyehooks that came."

"Oh, right. Ersen strikes again. According to him, he ordered rib cutters, and those came by mistake. I made him send them back."

Rib cutters? Jennifer thought. *How does anyone confuse eyehooks with rib cutters?* The phone on Clover's cluttered desk rang.

Winking at Jennifer, Clover answered the phone in her best official voice. "Kings County Morgue, you kill 'em, we chill 'em."

Jennifer rolled her eyes and was halfway out of the office when Clover's voice changed. "What? Say that again?"

Turning, Jennifer saw the shock that was spreading over Clover's face. Clover stared at her, with the phone still at her ear.

"Angel's dead."

***

By 9:30 that morning, the morgue was busy as usual. Jennifer wasn't used to seeing it during the day: coroners up and down the hallways and in and out of rooms, Ersen actually looking busy, other morgue attendants sliding gurneys by each other in the hallways.

Jennifer and Clover stood outside the autopsy room, looking through the glass as three detectives and the medical examiner crowded around the center autopsy table, examining a body they couldn't quite see. Jennifer recognized one of the detectives, who towered over the others. He was the one who had been raging about the lost body of his murder victim. Remembering she had promised to check into it, she hoped this new case would distract him. Jennifer's eye was continually drawn to him, the tallest guy in the room, the red hair, and not an ounce of fat on his body. This detective didn't have the steroid-induced weightlifter's bulk that Ersen dragged around with him; he had more of a sinewy strength. He seemed very confident.

Jennifer still hadn't gotten her mind around the fact that Angel was dead. She didn't know him well, choosing to keep her distance as she did with most people. Angel had seemed kind of sweet natured, but there was something about him that she found a little off-putting. A certain disingenuousness, like he was always hiding something behind his shy smile. She looked at Clover, who stood with Ersen at the autopsy room window, watching the group inside examine the remains.

"Did they say what happened exactly?" Ersen asked.

"Just that he lost control of the van and flipped it. With the body in it," Clover answered.

Ersen snorted, thinking that was funny. Jennifer and Clover glared at him. He cleared his throat. "Why so many cops?" he asked.

"I saw both bodies," Clover answered, her eyes on the cops. "I don't think a crash could cause all that, no matter how bad."

"Wait, what?" Jennifer asked. This was the first she'd heard of it.

"I'm just saying," Clover said. "Maybe an animal or something got into the van after the crash."

"What kind of animal?" Jennifer asked, chilled.

Clover stared through the glass. "A hungry one."

Inside the autopsy room, Marty and the other detectives crowded around the table, busy listening to possible explanations for these injuries from the medical examiner, a stern, pale man in his mid-fifties who slicked his hair back and wore clear-framed eyeglasses.

"There is no question in my mind that we're looking at some kind of animal attack. The remains of the male corpse are full of bite marks and claw marks. DNA and saliva will hopefully tell us what it was, but obviously this young man has been torn apart by something big and something strong."

All eyes around the table automatically went to Marty, who stood several inches above the tallest person in the room. He glared at them, and everyone looked away, embarrassed.

"What about the female?"

The M.E. looked haplessly at the body. "No bite marks that I could see. However, there are deep scratches, claw marks, but they're on *the inside* of the skin flaps."

Marty frowned at him. "What are you saying?"

Shrugging, the M.E. pointed to the body. "Look at the wound. It's ragged, with muscle, tissue, and bone damage. Bones and tissue are extruded. This massive wound was not caused by something going into her; it's from something coming out of her."

"An exit wound?" Marty asked, trying to get his head around this.

"An exit wound without an entrance wound," the M.E. said, as if trying to figure it out himself.

They turned their attention to what was left of Angel's body on the opposite table. They didn't notice the small black pool of liquid that oozed out of the dead woman's back, just below her shoulder blade. They didn't see that inky liquid slither down the leg of the autopsy table, and onto the floor.

The viscous fluid wended its way around the many feet arranged around the table and found the center drain. It seeped into the drain, and, deeper still, the dark liquid oozed onto the golden amulet, filling in the blank spot in the shape of an Egyptian dog.

Hardening, the liquid formed into the black onyx shape of the dog profile in the center of the amulet. It pulsed once; everything became still again.

***

A half-hour later, Clover straightened up as Detective Bell came out of the autopsy room. Ersen made a quick about-face, hurrying away from the detective and disappearing into the prep room. Clover still hadn't dealt with Ersen – she really did need to get rid of this asshole.

The detective turned to Clover and Jennifer. "I'll be back tomorrow to get statements from everybody, including the movie star." He looked around. "Where is Pryce?"

"He left. Our shift ends at 8 AM."

Bell looked down at his worn notebook. "I need to talk to the other two. Ersen Tekin and Otis Burke."

"We'll make sure they're here tomorrow," Clover promised.

"What about Sean Burrows, the MIA body?" the detective squinted at Clover. "You find him?"

Clover cleared his throat. "We're still checking."

The weary cop sighed, knowing that Clover was full of shit. "Well," Detective Bell said as he walked away, pointing his thumb at the autopsy room. "Do me a favor and try not to lose those two, okay?"

***

Later that night, things settled down and Jennifer and Trevor found themselves alone and doing their regular shift. Although there was no longer anything "regular" about Jennifer's job.

The Desecrated

Ironically, since the press and Trevor's fans never came during the day when Trevor wasn't there, the excitement around the two desecrated bodies was missed altogether by the media. Just as well, Jennifer thought. There was enough of a circus going on at night. In quieter moments, she could always hear the female voices shouting for Trevor from outside.

They sat in the office, watching the fish swim silently. Jennifer was exhausted. She hadn't bothered to go home and had been awake for a little more than twenty-four hours.

Looking over at Trevor, who sat on the tattered couch, staring into the fish tank, she thought he seemed uncharacteristically quiet. Usually when sitting around he was scrolling through his phone. For all his action star charisma, Jennifer thought that he looked more beautiful like that, still and thoughtful, than when running and jumping and fighting on screen.

He spoke quietly. "What was his name?"

"Angel," Jennifer answered.

"Hmmm. Did I meet him?"

Jennifer suppressed an eye roll. "He told you he loved all your movies, and that you're awesome."

"Ah – chubby guy, nose ring, small gun tattooed on his face?"

"Yes," Jennifer replied dryly.

"Damn."

"Right. One less fan."

Trevor took this in quietly "You know, I'm not completely without feelings."

She resisted the urge to say something sarcastic. He actually seemed sad.

"I'm used to fake death. Movie death. Then someone says cut and the stunt man gets up with a big grin and the crew applauds. It's never this . . . final."

Jennifer marveled at the thought of someone reaching his mid-thirties and having had such little experience with death. She was twenty and had already had her fill. Not liking where these thoughts were going, she stood.

"Look, we have to stay on this death certificate thing. I told Clover about it, but I didn't get the feeling it's a mystery she cares about solving."

"I know what you mean," Trevor replied. "It's hard to get excited about something that could require work. I speak from experience."

"I need you to dig into the paperwork. Pull up all of Ersen and Otis' intakes for the last year and see if you can find anything else that doesn't line up."

Trevor squinted at the ceiling. "I refer you back to my last statement."

"If Ersen is doing something illegal, and you help catch him, you can probably get your sentence reduced."

Trevor bounded up from the couch. "Brilliant!" He sprang out of the office.

She called after him. "Can I ask you something?"

He turned to her. Eyebrows raised in expectation.

Hearing the hesitancy in her own voice, she asked, "Have you seen anything weird around here? I mean besides the death certificate thing. Anything you can't explain?"

"Only your bulletproof resistance to my charm." He grinned and walked down the hallway, whistling.

The church bells tolled – time to feed the fish. Grabbing the shaker of fish food, she turned to the tank, and suddenly grew alarmed.

Where was Ziti?

The tank was crowded with fish, but Ziti was usually front and center. She studied the tank; he was nowhere to be seen. She looked at the other fish. "Don't tell me you bastards ate Ziti. He was trained!"

The fish paid no attention to her. Jumping when the

phone rang, she was amazed at how frayed her nerves had become. "Kings County Morgue."

"Um," the female voice said tentatively. "Is this the morgue?"

"Yes. That's why I answer the phone that way."

"Um. Can I speak to Trevor?"

"You've got to be kidding," answered Jennifer, pissed. "Are you a reporter?"

"No. It's Trevor's friend Meadow? Meadow Smith?"

"Look, you can't just call—" Jennifer stopped, impressed. "Wait. Your last name really is Smith?"

"Ye-ah," the young woman said, making two annoyed syllables out of the word.

"Huh. Anyway, you shouldn't be calling this number. Didn't he give you his cell?"

"He won't answer my texts and his voicemail's like full, " Meadow complained.

Jennifer didn't actually hear her because she was staring in shock at the fish tank.

All sixteen fish were lined up one by one against the glass of the aquarium. With the exception of the absent Ziti. All staring out. Dead still except for their twitching fins.

Jennifer hung up the phone, hearing the faint sound of Meadow's voice droning nasally on. Moving closer to the tank, she saw that the fish were completely focused on something behind her.

Hoping that it was Trevor behind her, planning some juvenile trick, she turned . . . but there was no one there. She saw the dimly lit autopsy room across the hall. Part of her brain screamed at her to get out of the morgue and never come back. Swallowing hard, she tried to calm herself. She was not going to give in to fear.

Walking out of the office, Jennifer stood in the hallway And listened to the eerie silence. She looked into the autopsy room. She knew what was in there and knew she should just turn around and go back into the office. Instead she stepped inside.

Standing completely still, she scanned the room. On one table was the sheet-covered female corpse that Angel had been transporting. On another table were several sheet-covered lumps. Jennifer shuddered – these were Angel's body parts. The question remained, what in this room could have possibly drawn the attention of a dozen fish?

She walked over to the table holding the intact body of the poor young woman who was now part of a police investigation. Jennifer lifted the sheet, The face was waxy and yellow-ish. Blue veins were visible along the cheeks and the forehead. Her eyes were open and fixed to the side, as if she were trying to look at something without turning her head.

Jennifer saw something out of the corner of her eye and pulled the sheet further back. She gasped out loud at what she saw.

The abdominal cavity of this corpse had been completely ripped out. There was a gaping hole from her groin to her solar plexus; and jagged bones from her broken rib cage jutted out of the opening, as if something had literally exploded out of her. Jennifer barely had time to take this in when she heard the sound:

Slurp.

It wasn't coming from the corpse in front of her; it was coming from the table behind her.

The table holding Angel's detached remains.

Slurp the sound came again. It was a wet, sloppy sound, and it was coming from under the round sheet that covered Angel's severed head. "You've got to be shitting me," she heard herself say.

She ripped the sheet off of Angel's head. She was no stranger to gruesome sights, but this one nearly made her cry out. Angel's head rested on the table, on his neck, which gave the impression that he was sticking his head through the table from underneath. His hair was matted and wet, his mouth slightly agape, his eyes at half-mast. Yellow tendons and severed, bent arteries extended out onto the table from the neck.

But what happened next almost made Jennifer fall down.

Something was inside Angel's mouth. Trying to get out. Angel stared impassively as his lips parted further, and after another loud slurp –

A fish slowly wriggled out of Angel's mouth.

The fish flopped onto the stainless-steel table.

It was Ziti.

Unable to move, Jennifer stared in shock at the fish as it violently flopped around, gills desperately trying to suck in water that wasn't there. Jennifer's eyes were drawn to Angel's head again. She watched in numb disbelief as his lips twisted and his mouth became distorted.

He was trying to speak.

Pinkish drool dripped onto the tabletop as a guttural, raspy sound came from the mouth, like a bad imitation of Angel's real voice. "Give it to them."

His still, half-open eyes made it seem like he was oddly disinterested in what he was saying. "Give it to them," he repeated wetly.

The sound of the fish flopping frenetically against the tabletop jolted Jennifer out of her shock. She instinctively reached for it, scooped it up in her hands, and rushed from the autopsy room and into the office across the hall. Sliding the heavy lid of the aquarium aside with her elbows, she dropped the fish in the tank. She watched Ziti twitch a couple of times and swim happily away from the little cloud of blood that lifted off of him.

Jennifer backed away from the aquarium. She was breathing hard. Maybe hyperventilating. Her hand flew to her chest; she had to get her heart rate under control.

A strong pair of hands locked themselves around her arms from behind.

ELEVEN

Jennifer spun her head around and found herself an inch from Trevor's face. He pressed his fingers to his lips. "Shhhhhh."

Once sure she'd be quiet, he let her go. Leading her out of the office and into the hallway, they tiptoed down the dim corridor.

"Where are we going?" she whispered.

Cupping his ear, he gestured for her to listen. As they got farther down the hall, Jennifer could just barely make out the sound of muffled voices. Trevor led her into the prep room and stopped by the gaping hole in the wall where she had heaved the cranial drill at him.

Pointing to the hole, he moved closer to it. She followed and found herself standing very close to him. The hairs on their arms were touching. They stood totally still, looking into the dark airshaft beyond the hole.

The voices came again. Clearer this time, but she couldn't make out what they were saying. Two male voices. One sounded angry.

She and Trevor both jumped when the deep thrum of machinery clanking to life filled the airshaft. Trevor backed up and stared at her. Jennifer, too curious not to, moved closer to the airshaft. When she squeezed the top of her head through the hole, Trevor hissed "No!"

Craning her neck into the tight space, the familiar panic came for her. Willing herself to stay calm, she tried to see as far as possible down into the airshaft. All she saw were shadows moving against a brick wall and some reflected light bouncing off of the tin of the airshaft. The cramped space became too much for her, and when her chest tightened and her breathing thickened, she pulled her head out.

Looking at Trevor, she whispered, "Give me your earbuds." He tilted his head at her quizzically. "Just do it," she insisted.

Reaching into his pants pocket, he handed her his knotted earbuds. Doing her best to untangle them, she inserted the lightning plug into the base of her iPhone. Swiping open her camera, she chose "video," and hit the record button.

She used the earbuds to slowly lower the phone down the shaft.

Trevor looked at her, impressed. "I'm going to remember this for my next—"

"Shut up" she hissed at him. She twisted the earbuds so the camera would rotate and show them as much as possible. They both listened to the sounds of the machinery and the men talking. Jennifer slowly pulled the phone back up by the earbuds.

She and Trevor stepped away from the shaft, and Trevor leaned over her shoulder to see her screen. His breath tickled her neck. He smelled good; she couldn't help but notice – not in a perfumey way, but in a clean, crisp way.

Playing back the video, they saw it was shaky and grainy; everything was very dark. There were shadows moving around and what appeared to be the silhouettes of two figures moving through the darkness.

They both stared in shock as another, more disturbing image appeared: a dark figure suddenly loomed at the top of the frame, only from the waist down, moving across from left to right, the feet seemingly floating high above the floor. The figure just as quickly disappeared. All they could see after that were shaky views of the airshaft as the phone was pulled back up.

Much to her surprise, Trevor laughed out loud.

She stared at him.

He grinned at her. "Okay, fair enough, we're even."

"What?"

"You're totally taking the piss. You're having me on. You made that video with some app and pretended you were shooting it just now."

"That's crazy. You brought me here. You heard the sounds."

Trevor shrugged. "Could be mice for all I know. Rats."

"When was the last time you heard rats having a conversation?"

"Happens every day in my business."

"Hey, you were just as scared as I was when we heard what we heard. Why don't you want to admit there's something weird going on in this place?"

"It's a morgue. Everything's weird."

"You know what I mean. What about the creepy things that keep showing up here? The PVC pipe, the hooks . . . and what about the missing jars?"

"I don't know anything about pipes or hooks."

Jennifer was pissed. "You saw the specimen jars the first night you were here!"

Trevor held out his hand. "Can I see the video again please?"

She handed him her phone. He smiled at her, and instead of tapping play, he tapped delete. "Oops. Sorry."

Jennifer grabbed the phone back. "You asshole! Why did you do that!"

"I don't like being pranked," Trevor answered, still smiling.

Jennifer got into his face. "Ulysses is right. All this weird shit started happening the day you got here. What are you doing? What the hell are you up to? Wait – is this whole community service deal just part of some fucked up reality show you're doing?"

"Ah, that must be it!" Trevor said as he yanked his earbuds out of her iPhone. *"America's Got Cadavers!"* Giving her a sly smile, he walked away.

Jennifer looked down at her phone. *Shit*, she thought.

***

Jennifer watched as Clover fitted a piece of sheetrock over the airshaft hole. Another day without sleep. She had again waited until well after her shift ended for Clover to come in so she could tell her about the voices and sounds she'd heard coming from the airshaft. It sucked that she had no proof thanks to Trevor, and she was loath to potentially reveal that she was slowly (or quickly) going insane, but she was also tired of shouldering this load herself. Her attempt to share this with Trevor last night had been a disaster. However, Trevor may have overplayed his hand by protesting too much. Assuming, that is, he actually had something to do with what was going on here.

The truth was that she had to stay anyway – as promised, the police detective was back, bright and early, and wanted to interview the staff in the employee lounge.

Trevor was in the midst of being interviewed, and Jennifer wished she could be a fly on that particular wall.

If she could only figure out how Trevor could benefit from gaslighting her, she might be able to understand what he was up to. Was this some reality-show bullshit? Was it Trevor messing with her, or her brain messing with her?

She was so deep in thought she had tuned Clover out. She was saying something about where the airshaft led.

"What?" she asked.

Clover coated the sheetrock with plaster. It wouldn't be a good match – the bright white plaster with the yellowed wall around it. Jennifer knew Clover didn't care, and she certainly wasn't about to paint it.

"I said this airshaft leads to an old basement. Boiler, pipes, stuff like that. It's been closed off for years."

"Have you ever been down there?"

"Hell no. It's enough that I have to come here."

Jennifer had to weigh how much she wanted to tell her. "Clover."

Clover arched her eyebrow at the sound of her name. *Uh-oh.*

Jennifer looked at her. "There's something you should know."

"What?" Clover asked, frowning, one hand holding a spackling knife in mid-air.

Searching her eyes, Jennifer asked herself if she really wanted to take a chance that Clover would think she was batshit crazy. "It's just that . . . I'm not sure, but I think there's something strange going on here."

Clover didn't miss a beat, continuing to smooth the spackle over the sheetrock. "Okay," she said evenly. "What do you think's going on?"

Jennifer knew she was patronizing her. She pressed on. "It might have something to do with Trevor."

"Look, I know you don't like that dude. Neither do I. But we have to—"

"It's not that. I mean, yes, I don't like him, at least not always. I just think he's up to something."

"What exactly?"

Having no answer, Jennifer thought she should quit while she was ahead. If she was ahead. "Never mind."

Looking at her, Clover saw her concern. "Hey." Clover smiled at her. "Stop worrying so much. He'll be gone in a few weeks, and this will all seem like some bad dream."

She laughed. "If you say so."

Clover found her eyes. Spoke softly. "Look, I know this isn't an easy gig."

Jennifer nodded. "It's a pretty easy gig. Usually."

"You're here by yourself. And when you're not, you're surrounded by men. And we're not talking Algonquin Round Table men. We're talking eighth grade level men. Their combined brain power couldn't charge my vibrator."

"Wow. Okay."

"I'm just trying to say that you're a survivor. Like me. You've been through a lot, but you're going to be okay."

"This is so unlike you. No offense."

"Hey, I didn't get to be a supervisor by being a cupcake. No woman can. But I can also give a little respect when it's called for. So," Clover nodded to Jennifer. "Respect."

Jennifer smiled.

Turning back to the wall, Clover observed her work. "It's not pretty, but no more hole." She packed up her tools.

Feeling a bit bonded with her, Jennifer thought she might push her luck just a little. "Clover? Have you ever heard anything from down there? Seen anything?"

Clover looked away. Hesitant. After a moment, she finally spoke. "I did. Once."

Jennifer leaned in. "What?" she asked, studying her face.

"More like who," said Clover.

Jennifer's heart almost stopped. "Who?" she whispered.

"Idris Elba. He asked me if brought the corkscrew and told me to turn out the lights."

Jennifer scowled at her. "You are such an asshole."

At that moment the door to the break room opened down the hall. Trevor stepped out from his police interview, looking as smug and confident as ever. Glancing back at Jennifer and Clover, he gave them a little sarcastic salute, and left the building.

The tall, red-haired detective poked his head out of the room. He spied Jennifer.

"Ms. Shelby?"

***

Marty watched Jennifer Shelby take a seat on the other side of the small Formica table in the tiny "employee lounge." As he closed the door behind her, she surprised him by asking if he would mind keeping the door open.

"If you feel it's necessary, of course," Marty answered, trying to keep the irritation out of his voice. Did she feel unsafe with him?

"It's just that I'm a little claustrophobic. I usually avoid this room." She caught his little smile. "Does my claustrophobia amuse you?"

He held his hands up. "Not at all. Sorry. It's just that my mother was very claustrophobic too. Severe. She couldn't go on subways, couldn't go on elevators, never went on a plane."

"For me it's more about super-tight spaces."

Leaning forward a bit, he looked at her. "When my mother died, it was in her will that the urn which carried her ashes had to be left open at all times. She didn't want to be closed in."

Jennifer nodded and smiled. "Okay. Hardcore."

He opened his notebook. A lot of his fellow detectives

had taken to using tablets; Marty remained old school. A well-timed pause to write down a note often made a suspect nervous, which was usually good for the process.

The process that morning had been particularly interesting. His interview with the movie star yielded nothing of importance, except some interesting gossip about his last female co-star. She was apparently so enamored with Trevor that one night she surprised him in his hotel room with two of her female friends. What made Trevor think Marty needed to hear about that was a mystery, not that Marty didn't have a moment of overpowering envy. Perhaps that was the reason Trevor felt Marty needed to hear about it.

However, his interviews with Ersen Tekin, the brawny dayshift assistant supervisor, followed by Otis Burke, the scrawny wannabe gangbanger were more promising. Ersen, who sulked and scowled his way through the interview, struck Marty as a monosyllabic moron, who apparently liked beards but not mustaches. There was also something cunning in his eyes; something – and this was a word Marty did not use lightly – evil. When Ersen said he was Turkish, Marty, trying to lighten the mood, smiled and said, "I thought you might be Mennonite." Ersen's eyebrows furrowed as he tried to process the foreign word. Marty helped him out by gesturing to his chin.

Ersen was offended. "American President Abe Lincoln had this beard."

Marty nodded, impressed, thinking that the beard looked more Wolverine than Lincoln, but why quibble?

Ersen thought way too long and hard before answering Marty's questions, which gave Marty time to wonder about the strange gurgling sounds coming from Ersen's stomach. Ersen was aware of the embarrassing grumbling noises, and he shifted in his seat. "Have not eaten yet today. Fasting," he tried to explain. Marty had an image of a bear hibernating while Ersen continued to parse his answers carefully. Marty understood that thinking was probably an exhausting process for him, but he also recognized that the man was worried about saying the wrong thing. Not because of his poor language skills, but because he had something to hide. Ersen would bear further scrutiny.

Otis was certainly a more entertaining interview, if only for the hilarious fake swagger and gang lingo he employed. Minus his tats, this pale kid could easily have posed for Picasso's painting "The Altar Boy."

After going through his movements with Angel that night, Otis offered little of interest, except the revelation that he tried to avoid working as much as possible. Other insightful observations he offered included his feeling that Angel was a dreamer, and, unlike Otis, was "soft." "I come from the streets, bro, you know what I'm sayin'?" he asked, with just the right defiant tilt of his head. "I live the life, son. Angel, he didn't wanna know about it."

Marty looked down at Otis' personnel file. "Hmm. It says here you're from Tarrytown, up in Westchester." Marty looked at him. "I've been to Tarrytown a couple of times. Nice antique shops up there. Good places for brunch."

Otis' acne scarred cheeks turn red. Looking down at the table, he rubbed his thigh nervously. "You don't know my life, bro," he muttered.

"Yeah, I pretty much do, bro." Marty answered, unable to help himself. "What do they call the gangs up there? The Tarrytown Unrulys?"

"Why you gotta be like that?" was the best response Otis could muster.

As buffoonish as Otis was, Marty sensed an underlying sinister, predatory personality. Marty believed this guy, like Ersen, was holding something back. Whether or not it was about Angel, Marty couldn't be sure, but Otis was on Marty's list now as well.

Marty heard Jennifer clear her throat impatiently. Looking up at her, he noticed she was squinting because of the daylight coming through the window. Of course. Like him, she worked nights. Did they call it the graveyard shift in the morgue? He too had trouble with daylight sometimes, and he liked that he was sitting across from a fellow vampire. "I've just spoken to Trevor Pryce. Not exactly your run of the mill morgue employee."

Jennifer just looked at him expectantly.

He smiled, trying to put her at ease. "Must be exciting for you guys, huh? Having a celebrity around?"

"Thrilling," she answered, looking at him dryly. He tried not to smile. Jennifer Shelby is okay by me, he thought.

"Me, I'm not impressed," Marty lied as he sat back. "These show-biz people mean nothing to me."

Jennifer didn't take the bait though; she just looked at him, waiting for a question.

Marty referred to his notes, even though he knew exactly what he was going to ask. "You were the last one to see Mr. Velez, correct?"

This seemed to startle Jennifer. "Well . . . I don't know. I saw him here, right before he left."

"Did he seem like he'd been drinking?"

"No."

"Did you know him to use drugs?"

"I didn't know him that well."

Marty looked at her with a pleasant smile and said nothing. People usually felt compelled to fill the silence, and sometimes they said more interesting things than if they had been prompted.

After a few long minutes of awkward silence, she spoke. "I saw his injuries. Clover said you guys don't think that could've happened from just a crash."

"Do you?"

She shrugged. "I've seen lots of car crash victims. I

know what metal and glass can do to a body. I think something else happened."

Marty nodded, looked at her, and kept silent. He had to admit he enjoyed looking at her. Jennifer was beautiful for sure, but there was something else, something in her eyes, or maybe it was the angle of her eyebrows . . .

Again, she filled in the silence. "Do you have a theory?"

"Well, there weren't any grizzly bear sightings last night, I can tell you that," Marty said with a conspiratorial smile. "How 'bout you?"

"What?"

"Have a theory?"

She looked at him, and he definitely saw something conflicted in her eyes. She was weighing something. "Not really, no," she said finally.

Time to shake this up a bit. Marty slid a file folder over to her. "We took these pictures off of Mr. Velez' phone."

Jennifer opened the file, and Marty's eyes went wide when he saw the 8x10 glossy photo of Trevor Pryce that he had asked Trevor to sign. Marty immediately sat forward and reached for the folder. "Sorry, wrong file."

But Jennifer was already reading the autograph out loud with a smile. " ' To Detective Marty Bell. He Always Gets His Man.' "

Marty grabbed the file back. Feeling his cheeks burn with his telltale blush, he slid the correct file over to her. "Just something for the guys back at the precinct." *Damn it,* he thought.

Jennifer opened the new file folder, saw the first photo and cringed. She flipped quickly through the rest of the pictures – a half-dozen naked shots of the young female corpse Angel had been transporting. Marty watched her reaction. It was genuine disgust. Quickly closing the file, she looked at him. Upset.

"Did you know about this?" he asked.

"Fuck no. I had no idea. Why would anybody do that?"

Marty slid the folder back to him. "I stopped asking that question a long time ago. Is this a 'thing' in your business?"

"I hope not," she answered simply.

"Seems like some strange things went on that night."

She looked at him again. Her eyes hinting at something she didn't want to say. Blinking, she glanced down. "No more than usual."

Another pause, and this time he didn't think she was going to fill it with anything that would help him. She looked tired.

"What does that mean?

"Nothing. Hey, I have to be back here in a few hours. I need some sleep."

Closing his notebook to signal he was done, he smiled neutrally at her. "Okay," he said gently. "Thanks for taking the time. If we need anything else we'll be back in touch."

Watching her walk to the door, he remembered something. "Hey, I forgot to ask – where was Angel taking the body?"

"To a funeral home," Jennifer answered.

"Which one?" Marty opened his notebook again.

"Drake and Sons, in Bay Ridge."

Holy shit, Marty thought, staring at the name of the funeral home as he wrote it down. He remembered where he knew Sean Burrows from.

***

Earlier that night, Ulysses had watched with alarm from the cemetery as an unmarked police car pulled up in front of the morgue. There had been a lot of activity lately; the night before there had been several police cars as well as this same unmarked car, parked out there for hours. Had something happened to Jennifer? He hadn't seen her all night.

It was time for him to pause his search for his daughter and help Jennifer. Ulysses was terrified of facing the specter of Death again, but if Jennifer was in trouble, he had no choice.

Stealthily, he approached the part of the morgue that bordered the cemetery. There were no windows on that side, no openings of any kind. He'd have to go to the rear of the morgue, and that involved hopping a fence. Even though he wasn't sure his sore feet were up to it, he would have to try.

It took an enormous effort and a lot of straining, but he made it over the fence, ripping one pair of the two pairs of pants he wore in the process. Regaining his balance, he steadied his complaining legs, and moved to the back of the building. There were some low windows, along the base of the building, and there was a service door, with a half-dozen garbage cans and recycling containers nearby. The door was metal, and although rusted and warped, it had no windows and was quite solid.

Ulysses put his hands on the door and tried pushing. He jumped back when a sudden deep *thrum* sounded from within. Like some giant piece of machinery had just started. The ground vibrated. Trying to steady his nerves Ulysses got down on his knees, wincing, bending over as far as he could to see through the dusty and clouded window.

The low, street-level windows were actually high windows looking down on the lower level of the morgue basement. Able at first to make out some shadows down below, it wasn't until Ulysses cupped his eyes and stared even harder through the thick glass that he saw something that made his heart race and his scalp tingle.

A naked pair of male legs floated by the window, toes pointing down, so close to the glass that Ulysses couldn't see anything higher than the thighs. The legs were spotted with age, with bumpy veins running like tiny rivers crisscrossing the calves and knees.

He craned his neck even farther to try to follow the legs, but they disappeared in the shadows.

Ulysses felt the evil.

It came over him like a heavy, filthy blanket, weighing him down. The air became foul. Something was off, though, out of balance – the powerful sensation of evil was coming from behind him.

He turned his body around and got to his feet by sliding up the wall. His breathing came ragged and heavy. He knew, felt, the evil was close.

He saw the same figure from last time.

A large man-like form came out of the darkness, toward him. The odd-shaped head. Yes – it was a hood, Ulysses was certain. It would make sense that Death would wear a hood. Ulysses pressed himself against the wall as the figure came closer.

It did not speak. Instead it reached him and slid a cold, clammy hand around the back of his neck. The wind got knocked out of Ulysses; this thing, this wicked fiend punched him in the stomach, while holding a vice-like grip around his neck. Ulysses barely felt the blows because of all the layers he wore, but as the punches rained on his body, his fear evaporated. This was no supernatural being, this was a human, a *man* just like Ulysses.

Armed with this knowledge, Ulysses suddenly slammed his forehead into the face of his attacker. Hearing the crunch of bone, he knew he connected with the bastard's nose. There was a yelp of pain, and the hand was no longer on his neck.

Ulysses pushed himself away from the wall. Feeling powerful, dominant, he was about to inflict some more pain, *serious* pain, on this pretend demon.

A voice came to him.

It was light, and sweet, and he knew it instantly.

"Dad?"

Turning in the direction of the voice, his eyes widened. They instantly filled with tears.

It was his daughter.

***

Drake and Sons Funeral Home was a converted Victorian house occupying an entire corner in a residential section of Bay Ridge, Brooklyn. A large canopy jutted out into the street, with the name embossed in a dignified but pretentious Old English font. Marty had grown up on these streets, and Drake's was a familiar sight. It had been the subject of many a ghost story told by his dad. The young Marty loved to be scared, and his mischievous father was always happy to oblige. His mother used to shake her head as Dad told Marty tales of the lonely ghost of Old Man Drake roaming the halls of the funeral home, trying to wake up the dead bodies so he could have some company. "You can stay up with him tonight when he has nightmares," his mom would scold. Most of the neighborhood residents ended up there, as did, eventually, his own mother, who was waked there just four months ago.

Marty, yet again working during the day when he should've been sleeping, entered the funeral home and headed to the office of John Drake, the owner and manager. Marty had never liked funeral homes, with their hushed atmosphere and cloying smell of flowers. In fact, being from the streets of Brooklyn, his only experience smelling flowers while he was growing up had been in funeral homes. For the rest of his life, even the nicest smelling rose or lily would remind him of death.

Before Marty could get to Drake's office, he spied the man he was really there to see.

Sean Burrows. Alive and well.

Burrows walked out of one of the visitation rooms with

a spray of colorful flowers. Wearing dress pants, with a white shirt and a muted blue tie, Marty remembered him from his mother's wake – he was helpful and efficient, and very dignified in that sympathetic but remote affect that funeral directors had. However, there was one thing missing:

No snake tattoo curled around his ear.

As Marty came closer to Burrows, the mystery was solved.

"Remember me?" Marty said with a smile.

Burrows looked at him blankly.

"Martin Bell. You handled my mother's wake," Marty reminded him. "And her cremation."

Burrow's eyes registered surprise, but his face stayed neutral. "Right. Officer Bell. Your mother was Regina."

"Detective Bell," Marty corrected with a smile. "You were very gracious to my family. We appreciated it."

"I'm glad you were pleased with our service." Burrows continued down the hall with the flowers. Marty followed.

"I assume you're here about my brother?" Burrows asked.

"It's my case, yes. My condolences. I would have come sooner, but there was no indication that he had a brother in any of the records we could find. A twin brother, no less."

They entered a small office, where Burrows set the flowers down, and woke up his computer. "He wasn't very close with the family."

"Including you?"

"Especially me."

Marty let the silence fall while Burrows worked the keyboard. He typed pretty fast.

"If you don't mind my saying so, you don't seem interested in how he died or who killed him. Families are usually all over the police for answers."

Burrows kept his eyes on the screen, typing quickly.

"You've probably found out enough about my brother's life to know the kind of people he associated with. Living by himself like a squatter in that awful movie theater. You've been there, I assume?"

"I have."

"Then you know what I mean. Crumbling and decaying, just like his life. The truth is, for us, he died years ago."

Marty took in the office. No personal touches, no photos. Neat and orderly, just like his brother's humble sleeping space in the theater's projection booth.

"Is that why no one's tried to claim his body?"

"The body is meaningless. Just an empty vessel."

"Did you know his vessel is missing?"

Burrows hesitated, without taking his eyes off of the computer screen. Marty saw his mind racing, even though his face remained placid.

When Burrows said nothing, Marty offered, "Just a mix-up at the M.E.'s office. I'm sure he'll be found."

"Good luck with that."

Marty studied Burrows' face. *This guy is really good,* he thought. "Any ideas about who may have shot him?"

"My guess is he's made a lot of enemies. But, again, we weren't that close."

"Yet you went to his workplace the morning after he was killed."

Burrows' eyes left the computer screen and locked on to Marty's. The surprise was obvious. After a small moment of hesitation, he looked back at the screen and continued typing. "I just wanted to make sure that anything personal of his was taken care of."

"You were seen going through his bosses' computer files."

"Just trying to purge any private information about Sean."

Bullshit, Marty thought. "How did you find out he was killed?"

Burrows shrugged. "One of his 'friends,' I'd guess you'd say, called me."

"What was his name?"

"He didn't give it."

"So you find out your brother's been murdered. You don't call the police for more information, you don't try to find out where his body's been taken, and instead your first move is to go to the nursing home where he worked to try to delete his personnel files."

"It's assisted living."

"I stand corrected. You get that this is all pretty suspicious, right?"

Burrows looked at him. "I get that you think it is."

John Drake, the octogenarian owner of the funeral home, appeared in the doorway of the office. He was tall and stooped, giving the impression that he could topple over at any moment. "Raffy?"

"Yes Mr. Drake."

Marty looked at Burrows.

"Short for Rafael," Burrows responded to Marty's puzzled look.

Drake squinted at Marty, and back to Burrows. "Raffy, tell your father you'll talk to him later. You're needed."

Burrows looked at Marty and said, softly, "He's losing it."

Damn right, Marty thought. He could understand being mistaken for a brother, or cousin, but father?

Burrows got up and gestured for Marty to follow him out of the office. Drake stepped aside and waited.

Marty looked at Burrows. "I'm going to have to ask you to come to the station and give us a statement in the next day or two." Marty wanted to give himself more time to check "Raffy" out.

"Of course," said Burrows. "You know where to find me."

The Desecrated

Marty watched Drake and Burrows walk to one of the many visitation rooms. The smell of flowers was much stronger in the hallway, and made Marty want to go somewhere else to breathe. Instead, he waited for Drake and Burrows to go into the visitation room and went back into Burrows' office.

The computer was still awake. Marty saw that Burrows had been working on a casket order: Cherrytone Solid Poplar Casket with Cream Velvet Interior. Sixteen hundred bucks. Ouch.

Marty went to the desktop and scrolled through the various folders, all listed by customer name. Too many to take in at once, so he opened up his Dropbox account, into which he dragged and dropped copies of all the folders.

Marty watched as his Dropbox filled up. Burrows stunk worse than the flowers.

***

Jennifer had given up on the idea of sleep as she opened her refrigerator and looked for something to graze on. The horrible pictures of that poor naked corpse kept flashing in her mind. She had no idea Angel had been some kind of a fucking pervy necrophiliac voyeur. It felt like everything around her was unraveling.

The urge to tell Detective Bell everything that had been happening to her was strong. He seemed like a guy who was hard to shock, but you never knew when it came to the supernatural. Cops were not known for their belief in ghosts and talking cadavers. And what exactly would be the point? He wouldn't know what any of it meant any more than she did, and he certainly wouldn't know what to do about it.

Jennifer kept going back to her meeting with Miss Nadja. At least the exotic Russian had reassured her that she wasn't crazy. Then again maybe Jennifer would be better off hearing that from an actual doctor, rather than from a dry cleaning psychic. *Stop fighting it and listen,* she had said. *You're more powerful than you know.* Psychic Bullshit 101, thought Jennifer. But still . . .

The sound of her doorbell made her jump.

***

Trevor opened the bottle of Sauvion Sancerre with his usual flair. Jennifer was somewhat embarrassed to have him in her modest apartment, but at the same time grateful for the company. At least her string lights, which were looped around the walls and molding, bathed the apartment in a flattering glow. Romantic even, if she were feeling so inclined, even with the daylight fighting to get in around the edges of her blackout blinds. She watched him pour.

"How did you know where I lived, by the way?"

"Clover has all of her contacts in a little folder on her computer."

"You hacked into Clover's computer?"

Trevor laughed. "Hacked is not exactly the word. We're not talking Edward Snowden here. I guessed her password on the first try. Although I didn't realize at first that Idris was all caps."

She smiled, shaking her head. He handed her the glass of wine and looked around.

"Love what you've done with the place."

Sipping the wine, she shrugged. "Thrift shops rule."

"I'm serious," he said, stepping closer to the string of lights on the wall. "Chili peppers." The lights glowed warmly on his face. "How'd you think of that?"

"My mother used to string lights like that on my bedroom walls when I was a little girl. She'd change them depending on the seasons. Santa faces, pumpkins, beach umbrellas, snow flakes . . ."

Trevor looked back at the lights. "Really."

"Didn't your mother do things like that for you?"

"Would've needed a long extension cord to reach boarding school."

Taking a healthy sip of his wine, he looked at her again. "You're an original, you know that, don't you?"

She couldn't help a laugh. "What's so original about me?"

"You're just not like anybody I know. And I know a lot of people."

Resisting the urge to make a crack about how many people she was sure he "knew," she instead looked into her glass and took another sip. There was a moment of silence. Jennifer wasn't quite sure if it was a comfortable or awkward one, but she was relieved when the sound of a bus squealing around the corner beneath her open window broke the quiet.

Trevor looked at her. "How do you manage sleep?"

"Rarely," she answered.

"Well, feel free to drop around mine any time. You hear nothing sixty-two stories up."

"Your apartment building has sixty-two floors?"

"Seventy-five actually. The top-floor penthouses were sold out by the time I wanted to buy. I had to settle for lower. Still eats at me."

"I feel for you."

He toasted her. "157 West 57th. Just say 'Poindexter' to the concierge and he'll let you up."

"Yeah, no. That's not gonna happen. I didn't realize you lived in New York."

Trevor shrugged. "I don't really live anywhere. I have houses all over the world, though."

"And what brought you to mine today?"

"A question. What was your father's first name?"

"What? Why?"

"Just tell me please."

"Rick."

"Richard?" Trevor asked.

Jennifer got a chill. She nodded her head yes. Trevor sat next to her and took out his iPad. "I looked up all of Ersen's intakes for the last year. And I found something straight away that looked weird."

He showed her a scan of an intake form and a Body Control Card. "Richard Shelby. The name jumped out at me for obvious reasons. His body was received on January tenth."

"That doesn't make sense. My father died in Elmhurst Hospital. I had the funeral home pick him up from Elmhurst. In Queens! He never went to a morgue, and there's definitely no reason he'd be sent to our morgue in Brooklyn—"

Jennifer stopped. The realization hit her like a ton of bricks. "Wait – what did you say the date was?"

Trevor looked at his iPad. "January tenth."

"That's impossible. He was buried on January ninth. Calvary Cemetery in Queens."

Trevor handed her the iPad. "Look at the cause of death."

Jennifer looked at the scanned form on the iPad. Cause of death: *Heart attack.*

She stared at Trevor. "He died of Covid."

"A different Richard Shelby?"

Jennifer looked at the body-control card again. "The height and weight is about right. Where are the pictures?"

"That's the other weird thing about all of Ersen's intakes. The photos are missing."

TWELVE

Julio the Hot Dog King glared angrily at Jennifer. "I'm an artist! You're asking me to be a hack!"

"A true artist knows simplicity is the best art of all." Jennifer was cold and tired and was in no mood for Julio's bullshit. She stood at the take-out window of the hot dog stand as a noisy truck coughed and rattled past her, sending grimy fumes wafting toward them.

Julio grabbed the relish and mustard-smeared hot dogs from the counter. "All right, all right. Two pedestrian hot dogs coming up. You're killing me." He angrily slapped two uncooked hot dogs on the grill.

Jennifer was reeling from the events of last night and earlier that day. Still trying to get her mind around Angel being dead, maybe murdered, she had to face the possibility that Ersen was somehow involved in all the crazy shit that had been happening at the morgue. Altered documents, a missing body, maybe her own father's identity somehow being used for . . . for what? She would have to take it all to Clover. It felt like she was trying to throw punches underwater.

"There!" Julio barked as he slammed down two new plain hot dogs. "As boring as I know how to make them. Anything else? Some watered-down orange juice maybe?"

Jennifer couldn't help a smile, giving him a ten-dollar bill. "Keep the change."

"I shouldn't take money from a cretin who doesn't appreciate condiments," he muttered, stuffing the hot dogs into a brown-paper take-out bag.

"Last time I checked, this is a frankfurter stand, Julio, not The River Cafe. Get over yourself." Jennifer took the bag of hot dogs from the counter. As she turned toward the street, she slammed directly into the man behind her, grunting as her face mashed into his chest. Pissed that anybody would stand that close to her, vaccine or no vaccine, she was about to get in their face when she saw who it was.

It couldn't be.

Neatly combed hair. Clean-shaven. The same clothes he had always been wearing, including the new Helly-Hansen boots Jennifer had bought him; but somehow everything looked neater and cleaner. Smiling at her with a row of even teeth, he looked healthy even in the garish neon of the hot dog stand.

"Ulysses?" she gasped.

The smile grew wider. "I've been looking for you."

"Wait – what happened? I mean, you look—"

"I know. It's okay! It's all good."

"What are you doing here?" She couldn't take her eyes off of his face – it was the same Ulysses voice, the same eyes, but he looked like a new, younger version.

"I don't know where you live. But I knew you'd come

here eventually. I have some amazing news."

She was crushing the bag of hot dogs. "What?"

Leaning closer to her, he smelled of pine. As if he had just come from a forest. "I found my daughter."

Jennifer felt a thrill go through her body. "What!! Get out! Are you serious?"

"She found me, really," he said, a huge smile lighting up his face.

Holy shit, Jennifer thought, *he's handsome as fuck*!

"Right behind the morgue last night. She's been looking for me all these years too!"

"Ulysses, I can't . . ." Jennifer didn't know what to say. Her heart was full; just looking at his beaming face made her want to cry. This was the last thing she ever expected.

"She got me all cleaned up. I'm gonna go stay with her. She's got a big house upstate, and she wants me to live with her. And her family. *My* family!"

"I don't know what to say. I'm so happy for you!" The tears came, along with laughter. "I have to be honest. I wasn't always sure you had a daughter."

"I have to be honest," Ulysses laughed. "Me neither!"

She collapsed against him, both laughing hard. He hugged her. She hugged him back.

"I didn't want to leave without saying good-bye." His voice cracked. "Without saying thanks."

Jennifer hugged him harder and closed her eyes against his clean neck. "Does this mean I'll never see you again?"

"That's my Jennifer," Ulysses chuckled. "Always finding the cloud in the silver lining." He broke the hug, held her by her arms and looked at her. "You will never be totally rid of me. That's a promise!"

Her eyes shone as she looked at him. Jennifer hadn't witnessed too many happy endings in her life. Not wanting to let the moment go, she whispered, "It's great to see you so happy."

Ulysses, his eyes full, gave her a final squeeze and turned away. He turned back to her just as quickly. "Ah!" he said, coming closer. "There's one more thing. Remember that amulet necklace?"

Jennifer frowned.

"The one the Movie Asshole said was an Egyptian Protection Amulet?" Ulysses prompted.

"Yeah?"

"Well, I hid it in the drain. To protect you."

Her heart sank a bit as the familiar manic quality was seeping back into his voice.

"What drain?"

He spoke faster. "In the morgue. In the operating room."

"You mean the autopsy room?" she asked, trying to follow.

"The thing is, I found out it's not what I thought it was. You should get it out of the drain as soon as you can."

"Wait – *what?*"

Ulysses gave her a dazzling smile. "Gotta go!"

"What do I do with it?"

"They'll tell you," he shouted, and turned and strode down the street like a man on a mission. Jennifer watched him go with a pang of sorrow, her head spinning. Feeling something in her hands, she looked down and saw that she had never given him the hot dogs.

***

Jennifer couldn't get to the morgue fast enough. *I hid it in the drain. To protect you.* It didn't hit her right away, but riding the subway into Brooklyn, she understood that a lot of the strange things she'd seen had involved the drain in the autopsy room. The gurneys arranging themselves in a circle around it, the ghostly figure of a woman with her hand

199

buried in it, the gurgling sounds coming from it . . . was all of it connected to that amulet? Was she so afraid of possibly being insane that she was willing to embrace an Egyptian relic as the source of all the terrifying things that had been happening to her? *Damn right*, she thought to herself.

They'll tell you.

Who?

Or had they already been trying to tell her?

***

Turning the corner on Winthrop Street, Jennifer broke into a run. It was nearly midnight, yet there was still a faithful contingent of losers milling around. Those who had nothing better to do than stand in front of a morgue hoping for a glimpse of the movie star who disdained them. She ran through them, possibly bumping one or two of them a little harder than necessary.

Not even bothering to take off her coat, she strode down the hallway, passing the break room where she saw Trevor's back, as he sat at the table with his feet up. He was Facetiming the barely legal Meadow, who was pulling her sweater up to show him her breasts. His name was written across them. Her ribs prominent.

"Eat a sandwich!" Jennifer yelled, passing the doorway. She was in no mood. In spite of brief flashes of humanity, Trevor Pryce was a perpetual naughty schoolboy. She walked into the autopsy room, where there were at least a half a dozen corpses on tables or gurneys around the chamber, waiting for their postmortems the next morning.

Pushing away the center autopsy table, ignoring the sheet-covered cadaver just inches from her face, she stared down at the drain. Getting down on her knees, she studied it closely.

The drain cover was rusted, dented, and had gross

chunks of red clots and fleshy bits that hadn't quite washed down. Jennifer paid no attention to this effluvium as she hooked her fingers through the grates of the drain cover and pulled.

Looking down into the dark hole, she saw light glinting off of something. She tried putting her hand into the drain, but it was too narrow to admit her entire fist. Rolling up her sleeve, she folded her thumb into her palm, and tried again, stretching out her four fingers and making her hand as thin as possible.

She kept going farther, until becoming afraid she'd never get her hand out again. Visions of a ghost woman's hand stuck in this drain, and its arm ripping out from its shoulder, flashed in her mind.

She made contact with the cool surface of the amulet.

Stretching and straining, the cuff of her shirt turning a disgusting rust color, she finally managed to ensnare the necklace chain between two fingers, and slowly brought the chain and the amulet up through the drain.

Out of breath, she sat cross-legged by the drain and cradled her prize in her lap. She studied it, angling it to get the best reflection from the dim yellow light from above. It was beautiful. At one time its gold finish must have been blinding. She hadn't really looked too closely when Ulysses had first showed it to her. Most intriguing was the black onyx profile of a noble-looking Egyptian dog of some kind. Unlike the amulet, it was unblemished and pure black, as if it were brand new.

The atmosphere changed in the room. There was an eerie sense of stillness. Jennifer froze. She began to have the distinct feeling she was being watched. She swallowed and slowly lifted her head to look up at the room.

Every corpse, on every table, sat up in unison.

Jennifer stared in shock – this macabre choreography was happening without sound. It was just a silent, synchronized movement of the dead. Like a decomposing gym class doing a ghastly sit-up in unison.

The white sheets slid off the cadavers and pooled on the floor. The dozen or so corpses stared lifelessly at her with their cloudy, blank eyes, their bodies in various stages of decay. Some had bullet wounds. Some had parts of their faces blown away by rifle shot. Others were diseased and putrefying. Still others looked like they had dropped dead of exhaustion. Jennifer recognized the corpse of the unfortunate young woman whom Angel had photographed, her abdomen gaping open, jagged ribs sticking out like broken tree branches. Jennifer flashed on the anorexic-looking Meadow.

Slowly, she got to her feet, clutching the amulet to her chest. She looked around at the bodies on the gurneys and tables; they surrounded her in a circle.

Again in unison, the arm of each body rose slowly and extended toward her. Their gnarled, papery hands reached for the amulet.

When the bodies leaned deeper into their reach, and Jennifer heard their crunching bones and popping joints, she unfroze and charged for the door, slamming into and knocking away the gurneys in her path.

She thought she heard a collective shriek over the sound of her own blood rushing in her ears.

Her knuckles white around the amulet, she reached the doorway, raced into the hall, and started to breathe again. Turning back to look through the glass into the autopsy room, she saw—

Every corpse was at rest, sheets over them, and every gurney was back in place. As if nothing had happened.

Jennifer took in the peaceful tableau. "Fuck this!" she shouted.

***

Click! She took a picture of the amulet with her phone.

Sitting at Clover's desk, she emailed the picture to herself, and downloaded it onto Clover's ancient PC, needing something bigger to look at than her phone screen. She fed the photo into Google image search.

Pages of text and images scrolled by. The words *Anubis, Guardian, Crypt,* featured repeatedly. There were also hundreds of images of the same black dog featured on the amulet – a dog called *The Anubis* in Egyptian mythology.

Jennifer clicked on a link called *Anubis – The Egyptian Guardian* and read as fast as she could.

Her arms bubbled with goosebumps.

Everything made sense.

"Holy shit," she observed.

***

Jennifer found Trevor in the body-storage room, and to her shock he actually seemed engaged in work, filling out a Body Control Card at the foot of a morgue drawer containing a wrapped corpse. She got over her surprise and approached, tossing the amulet on the corpse's legs. "You were only half right."

He looked at her in surprise. "That's exciting! I'm usually all wrong."

"This amulet." She pointed at it. "You were right about it being Egyptian—"

"Fourth-century Egyptian from the—"

"Yeah, yeah, yeah," Jennifer interrupted. "I'm impressed. But you said this amulet protects the living from the dead. It doesn't."

Trevor shrugged. "Okay . . ."

Picking up the amulet, she dangled it in front of his face. "It's meant to protect the dead from the living."

"What?"

She tapped her finger on the black onyx dog. "This is called Anubis. It's like an Egyptian guard dog that watches over graves and dead bodies. It protects the dead from grave robbers and . . . desecraters."

Trevor twisted his mouth in a halfhearted attempt not to smile. "Desecraters? Seriously?"

Jennifer wasn't going to let his sarcasm get to her. She was on to something, and she knew it. For the past hour and a half, she had schooled herself on the Egyptian god Anubis. The creature was depicted as a protector of graves as early as 3100 BC – the First Egyptian Dynasty. She learned that the Anubis was almost always represented as a creature with the body of a man, and the head of a dog-like jackal. Apparently jackals were known to scavenge for bodies to eat in ancient Egyptian cemeteries, so to turn a negative into a positive, they were assigned the duty of "protector of the dead."

The creature was always depicted as black, to represent the discoloration of a corpse after embalming, and the soil of the Nile. Ancient tombs had prayers to Anubis carved into their walls, and drawings of him were found in burial chambers from the Egyptian Old Kingdom.

Sticking the amulet in Trevor's face, she told him what else she'd learned. "When a dead body is threatened, the Anubis that's watching over it changes form and seeps inside of it somehow. It gets strength from the body's . . . I don't know, its mojo or whatever, then it's 'born out of the corpse.' "

"Come on!" Trevor exclaimed. "A dead body giving birth to a dog? This just gets better and better."

Jennifer got in his face. "It's a jackal, not a dog, and it tears out of the corpse and attacks the 'desecrater!' "

"Are you hearing yourself right now?"

"Maybe that's us. Maybe the dead think we're

desecrating them because of what we do here. Because of what you've done here."

"Ah. All my fault, naturally."

"I thought all this bizarre shit started when you showed up. But Ulysses hid this amulet in the drain your first night here. All this has been happening since then."

Trevor finished filling out the Body-Control Card. "You've lost the plot, love."

Jennifer grabbed his arm and made him face her, trying to dismiss the thought that his bicep felt hard as a rock. "Look, I saw the corpse that was in the van with Angel when he was killed. It looked like something exploded out of its middle!"

"Yes! Probably the engine block!"

"Right before they left, Angel took pictures of the corpse. Naked pictures."

"First of all, *ew*. Second of all, that makes him the desecrater, not me!"

"And that's why he was torn to pieces. By an animal! An animal with teeth and claws."

"The Anubis!" Trevor said with mock drama.

"That's why they want this amulet! They believe it can keep them safe from us."

"They who?" cried Trevor, confused.

"Hello! Are you even listening? The dead! The ghosts of the bodies here in this morgue. They want protection. From us. They sensed the amulet was here, and they've been asking for it this whole time."

Trevor moved her out of his way and slid the morgue drawer closed. "Right. Well, whatever you're taking, get me a gram or two."

Jennifer had had enough. She hated it when men dismissed her, when they acted like her ideas weren't worth listening to. She didn't take mansplaining from anybody; she certainly wasn't going to take it from this asshole.

She turned and walked away. He watched her.

"Come on, don't go away mad."

"Just go away, right?"

"I don't always mean to be such an asshole."

"Nevertheless, you are." She continued walking down the hall. He ran to catch up to her.

"I'm sorry. Finish your thought. I want to hear it."

"Don't patronize me! And don't forget, you're the one who said it's an Egyptian protection amulet."

"I had no idea what it is! It was all bollocks, I took a guess to impress you." He stopped her in the archway. "I also told you my new girlfriend's last name was Smith. Doesn't make it true."

"It is Smith."

Trevor blinked. "Really?"

She found his eyes. "This is the only thing that makes sense."

"It's the last thing that makes sense! Look, if there's something going on in this morgue, it's to do with Ersen, and, I don't know, identity theft or something, maybe even some kind of a cult thing, who knows? It's not about ghosts or Egyptian curses."

At that moment the lights in the morgue flickered. A row of overheard fluorescents made loud popping sounds, and several of them exploded in a shower of sparks. Trevor jumped.

Jennifer held his gaze. "You were saying?"

Trevor looked hard at her. Searched her eyes. He surprised her by speaking quietly. "Maybe you know this thing . . . this creature . . . better than you think."

"What does that mean?"

"Maybe you know where it lives."

She stared at him. How could he say that? Why would he say that?

Before she could follow up, they both jumped at the

loud, echoing sound of a door opening down the hall. Footsteps followed, along with the squeaky sound of something being wheeled toward them.

Of all the strange things she'd been hearing and seeing, this sound was at least routine – yet it scared her. "What is that?"

Breaking away from her, he looked down the hallway. "The Ghost of Christmas Past come to show me what my career would be like if I hadn't turned down the first *Avengers*."

Jennifer followed him into the hallway, where they saw Otis pushing a gurney toward them. Otis' head was bobbing up and down to the unheard tune in his earbuds. The body on the gurney was in a black rubber body bag, which meant it had been taken from a crime scene.

Jennifer slipped the amulet into her pocket. "Otis," she said with concern. "How are you doing?" Otis and Angel had worked together; he must be hurting, she thought.

Otis shrugged, speaking a little too loud over the hip-hop in his ears. "Okay, I guess. I miss Angel. Word."

"You guys were close?" Trevor asked.

"Nah. I just hate doing all this shit by myself."

Trevor looked at Jennifer. "Poignant."

"Don't dis a gangsta, yo," Otis warned Trevor.

"Wankster, more like," Trevor answered.

Otis glared at Trevor and handed Jennifer a pack of paperwork. "No ID, so he's all yours till someone claims him," he said sulkily.

Trevor perked up. "No ID? So he'll need a name!"

Jennifer glared at him. "No."

"This is just what we need to cheer each other up. A body naming!"

Jennifer was not in the mood. "Come on, I know we just had a brief moment there where no one was paying attention to you but get over it because I'm not naming a body tonight."

Trevor laughed and walked over to the gurney. He seemed to actually like it when she made fun of him; something else about him that drove her crazy.

Jennifer walked away; she was not going to participate in this.

Otis snickered and watched Trevor unzip the body bag. Trevor looked inside, and the smile faded as he froze in place. Otis noticed the look on his face and took out one of his earbuds.

"Yo dude, 'sup?" he asked.

Jennifer heard the alarm in Otis' voice. She looked over at them. Trevor finally tore his eyes away from the body in the bag and looked at her. The color was gone from his face.

Jennifer felt her heart drop. "What?"

Trevor tried to say something but couldn't seem to. Jennifer walked over to the body bag, keeping her eyes on Trevor. Looking away, he stepped back.

Jennifer looked down at the body – and stared into the dead face of Ulysses.

And not the clean-shaven, well-groomed face she'd seen at the hot dog stand. It was the old Ulysses. The bearded, dirty Ulysses. Blue, veiny skin. Mouth pulled back in a grimace. Yellow teeth bared. His eyes were open and bulging.

He died frightened.

Jennifer shook her head violently. "No. This is not him. This is not Ulysses. He doesn't look like this anymore. It's not him!" She shouted, her voice echoing off the metal lights above. Trevor and Otis looked at each other. Trevor looked back at Jennifer and spoke gently.

"It is him, Jennifer."

After a frozen moment, Jennifer grabbed at the body bag, zipping it open further, seeing the oblong stab wounds in the chest area of his coat and layers of shirts.

The tears came. Feeling out of control, her breathless

sobs made it almost impossible to speak. "No. I just saw him a few hours ago. He was fine."

"He's been dead since last night," Otis said.

Her head snapped toward him. "How do you know that?"

Otis stammered. "The 5-0 said it. They found him in an alley a few blocks from here. They said it looked like he was iced somewhere else and dumped there."

Jennifer couldn't keep her eyes off the terrified face of her dead friend. Her voice came out in a broken whisper: "He just found his daughter."

With a burst of rage-fueled adrenaline, she pushed the gurney into Otis, and ran down the hallway. Slamming through the front door of the morgue, she pushed her way through the crowd and into the night.

THIRTEEN

Jennifer had no idea where she was going, just as long as it was away from the morgue. A realization hit her with sudden clarity: she could never go back there. She was done with the morgue. She could never walk through that door and smell those smells without thinking of Ulysses' face, staring up at her from that gurney, almost like he was asking her how she could have let him die.

Jennifer hunched her shoulders against the chilly autumn air. The streets were strewn with leaves as she watched the brilliant, gold foliage silently float down around her. Fall was always a happy season for her. In spite of the fact that it signaled the coming of winter, she always found it a time of renewal, a time to get re-energized about life.

Not so much anymore.

Her lab coat was thin. Wishing she had thought to bring her jacket, she jammed her hands into her pockets and felt something with a sharp edge. Pulling it out, she looked down at Detective Marty Bell's card.

***

Ersen was on his way to his night job. His nose throbbed. He probably should've gone to a doctor, but who needed all the questions? One of his eyes was turning black. It was still hard to believe the old man had gotten that shot in – not that it had done him any good in the end, but Ersen hated himself for not seeing it coming. Plus it really hurt.

He was still pissed about his confrontation with Clover that night. She'd had the nerve to break his balls about the missing Sean Burrows body. Why did he always get the blame when things went wrong at the morgue? Granted, Ersen was usually at fault, but still, why did Clover always assume that was the case? Clover made threats about firing Ersen. That could never happen. It would sabotage everything that Ersen was working toward. He saw Clover as a threat.

It was no wonder that Ersen made the odd mistake. After his day shift in the morgue, he had only a couple of hours to have some dinner before it was time to head back out to his secret place of employment. On his "fasting" days, dinner consisted only of water and a few almonds. Ersen had grown to despise his two fasting days per week, which usually ended in him knocking over furniture in a desperate attempt to get to the refrigerator and stuff the first edible thing he could find into his hungry mouth.

They were incredibly busy at his night job. He had thought it would've slowed down after the Covid vaccine became available everywhere, but there still didn't seem to be enough hours in the day to keep up with demand. Who knew he would ever be willing to work this hard, juggling a day job that was really just a cover for his night gig? The lack of sleep was more than made up for by the fact that he was quickly growing rich. He, Ersen Tekin, was making a fortune. Oh, how he wished some of the people who grew up with him in Turkey could see him. How he wished his rotten, stingy, violent parents could see him. How he wished they would ask him for something. For money. For anything. There would be orgasmic pleasure in saying *Yok*. No.

Growing up on the streets of Istanbul, Ersen had always scoffed at education. He had been thrilled to quit high school after managing to talk himself into a job as a gravedigger in the historic Eyüp cemetery on the edge of Istanbul. While completely oblivious to the ornate tombs of sultans, scholars, and poets of the Ottoman Empire, he did become fascinated with the blank tombstones of the "Executioner Cemetery," on the adjacent Karyagdi Hill. Executioners were not allowed to be buried in public cemeteries, so they were buried on a hill next to Eyüp in the dark of night, secretly, with no names on the headstones, just to be sure an angry relative or friend of an executed prisoner wouldn't disrespect the executioner's stone by tearing it down or peeing on it. Not that Ersen really knew any of that; he just liked the idea of standing over men who had actually executed people.

Ersen fantasized about being an executioner, a man of mystery, wearing a black hood and doling out revenge and justice. Maybe women would finally find him interesting. Like most of his thoughts about a possible career, this one faded too, especially when capital punishment was outlawed in Turkey. Ersen saw this as another example of how society was doing its best to hold him back.

However, opportunity knocked as the fabled Eyüp cemetery become more and more a destination for drug dealers and prostitutes. The area was never monitored by police, and robberies and murders became commonplace. For once in his life, Ersen was in the right place at the right time. While always happy to take part in the odd mugging, his particular pot at the end of the rainbow came to him when he thought of something none of the other lowlifes had: what if he dug up graves and stole whatever valuables the corpses had buried with them?

Once again, Ersen's resistance to learning foiled him. Eyüp is a Muslim cemetery, and its residents are buried with nothing of value except a blindfold, and a piece of fabric to tie their jaws closed. Unaware of this, he dug up some dozen or so graves, cursing at the lack of treasure, before someone finally figured out what he was up to and fired him. That was fine with Ersen, for it let another of his ambitions move to the front burner: America. He became obsessed with the idea of going to the United States, a place where he was certain it was possible to get rich while avoiding work, and also where women might find him attractive because of his accent.

Finding a way to sneak onto a merchant ship, he made the long crossing and found himself stepping onto a Boston dock, with a song in his heart and a spring in his step. He was ready to start his new life – as soon as he could find someone or something to rob. Never what anyone would call a criminal mastermind, Ersen consistently aimed low: 7-Elevens, the occasional Taco Bell, a pretzel cart on Boston Common.

Not long afterward came the Uber Heist fiasco in Boston, his prison stint, and the INS mix-up that allowed his hasty relocation to New York. But that was all in the past. After spending some of his hard-earned cash for a fake social security number, he became an employee of New York City. Even more delightful, he had excellent medical coverage and several sick days a month! Who said crime doesn't pay? His experience and willingness in dealing with the dead made him a natural candidate for the morgue system, which sometimes had a hard time attracting employees.

All that would have been success enough for many; certainly it was more than Ersen ever really believed he'd attain. But his other job, a profession that had literally fallen into his lap, was the crowning achievement in a life totally devoid of any desire to do good.

He treasured his night job.

He was even willing to kill for it.

It was true he had a certain amount of hesitancy when it came time to kill Sean Burrows. His hands shook, and he came very close to peeing his pants. (Next time he killed someone, using a rest room first would be key.) Taking deep breaths and steeling himself by remembering what was at stake and the threat that Burrows posed, he found the strength to pull the trigger. Unable to bear being too close to Burrows, and in an unwitting nod to social distancing, Ersen shot him from much more than six feet away.

But the homeless guy, that crazy skell who kept snooping around the edges of the morgue – Ersen did him with a blade, up close. After getting clocked by the old man's forehead, he didn't have any trouble stabbing him, didn't even hesitate. Maybe it was because he wasn't about to take any shit from a hairy loser who lived in a mausoleum. Or maybe it was because he wasn't going to take a chance that the creep would stumble on the source of Ersen's treasure and babble about it. Not that anyone would probably believe him, but still. No room for sloppy thinking.

Or maybe Ersen was just getting tougher. That was his favorite theory. A theory he would soon test out on Clover.

Ersen had always dreamed of being an executioner.

***

"I'm sorry about your friend," Marty said to her, "but I didn't catch that case. I don't know much about it."

He didn't like it when people came to see him at his

desk at the Brooklyn South Homicide Task Force. The building was old and decaying, the second-floor bullpen was always cold, and everyone looked a sickly yellow under the bad fluorescent lights. The walls were full of out-of-date notices from the city and the department. They were kept hanging to hide the cracks in the plaster behind them. Considering himself a street cop, he preferred to interact with people in his natural habitat. But that night he was deskbound, pouring through the voluminous funeral-home files pilfered from Raffy Burrows' computer. Looking for connections. Wondering if there was some link between the River View Assisted Living Facility where Sean Burrows had worked, and the Drake and Sons Funeral Home, where Sean's twin Raffy worked. It was a long slog and Marty's eyes were burning. He had longed for a break.

Instead, Jennifer sat across from him at his cluttered desk. She had the most intense way of looking at you. Looking into you. Marty pitied anyone who tried to withhold something from her. Glancing at his bulletin board, he wished he had taken down the autographed headshot of Trevor Pryce. Hopefully she wouldn't see it.

At first, when taking her call, he'd hoped she had decided to level with him, to come in and tell him whatever it was he knew she was hiding. It might be a big thing, it might mean nothing, but he'd like to know. However, sitting in front of him, she was clearly devastated by the loss of her friend. Marty had only heard about the case in passing, just part of the usual body count.

"Does it bother you that two people who were connected to the morgue have died violently?" she asked, looking at him with those bottomless dark eyes. Watching her had the odd effect of making Marty wish he were twenty years younger, and at the same time glad he wasn't.

She reminded him of a woman he was in love with back in his rookie days, when he was about twenty-two or twenty-three. Lisa Rivas. A dark beauty, much like Jennifer, with the same kind of fierce intelligence. Lisa was a couple of years older, and a struggling actress. Marty knew nothing about the arts, still didn't as a matter of fact, but after running down a purse-snatcher for her on the street one day, he decided to ask her out. The memory made him smile inwardly at his younger self; he'd never have the balls to do that today.

It was the classic working-class guy meets the uptown girl. She had never known anyone like him; a tough cop who worked the streets and was handy with his fists when he had to be, who could also make her laugh and feel safe and listened to. And he certainly had never known anyone like her, for while she lacked street smarts, the breadth of her knowledge and her curiosity about life and people held him in awe. She saw things in him he didn't know had value. Having not even gone to college, Marty often felt a chasm between them; one that Lisa seemed to ignore.

Invited to her play rehearsals, he'd watch her perform, marveling at her courage; the way she exposed her inner self, her soul, in ways he never could. Nevertheless, their differences finally outweighed their similarities, and it ended. Badly. Marty told himself that he was out of her league, that he didn't like her whip-smart friends and their intense and complex conversations at dinners that he could barely keep up with. Everyone loved to hear his cop stories, of course, but telling them and watching their reaction only underlined the differences between them. At the time, he convinced himself she wasn't "real;" she was a self-absorbed "artist" living in a bubble, but Marty knew the truth. He was afraid of her, afraid of the intensity of their relationship and what he might have found out about himself if he was as fearlessly self-examining as Lisa was.

Marty often wondered what bend his life might have taken if he'd had the guts to commit to her. To commit to what it would've taken to be with her. Was she the change he had always waited for? The transformation he always saw coming for himself, and always ended up avoiding? The change he had missed?

"Detective?"

Snapping out of his mini-reverie, he realized Jennifer was waiting for a response. He seemed to be doing that a lot – getting lost in the past. Did it have something to do with turning fifty soon?

Marty cleared his throat. "It bothers me when *anybody* dies violently. But first of all, we don't know your transport guy Angel was murdered. It's a suspicious death for sure, but it hasn't been classified as a homicide yet. And what exactly was your homeless friend's connection to the morgue?"

"Me," she said simply. "I helped him when I could. He'd come by when my boss wasn't around, and I would give him things he needed. Sometimes just a Band-Aid. I used to visit him in the cemetery next to the morgue."

"You went to a cemetery to see him while he was still alive?"

"He lived there. In an old mausoleum."

Marty nodded and made a note on the yellow pad on his desk. Not thinking there was any reason to follow up on this, he would probably tear it up when she left, but people felt better when notes were taken.

"Okay. The thing is, other than the coincidence of this homeless guy's proximity to the morgue, there's nothing connecting these cases."

"His name was Ulysses."

"I think with Ulysses we just have a garden-variety homeless killing."

He regretted saying that the instant the words were out of his mouth, and by the expression on her face it was obvious she didn't approve. "I didn't mean it like that," Marty said, shaking his head and sitting back in his squeaky chair. "But there's a lot of crime against the homeless; beatings, rapes, they've even been set on fire. It's horrible but it's a fact."

"One of the cops told Otis that it looked like Ulysses had been killed somewhere else and dumped there. Doesn't that sound a little less garden-variety?"

"It sounds like you know more about this case than I do," he said, thinking to himself that cops should keep their fucking mouths shut around civilians. Leaning forward again, he found her eyes. "Look, I know what you're hoping for. I see it every day. We all want there to be a reason for the things that happen. We want it to make sense somehow, even if it's horrible sense. And sometimes we're looking for a reason for the shit that happens just so we can feel safe, so that it doesn't apply to us. 'He walked alone in a dangerous neighborhood' 'She smoked two packs a day.' 'He ate nothing but cheeseburgers.' But if I've learned one thing from years of doing this, very little makes sense. Very little happens for a reason. Bad shit comes out of nowhere, random people destroy other random people for no reason and half the time we never know why."

"So you're saying it's all out of our control?"

Looking at her, Marty knew he should follow his own advice about talking to civilians. Leaning back again, he regarded her. "What exactly do you want from me?"

"I just want to feel that somebody gives a shit that Ulysses was murdered. He should matter. His death should matter."

"Fair enough. Can I tell you what I'd like from you?"

She looked at him, surprised. Defensive.

Marty decided to go for it: "The truth. I know you're holding something back. There's more to what's going on here and you're not telling me. I can't help you if you won't help me."

She stared at him, her jaw working. It was clear to him

that there was more, and she wanted to tell him.

"If I told you everything you'd think I'm crazy."

"I'm a detective in New York City. I live in the crazy."

Holding her gaze, he saw her mind turning this over. Would she trust him?

He just waited.

"You're a cop. You probably only believe in things you can see and touch. Correct?"

Uh-oh, he thought, not expecting this. Was she going *Twilight Zone* on him? "Try me," he said, keeping a neutral tone.

Her eyes flicked to the side for a second, as if she were suddenly distracted. Then she looked at him and took a breath. "The murder victim whose body we lost."

"Sean Burrows."

"Do you really think that was just a clerical error?"

He couldn't hide his surprise. "Wasn't it?"

Staring at him, she tried to figure out how far to go.

He pressed. "Are you saying someone made it disappear?"

"Maybe some *thing.*"

Marty stared back at her. He wanted to smile, but something about the look in her eyes made the hair rise on his neck. She was serious. Another long pause, she looked deep in thought. Keeping his mouth shut, he waited for her to say more. His strategy backfired when she suddenly shook her head and got up.

"Never mind."

"Really? You drop that on me and now it's 'Never mind?' "

Looking away, she said, "I don't really know what I'm talking about. Yet. Thanks for your time." As she turned from the desk, her eyes fell on his bulletin board. She looked back at him.

"I'll let Trevor know you're a big fan."

Shit. Before he could think of a witty response, she was walking away from his desk.

The room seemed a little dimmer.

***

Jennifer left the precinct house and walked, not knowing where she was going. The crisp air felt good, and her legs needed stretching. She had come close to telling Bell what she thought was happening at the morgue – at least he acted like he'd be open to listening to her. Still, this detective had no way to anticipate that this was going to take a left turn into the supernatural. She was afraid that whatever credibility she had would vanish.

When he'd said, "Try me." she flashed on a memory with her father. In the depths of his insanity, when he was trying to convince her that one of his hallucinations was real, she would listen patiently and try not to seem judgmental. When he prefaced it by saying, "I know you're not going to believe this," she'd always responded, "Try me."

She had probably looked at her dad the same way Detective Bell had looked at her, making an attempt to arrange her face so that she seemed willing to believe. *Tell me anything.* But she'd seen the fear in her father's eyes; heard his certainty that the things he saw were real. That all the horror in his mind's eye was actually happening to him. That she herself was trying to kill him. Her face must have finally reflected her own fear and horror, and the grief of seeing him come to this.

She was not going to take a chance on seeing a similar look on Bell's face.

Walking the streets, hugging herself against the chill autumn air, she began to think maybe the detective was right. Ulysses being killed didn't have anything to do with what was going on with the morgue. She would have to live with the thought that he was murdered by some random asshole.

Jennifer had fought against the idea of randomness all her life. She strove to find reason and meaning in the things that happened to her. To those around her. Maybe there was no meaning. Who would know that better than a cop?

No matter. She was done with the morgue, and with that chapter of her life. She decided to go to the cemetery and say a final good-bye to Ulysses. She would make peace with his death.

***

Lighting the candle, her tears blurred the flame, and she had to squint to be sure her match touched the wick. Once lit, she used that candle to light the others all around the mausoleum. All around Ulysses' home.

She took in the cluttered space in the dancing candlelight. Each thing she saw made her heart ache. His sleeping bag, his shelf of neatly stacked canned foods, his paper towels. His bags of popcorn. He loved popcorn.

Jennifer saw the board with trinkets and pictures and articles pinned to it; it was way back in the shadows, so she had to go close to see it. Bringing the candle with her, she looked through the pinned newspaper articles that he hadn't wanted her to touch the last night she'd been there with him.

Lifting some of the articles from the board, she fingered them carefully; they were old, brittle, torn up around the edges. One article in particular gave her pause, from the *Rockland Journal News*. It was from eight years ago.

She read it, all of it, and her heart clutched. "Oh shit."

Just then there was a loud commotion from the street in front of the cemetery; she carefully pinned the article back to the board and looked out through the wrought iron barred opening in the wall of the mausoleum.

The Desecrated

She could just about see the street from here, and her eyes widened when she saw Trevor leaving the front entrance of the morgue and wading into the crowd of fans. *Don't tell me he's that desperate for attention,* she thought. His fans went berserk, grabbing at him, sticking phones in his face and taking pictures, begging for selfies, pushing pens and paper at him, nearly stabbing him. But she could tell that there was a purpose – he kept moving through the crowd, laughing and smiling and nodding, until reaching the liquor store across the street from the morgue. Quickly opening the door, he entered, as the two startled clerks looked on in shock, first at him, than at the crazed army headed toward the store.

Jennifer watched as one of the liquor store clerks had to hold the door closed behind Trevor to keep out the boisterous crowd. Camera flashes popped like hundreds of little lightning strikes. She saw Trevor talking to the owner of the store, an older man with a shiny bald head, wearing a Hawaiian shirt, looking at different bottles of liquor. Finally, Trevor nodded his head and handed over some wadded cash from his pocket to the storeowner, whose face lit up with joy when he looked at the bills.

Lots of laughter and back slapping, and Trevor again came back out onto the street, carrying his bottle in a brown bag, wrapped tight at the neck. The frenzy was even worse this time. A blond in a tank top tore at his shirt, one frizzy-haired woman in her forties grabbed at his crotch, and one teenage girl jumped on his back and tried to lick his face. The few reporters who were still manning the front were thrilled that their vigilance had paid off. They took pictures and shouted questions Jennifer couldn't hear and pushed and shoved with the best of them.

Trevor finally made it to the curb, stumbled into the front door of the morgue, and managed to close the door behind him before anyone could follow him in. There was a collective disappointed groan from the crowd.

Jennifer was puzzled. Did Trevor want a drink so badly that he'd run the crazed-fan gauntlet, and risk having pictures of the DUI convicted movie star buying liquor during his community service?

The heavy side door of the morgue groaned as it opened. Trevor emerged, holding the bottle, and made his way through the small parking lot, and into the cemetery. Jennifer stood back in the mausoleum, not sure if she wanted him to see her. Had he decided to have a drink in the quiet of this old graveyard? She became even more puzzled when Trevor headed directly to the mausoleum.

His hair was a mess. His clothes torn. Seeing her, he grinned, holding up the bottle triumphantly, along with two paper cups from the morgue. "I had to explain what Macallan single malt was. Although he was delighted to discover that it cost two-hundred dollars."

She had mixed feelings about Trevor being there. She wanted to be alone, but she was also craving some kind of human contact. He would have to do. "How'd you know I'd be here?"

Coming into the mausoleum, he gave her a sheepish look. "I followed you once."

"Stalker."

"I prefer to think of myself as curious." Setting the cups down on the stained marble floor, he twisted open the bottle of rare scotch with a grin.

A grin she knew she needed.

***

Back at his desk, Marty yawned. Going through the voluminous files from Drake and Sons Funeral Home was less than riveting. He was learning things about the funeral business he never knew, like how much money people were willing to pay to be sure they were not eaten by worms. Burial vaults for caskets, concrete coffin liners, watertight caskets (The Lady Guadalupe Blue Steel Model – Airtight and Waterproof!) Drake and Sons sold a ton of these things for the discerning mourner, who obviously didn't believe in the whole "dust to dust" thing.

Marty figured when his time came, he would go the cremation route, as had his mother. Her funeral had been a sad affair; she was deep into her upper eighties when she died, and there were very few friends left to mourn her. Marty was the only child; his father had gone years before, as men so often do. And now his mother's ashes (urn open, always) sat on his mantle, keeping a lonely vigil over his apartment. Who would mourn him, he wondered? Who would take possession of his ashes? After Lisa Rivas, Marty had been in love plenty, but had never married. He liked being free, not because he was a womanizer, he wasn't, but because he always believed in change. Change was good, and settling into a dull routine, even with someone you loved, was ultimately soul killing. Every time he entered into a relationship, he could never shake the suspicion that change was right around the corner, and that change would bring something real to him: real love, real friendship, a real career.

Marty also knew, deep down behind his left kidney, that he had always been waiting for another Lisa Rivas to come along. And should that happen, he hoped he'd be ready.

Approaching fifty, he was beginning to understand that the missing ingredient in this change was him. Only he could be the agent of his own transformation. There would be no *deus ex machina* (a phrase he'd often read but never had occasion to speak out loud). There would be no sudden variation he didn't see coming. His life was just going to keep chugging along exactly as it had been. At age twenty-five, the irony of this would've killed him. All this resistance to a linear life, to lasting love, the successful design of his existence so as not to be weighed down by commitment, would ultimately lead to him being alone and living a fairly routine life, all of which would have been anathema to him in his youth.

At forty-nine, he was kind of fine with it.

Yawning again, Marty tried to focus on the computer screen, not even sure what he was looking for. There had to be a reason Raffy Burrows had been rifling through the files at River View, and it wasn't to protect the privacy of his departed brother Sean. What was the connection? Would he find it in the myriad records of a local funeral home?

Marty sat up when he saw a funeral folder labeled *Regina Bell.*

His mother.

Hesitating, he wondered if he should open it. Somehow, it felt as if he'd be invading her privacy, but of course that was crazy. There could be nothing in that folder that he didn't know. Or hadn't arranged for. Most of these folders contained pretty dry files; dates, services rendered, charges, etc.

He decided to keep scrolling.

He stopped, scrolled back, and opened it.

Glancing at the cryptic notes in the file, it seemed routine: his mother's full name, date of birth, date of death.

Services rendered: Funeral Services, Embalming, Cosmetic Services, Hearse and Limousine Transport to the church for funeral mass (Regina had considered herself a good Catholic, even though she had not attended Mass in decades), *Document Filings: Death Certificate and Obituary (Regina is survived by her only son, Martin, an NYPD Detective), Viewing Room, Cremation Services, Urn . . .*

It seemed to go on and on; a macabre catalog of life's final checklist.

One last line item caught his eye: *Misc. Transport.*

He scrolled under this cryptic entry, preceded by a date: *March 31ˢᵗ, Transport to 599 Winthrop.*

Marty was very awake now. Staring at the screen. There was that address again. 599 Winthrop was the morgue in Brooklyn. The morgue that had lost his murder victim. The morgue where another victim of a mysterious crash lay on a cold table. He had found a connection all right. Not between the funeral home and the assisted living facility, but between the morgue and the funeral home. Why would his mother have been sent to a morgue? She had died at a nursing home that had nothing to do with River View, and she'd been picked up from there by Drake and Sons. Marty had arranged that himself. There was never a need for a stay at a morgue.

Was he looking at a clerical error? An entry mistakenly made that was meant for another dead person's file?

He remembered what Jennifer had said to him just a few hours before: *The murder victim whose body we lost. Do you really think that was just a clerical error?*

An electric jolt shot through Marty's body. He checked the date again. March thirty-first.

There had been no need to send his mother to a morgue after her funeral. And certainly no need to send her to a morgue the day after her cremation.

***

Nearly an hour later, the bottle of Macallan was half gone and Jennifer noticed her eyes were blinking very slowly. She looked at the golden-brown liquid in her cup. "This stuff is amazing." She slurred the "Z" in amazing, like she couldn't quite figure out when to stop pronouncing it.

"Pays to buy the best, I always say," Trevor said, seemingly unaffected by the scotch.

She looked at him. He seemed completely at home here in this tomb, slouched across one of the benches, long legs extended, totally relaxed and at ease, just as he always was. Never had she encountered someone so effortlessly sexy. Looking up through the open roof of the mausoleum, he seemed to be interested in and amused by the swaying tree branches above him.

"I saw you go to the liquor store. People were taking pictures. Reporters were taking pictures. Won't that get you in trouble? When they see you buying booze?"

Trevor shrugged. "Probably." Taking another sip, he poured more for the both of them.

"Is that what it's always like for you? Just going outside?" she asked.

"Pretty much," he answered lightly.

"So . . . you never really get to take a walk?"

Trevor looked at her. Laughed. "Walk to the pub. Jog around the park. Go see a movie. Haven't done any of it in years." There was that grin again. "Poor me, right?"

She raised one shoulder. "Kind of." He looked away. "Don't you feel like a prisoner?"

"I am a prisoner. A golden cage I grant you, but I despise it. And I'll despise it right up until the point where no one notices me anymore. Then I'll despise that. I'm basically fucked. It's that simple."

"I don't know why anybody would want to be famous."

"You mean besides scads of money and shagging at will?"

Jennifer smiled. She looked away. She felt Trevor's eyes on her. "You do like acting though, right?"

"Yes. And I also like what I do."

She laughed.

"I love it, actually," he said quietly looking out over the cemetery between the iron bars of the mausoleum, studying the rows of gravestones. "I like that I get to make believe I'm somebody else for a little while. Anybody else, as long as it's not me."

Watching him, she saw a little glint of sadness in his eyes.

"It never lasts long enough though," he added. "Before you know it, I'm stuck being me again. When Covid shut everything down and no movies were being made, I was stuck being only me for over a year." He smiled thinly at her. "I pray that never happens again."

Jennifer took this in. They were quiet for a moment. Looking at her, he held up the bottle; she leaned toward him with her cup so he could fill it again.

She swirled the rich golden liquid thoughtfully. "Can I ask you a question?"

"Absolutely."

"How come you never really seriously hit on me?"

He grinned. "Ah. Disappointed?"

"Relieved."

Laughing, he shrugged. "The naked truth is that I know I don't have anything . . . real to offer someone like you. Except, probably, more hurt."

Jennifer watched him drink.

He looked at her, this time without the grin. "And if I had?"

"You would've wasted your time."

"Really? No desire to be with a real-life movie star?"

"No desire to be a notch."

He nodded, taking this in with a little smile. He raised his cup to Jennifer. "Anyway, here's to Ulysses."

"You didn't even like Ulysses. You were rude and nasty to him."

"I'm rude and nasty to most people."

They touched cups and drank. Changing position on the bench, he hunched his shoulders and leaned closer to her. "The thing is, and I mean this with all humility, I am most often smarter than anyone I meet. And I meet a lot of people. After a while, one loses patience."

"And humility."

Trevor smiled and toasted her again.

As he drank, Jennifer put her head back. Hearing the wind in the trees and the muted crickets made her think of her last time here with Ulysses. "He was so alone," she said, almost to herself.

"As are you," Trevor observed.

"What does that mean?" she asked, defensively.

"Oh, don't get me wrong. I admire it. I envy people who know how to be alone. Who are comfortable with it. Who seek it."

Jennifer looked at him. Absorbing this.

"For me, the thought of being alone, even for an hour, is terrifying."

Tilting her head, she tried to fathom him. Had he just made himself somewhat vulnerable? "I can't figure out if you're a smart guy trying to act like fool, or a fool trying to act like a smart guy."

"If only I were that complex."

Jennifer leaned forward, her forehead only inches from his. He'd let her see something inside of him, so she decided to take a risk herself. "I saw Ulysses. Tonight. He was like a whole new person. He told me his daughter found him."

Trevor looked at her steadily and tried to keep judgment out of his voice. "But Otis said Ulysses has been dead for a day at least."

Jennifer got up, immediately felt the effect of the scotch, and steadied herself against the mausoleum wall. She glanced at Trevor, but instead of the expected snicker he just seemed interested to see what she'd do next.

Reaching over to Ulysses' board, she gently removed the *Rockland Journal News* article she had read earlier and handed it to him.

He took in the picture of an adorable twelve-year-old girl. " 'Middle schooler killed in bus crash,' " he read.

"Ulysses told me he was put into an institution about eight years ago. See the date on the article?"

"October tenth. Eight years ago." He looked at her. "His daughter's been dead all this time?"

"That's what sent him over the edge. It broke him. That must be why his wife put him away."

"To quote Jennifer Shelby: 'We don't die all at once, we die little by little.' "

They looked at each other. Jennifer finished her drink. Trevor lifted the bottle, but she waved him off. She was too dizzy.

"You said he found his daughter," said Trevor.

"That's what he told me. I think his daughter came for him when he was killed."

"Her ghost came to him, you mean."

Jennifer looked at him; waiting for that twisted grin; the sarcastic remark. But he was just returning her gaze. Interested. Engaged.

"And he came to me to warn me about the amulet."

"You're saying that Ulysses was dead when you saw him."

Jennifer nodded and sat back. She watched Trevor process this.

"You know how this sounds, don't you?" he said.

"I'm not my father. I know what I saw." The tear rolled down her cheek before she even knew it was there. Turning quickly away, she wiped it.

Trevor cocked his head and looked at her. "What?"

"Here we are sitting in a cemetery. Monuments to the memory of the dead all around us. And he's not even gonna get a funeral, or a real burial. No one's gonna even claim his body."

Trevor looked at her. Something danced in his eyes. "Let's do it ourselves."

"Do what?"

"Give Ulysses a proper sendoff."

"How?"

Trevor came close to her again. Excited. "I can get a limo here in ten minutes. We take his body, and . . . I don't know, give him a burial at sea! A Viking funeral maybe!"

A smile finally slid onto Jennifer's face. "Coney Island!"

"Yes!" Trevor cried. "A final ride on the Wonder Cyclone!"

"You mean the Wonder Wheel."

"That too! We'll set him free from this awful place."

Jennifer looked back at the drab brown and gray brick of the morgue building. "On one condition," she said, looking at Trevor.

Trevor was already standing up. Man on a mission. "Name it."

"After the funeral, we never set foot in that *fucking* morgue again."

Trevor jumped for joy. "Greatest plan ever!"

They grabbed the nearly empty bottle and their empty cups, and ran, laughing, back to the morgue building.

***

"Where the hell is he?"

Jennifer and Trevor had come back into the body-storage room only to find no sign of Ulysses or the gurney that carried him.

"He was right here," Trevor said.

"What about Otis?"

Trevor looked at her. "After you left, he and I wheeled Ulysses into this room. Then Otis took off. Ulysses was right here when I went to the off-license."

"Where?" Jennifer asked, puzzled.

"To buy the scotch."

"This is crazy," Jennifer said. " He's got to be here."

They searched every room in the morgue. The prep room, the autopsy room, even Clover's office and the "employee lounge." They checked every gurney, lifting sheets and unzipping body bags. They even slid out every tray from the refrigerated drawers.

No Ulysses.

They looked at each other. "Missing body number three," Trevor said.

"Maybe number four," Jennifer said with a shudder.

"What?"

"You saw it yourself. My father was sent here after his funeral. For no reason that makes sense."

Trevor swallowed. "You think something's being done with these bodies?"

She shrugged. "What do you think?"

He thought for a moment and then looked at her, a sparkle in his eye. "You said your father is buried in Queens."

"Right."

"And what's a 'Queens'?"

"It's a place. A borough."

"Near here?"

"Near enough, I guess. Why?"

He looked around. "Do they keep shovels here? Maybe for snow?"

She stared at him. "No. No way."

Taking her by the arms, he looked at her. "It's the only way to be sure. If they're doing something to the bodies, shouldn't we find out? Don't you want to know if . . . if they did something to your dad? Something you can take to the police?"

She looked away. "I'm not digging up my father."

"Of course not," he said, surprisingly gently. "I'll do it. You just show me where."

***

Marty was so rarely in his apartment during the nighttime hours that it looked somehow unfamiliar to him. The shadows fell in odd places that made it feel like his furniture and bookcases were trying to hide from him. No matter, it would be a quick stop.

Walking into his living room, he faced the mantel where the urn (open) containing his mother's ashes rested. He gazed at it for a moment, picked up the cork-lined lid and sealed the urn.

"Sorry Mom. We have to go for a ride."

Out of respect for his claustrophobic mother, he avoided the tunnel on his drive to the police lab and took the Brooklyn Bridge.

***

A brisk, biting wind blew through Calvary Cemetery. The warming effects of the Macallan had worn off as Jennifer leaned against a headstone, hugging her elbows against the chill. She looked up. There was a spectacular blanket of stars above her – an incredibly clear fall night. Or morning. Checking her watch, she saw it was nearly 4 AM.

Doing her best to block out the sounds of the shovel, she tried to concentrate on the more comforting sound of the wind in the trees above. Watching the brown leaves fall gently around her made her think of a similar night when she was a little girl. Always trying to cheer her up after the death of her mother, her dad had taken her to Amagansett on the Long Island shore. He'd rented them a cheap, off-season cabin right on the water. Just the two of them. One night he woke her up well after midnight. "Get dressed. I want to show you something," he whispered.

Groggy and cranky, she did as she was told, and her father took her by the hand down to the beach. She felt the warm breeze, and she could still feel the rough skin of his palm clutching her tiny hand. Being a city girl, she couldn't believe how dark it was – there were no lights anywhere.

They got to the beach, and he pointed to the sky. "Look."

Her breath caught at the sight of the sprawling canopy of stars above her, an explosion of tiny twinkling lights so near she could almost reach out and touch them.

"We can't see this where we live, 'cause of all the lights in the city," her father whispered. She didn't know why he was whispering, but she loved the conspiratorial feeling it gave her. Like a secret they were sharing. "You have to come to a place like this, where it's just nature," he said, "to really see the stars."

Holding her hand tightly, they both just stood there, looking up at the night sky, and the amazing, unfathomable banquet of constellations and stars, for a long time.

"Almost there," Trevor said from the other side of the tree that separated her from her father's grave. She shivered. She didn't want to see it; didn't want to see the mound of dirt growing beside it, didn't want to see the gaping hole that was never meant to be open again. She didn't want to see the shoddy coffin that was the only one she could afford, remembering the small, judgmental *sniff* from the undertaker.

"I just had a rather disturbing thought." She heard the effort in his voice as he wielded the shovel.

"Just one?" she asked, raising her voice so she could be heard beyond the tree.

"Does this officially make us 'desecraters'?"

"What's this 'us' shit?" she asked, hoping to lighten the moment. "You're the one digging."

"Good point," he said, out of breath. "I haven't worked this hard since I tried to seduce Zoe Kravitz. Long story."

"I'll bet."

"Total failure, if I'm honest. Although I did manage to—"

"I don't need the details, thanks."

"Well it was all sort of—" He was cut off by the loud sound of metal meeting wood.

The shovel had struck the coffin.

Jennifer backed away a few feet and hugged herself tighter. Trevor grunted, and there was the sound of wood cracking.

Silence.

"Trevor?" she called out.

His face appeared above the slight hill near the tree. His shirt was off, and his body glistened with sweat in spite of the chill. His face and hands were smudged with dirt. He looked at her. "You should see this," he said quietly.

"Can't you just tell me?" she pleaded.

Turning away from her, he leaned on the shovel, looking down.

Taking a breath, she started walking toward him. Her legs felt weak. She passed the tree, and saw the large yawning, ragged hole Trevor had dug beneath her father's headstone. She looked up at the sky again, at the stars winking down at her, and took a few more steps to the edge of the grave to see into it.

Trevor looked at her. "I guess the good news is, we're not desecraters."

Jennifer looked down at the dirt-smeared, worn coffin that Trevor had broken open.

It was empty.

***

"I've had a lot of weird requests here, Bell, but this is a first," Amina Mahdi said as she squinted through a microscope at the NYPD police lab. Amina was in her late thirties, with jet-black hair. Holding her eyeglasses in her hand as her upper lip curled toward her nose, she kept her eyes glued to the double-barreled eyepieces.

To his left, Marty watched the large, bright monitor that mirrored what Amina was seeing. He noticed Amina straining to see through the microscope. "Why don't you just watch the monitor?"

"Old school, baby."

Amina had worked nights at the police lab for years. Like Marty, she had grown used to the upside-down quality of life on the night shift and wouldn't know how to work days. Marty liked Amina; she was smart as a whip, and not all that bound to the rules. The diminutive lab tech had done many favors for him in the past, mostly because Marty had done her one giant favor several years ago. When Amina somehow attracted a stalker, Marty, on his own time, had tracked him down, unmasked him, and in a face-to-face meeting, Marty's sheer size and intensity had persuaded this lovesick loser to leave Amina alone. Ever since, when Marty needed something expedited through the byzantine lab bureaucracy, Amina was happy to help.

Which is why Amina studied the ashes of Marty's dead mother. Marty had to be sure. There were the weird connections he'd been finding lately, along with the recent dreams of his mother in a flaming building. He flashed on that Google hit he had found – *fire can represent transformation. Something no longer in its original form.* Not to mention the fact that his mother may have been sent to the morgue in Brooklyn after her wake. The morgue that more and more seemed to be the centerpiece of a lot of bizarre shit.

"May I ask what case this is in reference to Marty?" Amina asked, eyes still glued to the microscope.

"You may not."

"It is a case, though, correct?"

"Define 'case.' "

"Uh-oh. Am I going to get rendered to Guantanamo for this?"

"Only if you don't hurry it up."

Amina leaned back from the microscope, two circular indentations ringing her eyes, and looked at the tired detective. She put her glasses on. "Do you have pets, Marty?"

"What? No."

"Well, this is cat litter. Cat litter and flour. Dark rye flour, to be exact. These are not human ashes."

Marty's heart skipped a beat. He understood exactly what was happening.

***

Jennifer and Trevor had rushed back to the morgue. She felt ridiculous riding in the limousine Trevor hired, next to a dirt-smeared movie star, with a filthy shovel between them. Her heart was racing and had been since she had looked into the empty casket of her father.

Where was he?

What had been done to him?

While she was grateful not to have cried in front of Trevor, it was now all she could do to tamp down the growing rage that was burning up her insides. It was bad enough the way her father's life ended, and the months leading up to that end. To discover that his body had continued to have some kind of indignity inflicted on it after he was dead was too much to even contemplate.

Trevor was uncharacteristically quiet as they drove along the nearly empty Brooklyn Queens Expressway. He seemed to sense, for once, that it was not a time for jokes. Jennifer remembered something he said earlier that had bothered her.

"When I first told you about the Anubis, you said I may

know this creature better than I think. What did you mean?"

Trevor shrugged, looking out of the limo window. "I don't really know. It's just that – it seemed like the angrier you became, the more upset you were, the crazier things got in the morgue."

They both fell silent again as Jennifer took this in. Was Miss Nadja right about her feelings being more powerful than she knew? Was her own fucked-up psyche causing all this? Trevor interrupted her train of thought when he suggested quietly that they call Detective Bell.

Jennifer had thought about that already. "Not yet. It's all too random. I want to find something real. Some proof." *If there is such a thing as proof,* she thought.

"Of what?" he asked, looking at her.

She turned to him. "Of whatever's going on in that fucking morgue."

***

Their footsteps echoed as they walked down the tiled halls of the morgue. The gothic arches of the doorways, the institutional green walls, and the eternally buzzing fluorescents all took on a creepier, more menacing atmosphere than usual. Who knew what had happened to the other missing bodies, her father's included? But Ulysses' body had been there just hours ago . . . while she and Trevor had sat in his mausoleum and talked, they hadn't seen any vehicles or people approach the morgue. His body had to be close by still.

Without speaking, they again checked every room, every supply closet and maintenance closet. Trevor returned the shovel to the last one they checked and slammed the door.

When they passed the wall that Clover had recently sheet rocked, she stopped.

"Wait. Clover told me there's a basement below us. Just pipes and plumbing and stuff. She said it's not used anymore."

"Let's take her word for it. I've had enough dank dark places for one night."

"We have to check it."

"How?"

He had a point. She had never seen a staircase, or an elevator, or any way to get to a basement.

As if reading her mind, Trevor said, "Maybe the entrance to the basement is outside."

She looked at him. Of course. There was a side door that led to the small parking lot, but there was also a rusted door and a bulkhead behind the building. She had barely noticed them the few times she had to take something to the toxic waste receptacles back there.

"Follow me," she said, leading him to that rear door, which was down a little-used hallway on the other side of the morgue. When they stood at the beginning of that neglected hallway, they saw that most of it fell off into shadows. Jennifer tried the light switch, clicking it up and down uselessly. Opening her phone, she tapped the flashlight on as they walked deeper into the hallway, looking for the metal door she knew was there somewhere.

Up ahead, where the hall dead-ended, Jennifer saw something in the shadows. She aimed the light at the dark corner. Trevor followed her gaze. They were looking at a gurney.

A gurney with a body bag resting on it.

"Is someone having us on?" Trevor asked nervously.

Jennifer wondered if Otis had somehow thought it would be funny to come back and hide Ulysses' body on them. That was extremely unlikely, she knew. Otis would never come back to the morgue so soon for fear of being given something to do, and he had also never exhibited anything even close to a sense of humor.

After hesitating a moment, Jennifer walked cautiously toward the gurney, Trevor following.

As they got closer, they saw the body bag was unzipped. And gaping open.

Empty.

Trevor swallowed. "Why would this end up here?"

"I don't know," Jennifer answered, shining her light in all corners of the hallway.

"And who would take the body? It's just us here, right?"

"I hope so," Jennifer said.

"He didn't just get up and walk away."

When Jennifer didn't answer, Trevor stood in front of her. "Right?"

"Don't be an idiot." She pushed the gurney aside to see if there was anything under it.

The corner of the gurney banged into the wall, and an unseen panel depressed when it made contact.

Jennifer and Trevor jumped at the loud groan of metal that filled the hallway. So loud they looked around frantically trying to fathom where it was coming from.

Jennifer aimed the dim light beam up at the ceiling. Trevor followed her gaze. So they were both taken even more by surprise when the floor below them fell away.

The floor separated into two giant panels, which swung down on hinges, plummeting them into the darkness below.

FOURTEEN

The wind was knocked out of Jennifer as she hit the floor hard. Feeling the dirt and grit under her hands, she scrambled to get back on her feet. She didn't know if anything was broken, but her shins and knees were on fire.

Trevor rolled onto his back. He sat up, like her, totally disoriented. It was pitch dark, with only a dusty column of light filtering down from the trap doors above.

Before they could really figure out what just happened, they were startled by a loud crack from above them. They jerked their heads upward, where a ceiling panel opened above the swinging trap doors, and two large, metallic objects hurtled down toward them. Trevor literally tackled Jennifer just before the mass of falling metal crashed into the floor where she had just been standing, raising a cloud of dust.

He helped Jennifer up as they stared at what looked like two giant hooks. The hooks were actually connected to cables, which ran up into the ceiling of the floor above them. Jennifer recognized these hooks.

Eyehooks.

"Hooks like these were delivered here a few days ago. I asked Clover what they were, and she said Ersen ordered them by mistake."

Trevor picked up one of the hooks; it took both hands. The end of it was incredibly sharp. They both noticed some kind of debris on the edge of the hook. When they looked closer, Trevor gasped.

There was blood, and what looked like bits of flesh on the edge of the hook. Trevor dropped it as if it were on fire. Jennifer thought he might start hyperventilating.

"Okay. I'd like to get out of here now, thanks." There was panic in his voice.

"How?" she asked. They looked above them; they were too far below the trap door to get back up. Jennifer aimed the light in every direction, but there were no handholds, no way to climb. The shaft was meant to receive something heavy, which would be lowered from the hooks above – no one was supposed to fall through it.

"I'm calling Clover." She punched her number in, and nothing happened. Checking the signal, she saw there were no bars. She didn't understand; they weren't that far down. "Okay," she said, taking a breath. "There's got to be an exit. A staircase. Something that leads outside."

Trevor looked past her into the darkness that stretched beyond. "I'm not going."

"We have to."

"Look, I was in three horror movies. This is the exact moment where the main character makes the wrong choice and dies a horrible death. I think we should stay here in the light. Someone will come."

"No one's gonna be here for hours. I'm not waiting." Jennifer moved away from him. "And who says you're the main character?" she added while moving deeper into the blackness ahead. Trevor looked back up at the morgue looming above him, and ran to catch up with Jennifer, adding his phone light to hers to help them see.

Their footsteps echoed as they walked. The shaky beams from their phones danced across the ceilings and walls, playing hide and seek with dusty, nineteenth century fixtures, complete with old sconces and candleholders. The cold-looking, moist walls sweated condensation. They were made of old, institutional tile, stained and cracked. Rusted drainage vents were cut into stone floors.

Up ahead, the hallway snaked around a corner, and when they cautiously turned it, they saw a series of doorways lining the cobwebbed corridor. They paused in front of one of the rooms. In the dim beam of their lights, they saw a row of ancient, wooden, morgue drawers and an old and rusted autopsy table, with drainage indentations at the head and foot.

"This isn't just a basement, It's another freakin' morgue," said Jennifer.

"Stop trying to cheer me up," Trevor said, his voice a little shaky.

"It's old. They must've just built the new one on top of this."

"One morgue – not creepy enough. There have to be two morgues," he said. "What if there's no exit? What if it's all been sealed up or something?"

Jennifer had no answer. "We have to check it out."

They kept moving. Trevor's light was jittery; his hand was shaking. Reaching out, he stopped her, his eyes wide. "Did you hear that?" he asked in a whisper.

They were quiet, and Jennifer heard it, too. A footstep. Or maybe it was something being moved on the wet stone.

They looked at each other; the sound didn't come again.

When they turned yet another corner, Jennifer began to worry about how they would find their way back if they had to turn around. They saw a bright light coming from a room at the very end of the dark passage. They stopped. Looked at each other. It was eerie. Incongruous, hot-white light spilling out from an otherwise unseen room, cutting the darkness ahead like a knife. They kept moving toward it.

Before they could reach the room, Jennifer stumbled over something and gripped Trevor's arm; he grabbed her just as she was about to fall. Regaining her footing, they both shone their lights at the floor to see what she had tripped over. What they saw made Jennifer's throat tighten.

It was Ulysses' brand-new boots, lying on the stone floor, the yellow and black laces undone. When Jennifer looked up at Trevor, he was looking past her into a room right behind them. In the creepy spill of light from her phone, which sent shadows up and across his face, he looked terrified, gesturing with his chin toward the room.

Following his gaze, she saw an old, porcelain autopsy table in the far corner. A body lay on it.

Jennifer entered the room. Trevor took her arm, trying to hold her back. "No," he hissed.

Tearing her arm away, she moved to the table. She knew it was him. She came closer and pointed her light at his face. Ulysses stared up at the ceiling with his bulging dead eyes. He was naked.

"What the hell is he doing here?" Trevor whispered.

Jennifer jumped, not expecting Trevor so close behind her. She noticed something on Ulysses' arms.

Her blood froze.

Trevor, seeing the look on her face, pointed his light down at Ulysses, and saw what she saw:

Thick, raw incision wounds on both of his arms.

They seemed fresh; hastily sewn up with heavy sutures.

244

Jennifer looked lower. The same black sutures ran up and down both of his legs.

"What the *fuck*," observed Trevor.

Jennifer reached out to touch Ulysses' arms.

Trevor's hands flew to his mouth. "Don't!" he cried.

Remembering her pre-med days, Jennifer ignored him and gently placed her hand on Ulysses' dead arm. Then, not so gently, she squeezed the arm.

There was something wrong.

The arm squished under her grip, almost like it was hollow. Reaching for his leg, she squeezed it, and it too just caved in under her hand like so much dough. Putting one hand under his thigh, and the other on top of his shin, and she bent the leg.

Trevor looked like he was going to pass out. "Bloody, fucking bollocks."

The papery skin under Ulysses' knee creased and tore open.

Something pierced the skin and stuck out like a broken twig.

"No *fucking* way!" Trevor exclaimed and took a step back.

Jennifer leaned forward. Directed her light at the object. It should have been a tibia, but Jennifer knew it wasn't. There were little blue letters stamped on it:

Nat'l Pipe and Plastic

"It's not bone," Jennifer said, touching the white plastic rod. "It's PVC pipe."

There was a sickening, sticky sound as she pulled the plastic pipe out further. Trevor gasped. She knew this was the same pipe that had been delivered to the office.

She looked at Trevor, her hands bloody and sticky. "His bones have been taken out. Replaced with this." She held up the pipe for him to see. Bloody strings of yellow fat were clinging to it.

Trevor didn't even try to process this. "Right," he said shakily. "This is an exit cue if I ever saw one. It's time to get out of here. Now."

Jennifer looked back at Ulysses' face, her heart breaking. "What did they do to you?" she whispered.

For some reason she flashed on her father's face, in death, that same confused, panicked look in his eyes. Feeling a rush of sorrow, her eyes stinging with tears, she reached toward Ulysses' face, and gently closed his eyelids with her thumbs, just as she had done with her father.

"We have to go," Trevor implored.

Jennifer remembered the amulet, which she had stuffed in her pocket. Taking it out, she gently placed it around Ulysses' neck.

"You should have kept this," she said, her voice breaking, her face wet with tears. "Instead of trying to protect me."

Trevor shifted his weight impatiently. "Well, it's a little late for that now, isn't—"

Ulysses' body jerked violently.

Jennifer and Trevor jumped back as a loud, grinding motor started somewhere.

Ulysses lurched into a sitting position, his head rolling on his shoulders, his chin bobbing on his chest. His body started to rise from the table, in fits and starts.

Trevor cried out, and Jennifer saw that the cable, which had been coiled out of sight on the floor under the autopsy table, was being winched tight from the ceiling. She went behind the gurney, and, to her horror, her suspicion was confirmed.

There was a hook embedded in Ulysses' back, between his shoulder blades.

Like a marionette, he was being hoisted off of the table, his body suspended from the hook. His shoulders were pulled up even with his ears. His body shook and twitched as his legs left the table and his entire bulk was suspended above it. The hook and cable pulled his slack body toward the ceiling, his arms and legs dangling limply.

The unseen motor ground and shifted again, and the body shuddered forward. Trevor squatted down and covered his head as if afraid Ulysses would fall on him, while Jennifer squinted at the ceiling. Aiming the beam of her light upward, she saw the metal tracks that ran across the ceiling and out of the room. There was some kind of rail system at work there. The cable and hook moved along the track, transporting Ulysses across the ceiling, like a garment moving along a track at a dry cleaners.

They watched in horrified silence as Ulysses' body was pulled along the rails and out of the room. Trevor got to his feet, and with a shaking hand, dialed 911 on his cell phone. Nothing happened. Jennifer moved past him; he looked up in time to see her leave the room, following Ulysses.

"Shit," Trevor said. He trailed her out of the old autopsy room and back into the dark corridor. Ahead was the eerie sight of Ulysses' body dangling high above them, moving away from them along the ceiling track, silhouetted by the bright light coming from farther up the hallway.

Jennifer understood the illusion of a "floating body" they had seen on the cell phone video. She followed the body, while Trevor tried to keep up with her. Ulysses disappeared into the bright room ahead. Jennifer and Trevor reached the doorway of that room and huddled in it, staying low. Shielding her eyes from the blinding light, Jennifer looked through the doorway and saw another old autopsy room, with rusted and chipped tables and rickety porcelain carts and instrument cabinets set back in the shadows.

However, in the center of the room stood an incongruously modern, bright, operating room light, which shone down a shaft of dusty white light onto a new stainless steel operating table. The table gleamed under the harsh illumination.

A man stood at the head of the table, wearing a rubber apron, rubber gloves, and a black silicone facemask. His head was tilted toward the ceiling, waiting patiently for Ulysses' body to reach him. This hulking figure was muscular, bulked up, and it was clear he couldn't even rest his arms by his sides due to the oversized lats which were in the way. Thus he stood like a cowboy ready to draw.

Jennifer was familiar with that muscle-bound stance.

It had to be Ersen behind the mask.

Ducking low and moving deeper into the room, she hid behind a row of dusty shelves.

Trevor, desperate to get farther away, not closer, cursed and followed. He glared at her. "What if he sees us! We have to get out of here!"

Jennifer was totally focused on one of the shelves of the cabinet they were hiding behind. Something on it had caught her eye, but it was too dark to see. She looked at the rubber-garbed man at the table; his gaze was still fixed on the ceiling as he reached up and prepared to grab Ulysses.

While rubber man was distracted, Jennifer aimed her light at the shelf. On it were a row of specimen jars. The same specimen jars that had gone missing, although they were no longer empty. Jennifer moved the light closer to the nearest jar. It contained a thick, white, dough-like substance, packed in fluid. Looking closer still, she saw an image on the substance: a blue snake. It was the tattoo that had curled around Sean Burrows' neck and ear. When Jennifer moved the light lower, her heart began to pound.

She was looking at a human ear.

Dropping her phone in horror, she and Trevor both looked over at the table, but rubber man couldn't have heard anything over the sound of the motor as he lifted his gloved hands, preparing to receive Ulysses from the hook and onto the table.

"What is that?" asked Trevor, horrified, looking at the jar and afraid of the answer.

"Skin," Jennifer said. "Human skin. I saw that tattoo on the neck of the body that's missing. Sean Burrows, the guy who got shot."

Trevor looked like he might pass out, and Jennifer was feeling light-headed as well. She took deep breaths to stay conscious. She picked up her phone from the floor and aimed the light again at the shelf and at the other specimen jars lined up on it. Inside one, human organs floated in a cloudy liquid.

In another, they saw what appeared to be small wires and tubing. Blue and red. Trevor looked at her. "Is that what I . . ."

She knew enough anatomy to understand what they were looking at. "Veins. Arteries," Jennifer whispered, her eyes glued to the jars.

Trevor took a deep breath, deciding it was time to shake off his fear and take control. Grabbing Jennifer by the shoulders, he looked into her eyes.

"Right. I'm not dying today," he hissed. "Neither are you. Come on!"

"Are you kidding me?" Jennifer whispered, incredulous. "You said that in a movie!"

"You told me you hadn't seen my movies!" Clutching her by the hand, he pulled her out into the hallway. They ran into the darkness as fast as they could, hoping they wouldn't slam into anything. Jennifer tried to light the way ahead of them with her dim phone light but running so fast made it too shaky to really see anything.

Trevor thought he saw a bend in the dark hallway, and without slowing they turned the corner.

A familiar, angry face appeared briefly in the scattered phone light. Trevor made a horrible sound as Jennifer heard a whoosh of air escape from his mouth. Stepping back, she aimed her light at Trevor, and what she saw made her scream for the first time.

Trevor was face to face with Otis. They were way too close together. Trevor was holding his stomach, and when Jennifer looked down she saw a glint of light kick off the blade that was deep in his abdomen. Otis' hand was tightly gripped around the handle of the long knife.

Otis seemed just as surprised as Trevor; the stabbing had been born more of momentum than an actual attempt to kill. Trevor had literally run into the knife, but Otis covered his astonishment (and fear) quickly. "Who's the wanksta now, motherfucker?" he snarled.

Time seemed to stand still as Trevor stared in shock at Otis.

A fountain of blood gushed around the blade and onto Otis' hand. Trevor's legs went out from under him, and he sagged to the floor. His face turned bone white. Looking up at Jennifer, he shouted, "RUN!!"

In the autopsy room around the corner, the man in rubber heard Trevor's cry over the machinery. Ripping off his mask, he turned to the wall, punching a large button with the side of his fist. The motor stopped.

Ulysses' body jerked to a halt. Swaying and twisting on the hook, halfway to the operating table.

Ersen turned and cocked his head to listen carefully.

There were running footsteps in the distance. "Shit, what now?" he asked himself, throwing his mask on the table and lumbering out of the room.

***

Where the hell is everybody? Clover wondered, entering the main morgue upstairs. It was 8 AM, and she usually saw Jennifer and the Movie Asshole before they left, and she clocked in. In an hour, the place would be humming with coroners and autopsies and the usual daily routine. But Clover sensed something in the air that made her uneasy. Then again, since that asshole Trevor had started there, Clover had a constant uneasy feeling. That Hollywood shithead was causing a lot of problems. Clover liked to think she ran a tight ship and hated the thought that anything might upset the little world she'd created for herself.

Walking through all the morgue rooms and hallways, she called out to Jennifer. Jennifer wasn't picking up her cell phone either. *Shit.* That was bad. Had Trevor taken her somewhere? It wasn't like Jennifer to abandon her post. Clover wasn't even going to bother checking the back hallway but convinced herself she should be thorough.

Rounding the corner, she saw the abandoned gurney and body bag at the end of the dark corridor. Her mouth went dry as she got closer. Reaching the edge of the open trap door, she looked down into the darkness below.

"What the fuck."

***

It had started to rain. Marty was sitting in his car in Bay Ridge, listening to the strum of his windshield wipers sweeping back and forth. Watching the Drake and Sons Funeral Home across the street, he was pretty sure he had it all figured out but needed Raffy Burrows to fill in the blanks for him. Of course Marty had heard about this kind of thing, even read about it, but always thought it was just some kind of urban myth. The big question: how big was it? How far did it stretch? Marty suspected it was bigger than anyone could guess.

Burrows turned the corner, holding a black umbrella over his head. Neatly dressed in dark clothes, he carried a small paper bag from a nearby deli. Maybe he dresses nice, Marty thought, but he was just as dirty as his dead brother.

Marty got out of his car and crossed the street, getting pelted by the rain. He was on a trajectory to intercept Burrows before he got to the front door of the funeral home.

Burrows saw him coming. "Detective Bell. I was wondering when you were going to take my statem—"

Marty shoved him hard against the fence under the awning. Grabbed him by the shoulders and turned him around so he was facing the fence. The umbrella crushed against the bars and the paper bag went flying.

"Hey!" Burrows protested.

"You're under arrest," Marty said as he kicked Burrows' leg apart and quickly frisked him.

"What is this?" Burrows howled angrily.

Marty's handcuffs closed with a satisfying crunch around Burrows' wrists. Marty had always been good with handcuffs. He leaned close to Burrows. "I know what you motherfuckers are doing."

After reading Burrows his rights, Marty yanked him away from the fence and marched him toward his car. Burrows bent his head against the rain, as if trying to make sure it didn't ruin his hair.

Marty saw a quick flash of something in Burrows' eyes. Abject terror.

***

Jennifer fought panic as she raced blindly down arched hallways that seemed to lead to nowhere. Her strained breathing echoed off the walls. There was no hope now of retracing her steps and finding her way out. Worse, she didn't think she could find her way back to Trevor.

Was he still alive?

What kind of nightmare had she wandered into? Had Otis really just stabbed Trevor? What the fuck was going on? *What was happening down here?*

There was no time to dwell. She had to find a way out. There must be a staircase or some other way back upstairs. Or better yet a door that led outside. It was so dark she could barely see the walls, never mind a door. Not able to run anymore, she stopped, trying to catch her breath. If only she could—

Wait. Was that a footstep behind her? She tried to be as still as possible. There was water dripping somewhere; was that what she heard? Deciding that she couldn't just stand there, she felt along the walls, and when she touched a doorway, she ducked into another dark room.

Fumbling with her phone, she checked to see if she had a signal.

She didn't. Her battery was now in the red zone. She would have to ration that flashlight. Holding the phone high, she used only the glow from the screen to try and see where she was.

Turning, she suddenly found herself inches away from a dead, upside-down face.

Trying to back up, she bumped into something. Something that gave way. She forced her terrified body to turn and saw another upside-down dead face. She waved her phone around the room and saw that she was standing in a grove of dead bodies, hanging upside down, suspended on cables from the ceiling, attached by their ankles.

They twisted gently, arms dangling over their heads, in macabre silence.

Jennifer clamped her hand over her mouth as she tried to maneuver away from the forest of corpses. The close smell of rotting flesh was overwhelming; mixed with another familiar smell – formaldehyde. Had a half-hearted attempt been made to preserve these bodies? She recognized some of the faces. The middle-aged woman with the shock of white hair, who'd spoken to her in the autopsy room; the man with the bullet hole in his forehead; the corpse Clover had named Why Me.

Even worse, she saw that they were all in various stages of some kind of dissection. Some had their entire chest cavities cut out, some had their skin completely removed below their ears, some had veins hanging out of their necks and limbs like errant wiring.

She stumbled her way back to the doorway. Footsteps or not, she was not staying in that room. Seeing an instrument tray full of clamps and scalpels, she took a scalpel and slipped it into her pocket. As she felt for the doorway, she crashed into something else – more shelves, these holding rows of cardboard boxes, some of which spilled onto the floor.

Holding her ever-dimming phone up again, she saw they were sealed shipping boxes, and each one had *BioMed Tissue Bank* stamped in the return address spot. Each box was addressed to a different institution: medical schools, pharmaceutical companies, hospitals.

Jennifer tore open several of the boxes. They held specimen jars and plastic pouches containing what looked like human body parts.

Organic tissue.

Bones.

Joints.

There was also paperwork. Rifling through the boxes, she ripped out the forms from several of them, scanning them quickly. There were death certificates listing the "donor's" age, cause of death, etc. And just like the paperwork Trevor showed her earlier, the ages of the donors were all listed in their fifties or younger, and there was no mention of any kind of disease in the causes of death.

Jennifer understood. Ersen and Otis were running some kind of illegal body parts-harvesting operation. They were stealing bodies from the morgue, cutting them up, taking anything they could sell: bones, veins, tissue, and then replacing the bones with PVC pipe and sewing them back up.

They made the "donors" all look good on paper. Not sick, not diseased, not too old. The bones and tissues were being sold to hospitals and implanted in people who had no idea they could be highly toxic. Had Angel been in on this too?

It hit her like a hammer:

Was this the desecration the dead were rebelling against? Was this why they were imploring her to give them the protection of the amulet?

Was any of this real? Could it be real?

Jennifer stuffed the paperwork in her back pocket and found her way to the door. Stepping out into the hallway, she was not even certain what direction she had been heading when she'd ducked into this room from hell. She wasn't even sure it mattered, since she had no idea where she was going.

Turning blindly to her right, she started running, but immediately slammed into what felt like a brick wall. Stumbling backward, she fell hard on her ass.

Looking up, she saw it wasn't a brick wall; it was Clover, who was now standing over her, a completely stunned look on her face.

Relief flooded Jennifer.

"What the hell are you doing down here!" Clover asked, shocked.

Jennifer got to her feet. As she started talking, the panic rose. She was about to lose it. "Trevor. Otis stabbed Trevor!"

"What?" Clover barked, confused.

"It's Ersen too. They're cutting up bodies. Selling the parts." She knew she sounded insane.

Clover took her by the shoulders. "Whoa, whoa, whoa. Just take a breath. What are you talking about?"

"There's no time, Clover. We have to get out of here. There are bodies everywhere. We have to call the police!"

Clover looked stricken, staring at something behind Jennifer.

Jennifer turned.

Ersen stood there, rubber apron shiny with gore. His rubber mask was off, revealing his bruised and crooked nose.

Jennifer froze. Ersen looked at her and glared at Clover. "I told you we shouldn't work at night, when they're right above us! What happens now is on you, you greedy bitch."

FIFTEEN

Clover had gotten into the body harvesting business by accident. Or so she would tell herself. For years, she would meet her friend Patty Parmenter every Wednesday night for happy hour at The Ball Room, a male strip club in Queens. Pamela owned a funeral home on Staten Island, which had been a local mainstay for years. One of the few female undertakers in New York, Patty had built the business from the ground up, and after thirty years, had earned the trust and loyalty of the community.

Clover envied Patty; she lived in a big house in the Todt Hill section of Staten Island, cheek by jowl with the best mobster mansions. Patty always drove a new car, leasing them and turning them in every thirty-six months for the latest model. Going to Broadway shows with her husband, eating at great restaurants, Patty had a good life.

Clover wanted one just like it.

The Desecrated

Clover's divorce had been rancorous to say the least. Strapped for money, Clover couldn't afford a big-time lawyer, so she had to use a high school friend of hers who mostly did personal injury cases. Her husband's attorney, paid for by her father-in-law, who never liked Clover, came from a white-shoe Manhattan firm. The extremely competent lawyer saw to it that Clover was cut off from the marital accounts, lost her home, her car, and also her membership to the Wine Of The Month Club, the unkindest cut of all. Her husband, Mitch, didn't even like wine, but it was enough for him to know that she liked it, and so he happily took it from her. All because of Clover's torrid one-night affair with Bruno, a male stripper from The Ball Room. Well, technically, it was an eight-month torrid affair; the "one night" thing had been her attempt to convince Mitch it "meant nothing." That attempt failed, although, if Mitch had known about the eight months, he may have also taken her giant aquarium and the tropical fish in it. It was the one important thing (along with a beloved shag rug) she'd managed to wrest out of the marriage.

Patty felt for Clover as she watched her go through the divorce, although Patty had warned her that Bruno would only lead to trouble. Nevertheless, Bruno had begun sleeping with Patty, because Clover had no more money to spend on him and Patty had plenty.

However, before Patty took up with Bruno, or at least before Clover was aware of it, Patty took Clover aside one night at The Ball Room and asked her if she needed to make a little extra money. Clover assumed Patty was going to offer her some part-time work at the funeral home, maybe picking up bodies or driving for funerals.

What Clover didn't expect was the story Patty told her about a company called CBI Biologics. CBI was a Florida-based outfit that supplied human tissue and organs to hospitals for implant into patients who needed things like skin grafts, heart valves, bones, corneas, etc. It was a booming business, and CBI was only one of many suppliers trying to fill the ever-increasing demand for human tissue.

What made CBI special was their willingness to bend the rules. Frustrated by the cumbersome regulations put in place by the states for frivolous reasons like protecting the health of implantees, and annoying rules like needing to get permissions from families, CBI had begun to covertly outsource their "manufacturing." Patty, and many funeral directors like her, had been working with the medical company for two years. Patty would earmark a relatively healthy corpse and allow a CBI technician to come to the funeral home after hours to harvest whatever could be taken. Corneas, bones, teeth for dental implants, even tendons and ligaments, which were popular to help heal athletic injuries and get those players back on the field.

Afterward, they would stuff the corpse with fabric and PVC pipe to let the body retain some kind of shape for burial or cremation. Stuffing the body was the only real effort Patty had to expend, and for providing the corpse, she pocketed ten thousand dollars per body.

Business was good. Plenty to go around. So Patty looked at Clover, a supervisor of a New York City morgue, which handled thousands of bodies a year, and saw dollar signs. Patty offered to introduce Clover to her rep at CBI, who would no doubt be happy to have another source. Of course, Patty would need to get a ten-percent "honorarium" for every body Clover sold.

Clover wasn't sure. It was illegal. Also immoral. Although knowing full well she could live with the immoral, it was the illegal part that scared the shit out of her. The CBI rep Patty introduced her to was good. A jolly man in his sixties with tiny eyes and huge earlobes, Vince liked to laugh and loved to take Clover out to expensive dinners. Clover struggled to avoid glancing at his bad toupee, which fascinated her. The smooth CBI rep told Clover she'd be doing something noble, helping to harvest organs and parts that could save lives all over the world.

"One body can save a hundred lives!" The CBI rep assured Clover, between bites of steak. And the legality of it all – well, CBI made over two hundred million a year in the U.S. alone; that kind of money bought some pretty smart lawyers.

Clover went for it. It was easy. At first she only earmarked unclaimed and unidentified bodies. Virtually no risk. The hapless corpses would eventually be sent to Hart Island, the Potter's Field of New York, for mass burial, and no one was likely to notice that these particular dead no longer possessed their innards. For most of them, she didn't even bother with the PVC pipe.

The money rolled in. Thirty, forty thousand a month.

Clover, being a more gregarious soul than Patty, expanded the business, and recruited nursing-home attendants, other funeral directors, and hospital administrators all over the city. It was a windfall for everyone. Her enthusiastic collaborators would arrange for bodies to be clandestinely sent to the morgue on Winthrop St, where they would be stripped of their most valuable parts, stuffed, and sent back to the point of origin.

Then, along came Covid-19.

Dead bodies were filling up morgues, hospitals, and nursing homes faster than the system could handle. Hospitals had to park refrigerated trucks in their parking lots to handle the overflow of corpses; some hospitals told the families if they didn't have the bodies of their loved ones picked up in two days, they would be sent to Hart Island. That in turn quickly caused an overflow of bodies at funeral homes, which generally had no refrigeration, with some taking to storing bodies with tarps over them in their side alleys and garages. It was total chaos, and those enterprising souls who were willing to throw in with Clover made out quite well by sending her bodies and accepting them back hollow before anyone knew they had gone anywhere.

Overwhelmed by the workload, she eventually brought in Ersen, against her better judgment, doing it mostly because Ersen began to suspect something was going on and it was getting too difficult to hide it. And, as it turned out, Ersen had had some previous experience with grave robbing in his native Turkey, and he, like Clover, was untroubled by things like ethics or morality. And, having another pair of hands would certainly lessen Clover's workload. Not long after, when they got even busier, they had considered approaching Angel, but he had always given Clover the creeps. So they approached Otis, who, in spite of his ridiculous, white-boy gang persona, had turned out to be a diligent worker who did what he was told.

And while at first they made sure they sent back most bodies intact enough to wake and bury, Clover was becoming more fretful about the waste of saleable tissue. She literally salivated when an indigent and unclaimed body showed up. Such a body could be stripped of everything, even the skin, hair, and teeth. Every part of a body had a value. Bodies that were set for cremation also offered a bonanza – she would exchange five thousand dollars and some fake ashes with the funeral home, and they could use everything that body had to offer. Doing a real cremation was literally like sending two hundred thousand dollars up in smoke.

Even though she had been pleased overall with the business, like many greedy souls before her, Clover longed for more. She started taking chances, started harvesting more than was prudent from bodies that *had* been identified, which were going to be claimed by families and given wakes. Using Patty's connections, Clover would spread some cash around to other funeral homes to look the other way when it came to missing bones and corneas and such. It turned out that many funeral directors were happy to enlist in the noble cause of providing tissue for medical use, providing the price was right.

It got so busy that Clover needed to expand. It had gotten too difficult for her to hide her activities up in the main morgue, so she explored the old, abandoned morgue down below. She found some handy rooms where tables and equipment could be brought in. There was lots of space to create an efficient shipping center. Always looking for ways to streamline the work, particularly when it resulted in less toil for her, she pumped some of her profits into renovations, using her cousin, who gave her a good deal on the installation of the ceiling tracks and conveyors, and easing access from the back hallway of the morgue by cutting panels into the floor so they could lower bodies down below without anyone being able to see. Of course, she had cajoled Ersen and Otis into contributing five thousand each toward the renovations; not because it was needed, but because she thought it would help cement their commitment. Clover was also happy to let the money-hungry Ersen become the "face" of the operation, weird beard and all, letting him take over recruiting the outside help and keeping them in line. All of which gave Clover a chance to concentrate on the business end of things and some possible cover in case they got caught. Clover wouldn't think twice about throwing Ersen under the bus if it came to that.

When the Pandemic finally ended, and the vaccine became widespread, Clover needed to bolster her profits. At the same time, as preordained as these things tended to be, Clover began resenting the ten percent off the top that had to be paid to Patty. Especially when she finally understood that some of that ten percent was no doubt being spent on gold chains and speedos for Patty's new heartthrob, Bruno.

John Gray

And so it was that Clover went into business for herself. Giving her less than brilliant high school lawyer friend a chance to redeem himself after the divorce fiasco, she got him to form an LLC for her called BioMed. After cleverly picking the brain of the unwitting CBI rep for months, Clover had used that info to sell directly to hospitals and dental clinics and even plastic surgeons. (Some varieties of human tissue came in handy for plumping up lips and getting rid of wrinkles.) It was a steep learning curve, she had to admit, but worth it to be able to give a large "Fuck You" to Patty, and by extension, Bruno.

Clover relished the look of awe and envy in Ersen and Otis' eyes when she revealed to them that these corpses were earning her up to one hundred thousand dollars per body, depending on their condition. Always very generous with the profits, Clover paid her men so handsomely that the dimwitted duo often forgot to pick up their actual paychecks from the morgue on Thursdays. However, should Ersen and Otis ever find out that in reality Clover made more like two hundred thousand per corpse, and she could easily pay them a lot more, that awe and envy might very well have turned to anger and rage. Clover didn't relish confrontation, so better for all concerned if she kept the actual figures shrouded in mystery.

Since so many of the incoming bodies sent to the morgue were in dubious condition, diseased, elderly, who knows what else, Clover was frustrated that her price sometimes suffered. There was a good workaround for that problem – just have Ersen falsify the death certificate. Make 'em all younger. Healthier. In Clover's view, that was a win-win for everybody.

In fact, Clover soon stopped worrying about things like refrigeration, or how long the decaying bodies literally hung around before they were stripped of everything. Life was sweet. Sometimes she even fantasied about getting Bruno back. They saw each other at a stoplight one day, Clover in her teal BMW convertible (which she only drove on weekends) and he in his Ford Cavalier provided by Patty. Bruno couldn't hide the surprise in his eyes when he saw her, especially when Clover just looked at him through her Ray Bans without expression, like she didn't even recognize him, and peeled off. (Luckily, Bruno didn't see Clover fight to regain control of the car after she cornered too fast and almost sideswiped a Department of Sanitation street sweeper.)

Then things took a sudden turn. After the debacle of making Sean Burrows' body disappear before the autopsy, it was clear to Clover that Ersen had become a loose cannon. While it was true that Burrows had turned out to be a liability, he was a real value-add when Ersen first recruited him, sometimes sending two or three bodies a month from the assisted living facility that employed him. Not surprisingly, greed got the better of him, and he threatened to expose their operation unless Clover paid him thirty-five thousand dollars. How this idiot arrived at that number, Clover didn't know, and wasn't going to ask. It was just another example of the idiocy that always surrounded anything Ersen touched. Clover left it to Ersen to solve the problem, although she certainly didn't expect him to murder the guy.

Well, that wasn't quite true, Clover was pretty sure Ersen would kill Burrows. In fact she rather hoped he would, as that really was the best solution. But she'd never suggest such a thing.

And of course there had to be a fuck up involved. While the murder itself went pretty seamlessly, Ersen panicked when the cop Bell wanted to see Burrows' body. Afraid the detective might somehow trace Burrows' murder to him, Ersen deduced that it was better to make the body disappear than take that risk. Of course all it did was turn up the heat, a mess that still hadn't been put to bed.

Although in the back of her mind, Clover always knew her luck could run out someday, she never imagined it would involve Jennifer. She was the only person in Clover's life who was actually good, who, in spite of her razor mouth, did not have a cunning or dishonest bone in her body. Pardon the pun.

She needed to change that in a hurry.

SIXTEEN

Jennifer turned back to Clover. The expression on her face said it all: fear, guilt, anger. She couldn't meet Jennifer's gaze. Ersen looked on impatiently.

Clover faced Jennifer and held her hands up innocently. "I know what this looks like."

Jennifer was backing away. Rage rising in her like a violent sea. "What does it look like?"

"It's just a business. That's all. I know it's not pretty, but nobody's getting hurt."

"What about Trevor?"

"You shouldn't have come down here."

"It's not like we had a choice."

"Jennifer, you gotta understand. They're just dead bodies. Some of them won't even be claimed. Why let them go to waste?"

Ersen grunted impatiently. "Come on. We're wasting time."

"Was my father just a 'dead body' to you? Was he 'unclaimed'?"

Clover looked surprised. She looked at Ersen. Ersen shrugged.

"Jennifer, I swear, I would never do—"

"He was sent here! Without me knowing!"

"If that's true, it must've been before you started working here. If I had known—"

"Did you take his bones? Did you take his organs?"

"It's not like that—"

Ersen lost his patience. "What are you arguing with her for!"

Clover shot him a look. "Shut up." Clover came closer to her. Jennifer recoiled.

"Jennifer, we take from the dead and give to people who need. Living people. Tissue, stem cells. Arteries for bypass, heart valves, bones for fusing, even teeth." She searched her eyes, hoping for even a small flash of understanding, but saw only disgust.

"One body can save a hundred lives!" she proclaimed, giving it one more shot.

Jennifer advanced on her and poked her in the chest with her index finger. "You're selling diseased tissue! You're faking documents!"

Otis appeared next to Ersen. Holding the knife that was still dripping with Trevor's blood.

"I got him on the table," he said, and Jennifer shuddered, knowing he meant Trevor.

"Put that thing away!" Clover hissed at Otis.

Otis reluctantly stuck the knife in his side pocket, staining it dark red.

Clover turned back to Jennifer. "Please," she pleaded. "You can be part of this."

"What is wrong with you! These body parts could have bacterial infections! They could be cancerous! Do the doctors you're selling to know you're not testing them for pathogens? You don't know if they have HIV, Covid, hepatitis, or who knows what!"

Clover lowered her voice, getting desperate now. "Be my partner. With your medical knowledge, you can help us figure out all those things. You can make it better!"

"There is no better for this!"

Ersen snorted.

Clover pleaded with her. "You can make a fortune. I get two hundred K a body!"

Ersen and Otis' heads snapped toward each other. Clover pretended she didn't notice and went on. "I mean a hundred K. Someday maybe two, but now one hundred."

"I think I'm gonna be sick."

Clover got as close to her as she dared. "You can go back to school. You can get your tuition in a few months."

All eyes turned to Jennifer. Glancing at Ersen, she knew that he'd just as soon kill her. Or do other things to her. Needing to buy time, she took a shaky breath, and tried to arrange her face so that she seemed thoughtful. "If I did this . . . what about Trevor?" she asked.

Clover opened her mouth to speak, but Otis got there first.

"Trevor donated his body to science," Otis smirked. Ersen snorted again.

Jennifer tried to stay in the moment, but her eyes filled. When she spoke, her voice shook. "Don't you think someone might notice he's missing?"

Ersen shrugged. "Flaky movie star. They just disappear sometimes."

Clover tried to smile kindly at Jennifer and spoke gently. "In a couple of weeks he'll be in the bodies of a dozen people. That's a great finish for an actor, don't you think?"

Jennifer held her gaze. "What if I say no?" She thought she saw tears suddenly rim Clover's eyes.

Clover whispered in a shaky voice. "Please don't make me go there."

Jennifer knew. Knew that Clover would kill her. Or more likely have Ersen or Otis do it. She had to move.

"*Aarrgghh!*" Clover cried out in agony as Jennifer kicked her so hard in the crotch that it sounded like a tire had blown out. Otis jumped at the scream and couldn't get his arms up in time as Jennifer barreled into him, making him lose his balance. Ersen had to stretch over Otis to reach for her, managing only to grab her lab coat. She kept running.

Clover was on her hands and knees gasping for breath, looking up at Ersen and Otis. "Find her and bring her to me." Her eyes watering, she stared at Ersen. "I don't want her hurt."

Ersen looked down at her with disgust. "You're finished giving me orders." He nodded at Otis, and the faux gangsta obediently took off after Jennifer.

Ersen looked back down at Clover.

***

Jennifer ran blindly down damp hallways, feeling along the walls. She was afraid to use her phone for light and kill the battery in case there was a signal at some point, and she could make a call. But she needed to hide.

Feeling her way into a recess, she kept walking and could tell by her echoing footsteps that she had entered yet another room in the labyrinth. Moving in slowly, she held her outstretched hands in front of her. Her fingers found something - something fleshy, soft. She was feeling a nose and wet mouth. She was touching a face.

Jumping back, she waited to be grabbed, but nothing happened. Reluctantly, she pulled her phone out, and opened the screen just to give her enough glow to see what she was looking at.

It was indeed a face, a forty-ish man with his mouth open and his half-lidded eyes looking down as if he were ashamed. There were hooks behind both of his ears, connected to a cable behind his head that ran to the ceiling.

But it was what she saw below that head that made her stop breathing.

There was no actual body below the neck, no skin, no bones; just the man's spinal column dangling from the neck, nerves intertwined and drooping from it like tangled spider webs.

She backed away, but it was what she saw behind the ghoulish sight in front of her that drew her attention. In the other corner of the room sat a large, boxy structure that didn't belong. It was painted gray.

Holding her breath, she squeezed past the slowly twisting spinal column and approached the cube. There was a quietly humming generator hooked up next to it, and coiled, fat tubing running in and out of both sides of the square structure. She flashed on an image of a ventilator and shivered. There were digital dials and meters, all very modern looking in stark contrast to the nineteenth-century fixtures in the rest of the room.

Jennifer was looking at an industrial freezer.

The gray door and chrome handle beckoned to her. She could only imagine what was inside. Touching the handle tentatively – it was cold and slippery - she yanked the door open.

A vapor-like mist of condensation escaped from the dark freezer. With the cold air came a smell. It reminded her of the neighborhood butcher shop her father used to take her to. Shivering, she tried to take a step into the freezer, but felt her heart accelerating. Her breathing became shallow. Her claustrophobia rose up like an angry demon inside her. Attacking her will to move. It was dark inside – tight. Her mouth went dry. But when the footsteps echoed from down the hall, she knew it was time to move or die. Taking a breath, she pulled the heavy door fully open and stepped inside.

The cold air hit her full force, like an arctic blast. At first it felt refreshing after the stale air of the lower morgue, but she knew it would soon become painful if she had to stay in there too long. There was a dim blue glow that came from the floor of the freezer, throwing unnerving shadows against the walls and ceiling. She tried not to dwell on how close those walls and ceiling felt.

Checking to make sure that there was a handle on the inside of the door that would let her exit, she quietly shut the door behind her, praying that she would get out again. Her breath floated in front of her like vaporous clouds.

The claustrophobia hammered at her chest. It felt like she was smothering, like she had to burst through that door and get out of the freezer immediately.

Pushing those feelings away, she stepped deeper inside. It was about survival. Once her eyes adjusted to the blue light, she saw that she was surrounded by racks and shelves.

All contained frozen body parts.

A stack of arms here, a bundle of legs there – piled on the metal shelves like cords of firewood. She made her way past the racks, noticing that some of the limbs had been skinned almost to the bone.

At the rear of the freezer was the skinned flesh of what appeared to be an entire male body, empty of bones and organs, looking like a floppy dressmaker's pattern. The face was slack, and the eyeless sockets drooped onto sunken cheeks.

She stepped closer.

It was her father.

Staring in numb horror, she wanted to look away but couldn't. Seeing the empty sack of flesh that had been her dad was the perfect metaphor for the deflated, sad man he had become as his illness ate him up. What had happened to his Covid-infected insides? Had they been sold to the highest bidder? Were they going to be implanted in unsuspecting patients all over the city?

And what was meant to happen to his skin?

Her legs were shaking. Her breathing was ragged. For a moment it seemed that her body was going to rebel and just run out of there whether she wanted it to or not. She tried reminding herself that she had to hide. She had to survive this – if only to stop it.

There was a pronounced "click" from behind her.

She turned. The handle of the freezer door was turning.

Backing up against the rear wall of the freezer, she was uncomfortably close to the dangling outer skin of her father's empty body. There was a tiny space between the wall and the last rack. Swallowing her rising claustrophobia, she slid herself into the tiny space.

The freezer door opened, causing the frozen air to swirl. Jennifer squatted down as low as possible, her back pressed against the wall and her knees bent. Looking through the shelves, she spotted Otis silhouetted in the freezer doorway. His long knife was in one hand, a flashlight in the other. He trained the beam all around the inside of the freezer.

As the light danced across the rack of shelves she was squeezed next to, Jennifer saw a row of human heads on the top shelf. Some of these heads had also been skinned; leaving only raw muscle and gristle stretched over the facial bones.

She fought off the rising nausea.

On the shelves below were stacks of hands and feet, cut off at the wrists and ankles.

Otis entered the freezer.

Jennifer closed her eyes, hoping that he couldn't hear her pounding heart. Realizing that Otis might see her breath misting out of her mouth and nose, she breathed in silently and held it.

The beam from the flashlight swept the racks and shelves, at one point skipping along the tip of her sneaker. Otis kept coming in deeper. Jennifer opened her eyes; his elbow was just inches from her face. Her body was trembling; she was freezing and couldn't control it. Praying not to make any noise, she scraped her butt ever so slightly away from the shelf next to her, so her shaking body wouldn't rattle it.

Otis was absolutely still, scanning the room with his flashlight, and for a few awful moments Jennifer squeezed her eyes shut and waited for the knife to come.

Otis finally turned his back toward her and moved away, but not before accidentally bumping the shelves she was hunkered down next to with his hip. The heads on the top shelf rocked back and forth from the impact.

Jennifer looked up in horror, seeing the head at the end of the shelf right above her teetering on the edge.

Holding her breath again, her eyes were glued to the head. It finally toppled off of the shelf—

And directly into her lap.

A small blast of vapor escaped her mouth as she silently gasped. Cradling the head between her thighs so it wouldn't hit the floor and make noise was like trying to trap a freezing cold bowling ball between her legs. She stared at the head. The frosted eyebrows, and the half open, cloudy eyes looking at her with indifference were bad enough, but when she saw that the head was skinned below the eyes, her whole body tensed as if it had just been electrocuted. Clamping her hands over her mouth, she squeezed the head tightly between her legs to hold it in place.

Otis once more swept the flashlight left and right. Jennifer felt the head slipping. She knew from her pre-med classes that the head was the heaviest part of a body. She had certainly weighed enough of them at the morgue. If the head slipped from her grip, it would be like an eleven-pound block of ice hitting the floor. Otis would hear that.

She tried to work the head upward and into her lap. Bits of ice broke off of the nose and onto her pants.

Otis shivered in the cold air and walked out of the freezer, slamming the door behind him.

As if she were on springs, Jennifer arched her hips up and out to fling the head off of her lap. Hearing it hit the floor like a giant stone, and rolling away somewhere, she got to her feet. The shivering was getting worse, and she rushed to the freezer door, her lips numb. Waiting by the steel door, her hands trembling on the ice-cold handle, she listened for sounds from outside. She was aware of the ceiling getting closer to her head. And the walls, wet with icy condensation, closing in on her. Struggling to breathe, knowing she couldn't stay in there one more second, Jennifer took a deep breath that seared her lungs with frost, and opened the door.

Stepping out of the freezer, her body greedy for the dank warmth she'd hated a few minutes before, she quietly closed the door behind her and hugged herself to get warm, attempting to find her way back to a hallway. She stumbled down the corridor, trying to not let herself think about what Clover and the other two had been doing down here. Had Ersen and Otis been down there every night while she was upstairs going about her work? If she ever got out of here, would the police believe her? Would Detective Bell think she was in on it? How could she not have known?

Her thoughts were broken by the loud *thump* and groan of the machinery starting again. The cables were moving along the tracks over her head. Something was coming at her.

Pressing herself against the wall, feeling paralyzed, she had no idea which way to turn. She looked up at the shuddering mechanism, and down the hall saw the dim outline of someone suspended from the horrible hooks, shoes hovering five feet above the floor, being pulled along the tracks.

She tried to become one with the wall. Not wanting to look, her eyes nevertheless kept turning to the horrid sight before her. A fully dressed woman, head bobbing on her chest, body jerking with the motion of the cables, drifted down the hall like a gruesome float in a macabre, one-person parade.

The body passed right over Jennifer. She tried to turn away, but some kind of morbid curiosity made her look right up into the face of the dead woman being pulled along by pulleys.

It was Clover.

Her eyes stared sadly toward Jennifer, but not at her. Her throat had been cut, an inverted V of blood soaking her body.

Jennifer almost yelled out when several drops of the blood splattered on her face and lab coat. The body finally lurched past her, shoulders straining against the hook, moving along on its ghastly last journey.

Desperately trying to wipe the blood from her face, she heard a horrifying sound.

Church bells.

The loud gongs echoed against the stone walls. Jennifer fumbled for her phone, the word *Fish* flashing on the screen. She almost dropped the phone as she struggled to turn the alarm off.

Knowing that she had just given away her location, Jennifer shoved off from the wall, and ran in the opposite direction from where Clover's body had gone. Turning to glance over her shoulder, she saw nothing in the blackness behind her, so she turned back around—

And ran right into Otis' fist, which slammed into her forehead with astonishing force. The last thing she remembered was a flash of the ceiling as her body slammed to the cold, wet floor.

***

Raffy Burrows sat straight in the hard chair, his hands folded placidly in his lap. Marty had considered shackling him to the Formica table in the worn, dim interview room but thought it might be better to let Burrows relax a little. He had not asked for a lawyer, and Marty hoped to keep it that way. It was clear that Burrows had already tamped down whatever fear Marty had seen in his eyes when he arrested him. The funeral director sat there calm and in control.

Marty sat down opposite him and opened his notebook. Paging through it, reading earlier notes, he made it a point not to look at Burrows. The room smelled of stale coffee and sweat. Sounds from the busy Brooklyn South station leaked in. Laughter, phones ringing, squeaky shoes walking past the interview room, heavy equipment belts jangling. In his peripheral vision, Marty saw Burrows was unfazed. Safe to say this was not his first time within the walls of a precinct house.

"So," Marty began casually, "your brother was funneling dead bodies from the nursing home?"

"It's assisted living," Burrows said dryly.

"Correct me on that one more time."

Burrows registered the look in Marty's eye and turned away.

"How many people are involved in this?"

"Involved in what?" Burrows asked innocently, casting a glance at the large, stained mirror that covered the opposite wall, probably wondering who was behind it, watching him. Marty knew no one was, but it was good to let Burrows speculate.

"Could I get something to eat? Some French toast maybe?" Burrows asked with a smirk. Marty knew he was dealing with an oversized ego. Good.

"Okay, well, here's what I think, and you correct me if I'm wrong. You and your brother were sending bodies to the morgue on Winthrop Street. The bodies disappeared from there and were chopped up and sold for parts. You make a few bucks. Old Man Drake doesn't even know what day it is half the time, so it's all good."

Burrows shifted in the chair. His smile growing. "A few bucks?"

Marty shrugged. "I'm sure for a couple of small timers it felt like a lot."

Burrows laughed. "Let me tell you something. If any of what you say is true, and I'm not saying it is, there's nothing 'small time' about it. A thing like this, if it existed, could be huge. Citywide. Millions of dollars."

Marty smiled and went back to his notes. "Right."

He felt Burrows' eyes on him. "You don't believe me?"

"Sure. Sure I do. Millions of dollars," Marty said, continuing to write, not looking up. Burrows shifted again.

"You want to say my brother was small time, I can't argue with that. But don't—"

"Is that why you killed him?"

Burrows stared at Marty. Thrown. "I didn't kill my brother."

"Uh huh. Who did then?"

"My brother was an asshole. Any time he had a good thing going, he had to fuck it up. Like it was in his DNA."

"Sean wanted more money, threatened to expose you—"

"Not me."

Marty looked at him expectantly and said nothing. Burrows shifted yet again. Marty knew guys like him well. Guys who always believed they were the smartest people in the room. Burrows was trying to figure out how much he could say and still not incriminate himself. He believed he was the one playing the game.

"There's a guy named Ersen. Ersen Tekin."

Marty didn't change his expression.

"Ersen works at the morgue on Winthrop St. You might describe him as the mastermind," Burrows said, with a twinkle in his eye.

Marty remembered his interview with the steroid enhanced Turk. Mastermind was not the first word that came to mind, and by the look in Burrows' eye, he knew that too. Clearly Burrows was trying to make Ersen take the fall. Why? Because Ersen was the one who killed his brother?

"What else?"

Burrows settled in. "Well, what I've heard," he said with a self-satisfied smirk, "and again, I have no direct knowledge of this . . . but they might have a whole separate morgue setup. Just for this enterprise. Nobody knows about it. But it operates twenty-four seven. It's like the Amazon of body parts."

"This separate morgue. That's where the cutting is done? That's where the body parts are sold out of?"

Burrows shrugged with that shit-eating grin. Marty resisted the urge to crush Burrows' nose beneath his fist. *This scumbag sent my mother to that body farm.* But he couldn't lose his cool with this guy. Instead he leaned back. "And they chopped up your brother too? That's why you didn't bother claiming his body?"

Picking a piece of lint off of his pants, Burrows shook his head. "If that's true, it's the most useful Sean has ever been. Trust me."

"Where is this other morgue?"

"I think I deserve something for this information."

Marty wondered what had taken him so long to get to this. "Come on, I know you're not an amateur. If your info is good, you know the D.A. will cut you a deal." Marty had no idea if this was true, but Burrows beamed, thinking, because of the "not-an-amateur" line, that he had Marty's respect.

"Where's the other morgue?" Marty asked again.

Burrows smiled.

"You already know, Detective."

***

Marty raced out of the building. The rain came down harder, tearing up the streets, soaking him by the time he got to his car. When Raffy had told him where this other morgue was set up, it was a surprise to him, even though it made perfect sense. Marty had been in that building; it had never even occurred to him that there was a basement there. If traffic was on his side he'd be in Brooklyn in less than an hour. Hopefully in time to catch these fuckers in the act.

SEVENTEEN

The light was so bright it hurt her eyes through her eyelids. Her head was pounding. Wait – the bright light – was she . . .

Opening her eyes, she immediately felt an explosion of pain in her head. She looked around, trying to orient herself, but everything was out of focus and too bright. She was lying down and could barely move.

As her vision cleared, she understood why. Her wrists and ankles had been secured with thick electrical tape, her wrists bound over her stomach, and her ankles taped to the bottom corners of the old porcelain autopsy table she was lying on. Squinting across the room toward the light, she saw that she was in the "operating" room she'd seen earlier. Ersen, on the other side of the space, stood over the modern operating table, under the searing bright light that cascaded over his head and shoulders, giving him a glowing, almost angelic look. Except for the black rubber mask and gloves he was snapping on while gazing into the shadows. When Jennifer's eyes adjusted to the light, she saw the gleaming autopsy table that Ersen was looking at, and her heart skipped a beat.

Trevor lay on the table, his head grotesquely bent against a rubber body block. Ersen stretched his fingers in the gloves like a pianist about to go to work.

Jennifer shouted; her voice echoing off the walls and ceiling. "Leave him alone!" Knowing it was futile, even stupid to shout, she couldn't help herself. She was about to yell again, until Otis appeared beside her and slapped a huge piece of duct tape over her mouth. The adhesive pulled against her lips, and she smelled the suffocating plastic coating of the tape.

Otis walked over to join Ersen at the table. Jennifer, her forehead throbbing, dropped her head on the table hoping the pain would ease. Looking up, she tensed when she saw Ulysses' body dangling over her, still suspended by hooks from the ceiling. She craned her head farther and saw Clover's bloody corpse swinging next to him. Waiting their turn on the table, for the next phase of their harvesting.

Jennifer saw that the amulet she had hung around Ulysses' neck earlier was still there. Something wasn't right though. Lifting her head to get a better look, she saw what it was.

The black onyx dog was missing from its place on the amulet.

Ersen's voice distracted Jennifer. Looking over, she saw Ersen and Otis standing over Trevor's body.

"Oh shit," Ersen said, loud enough to make sure Jennifer heard, "We forgot to name him."

"Go for it," Otis laughed.

Ersen put his finger on the chin part of his mask, as if

he were thinking. His face above the mask brightened. "I didn't see that coming!"

Otis howled with glee. Ersen joined in with a maniacal cackle. Jennifer wished she could hold her ears against the demonic-sounding laughter.

Without missing a beat, and still chuckling, Ersen picked up a scalpel from the instrument tray, held Trevor's arm up, and sliced in one quick motion from the wrist down to the elbow.

Jennifer turned her head away. She shut her eyes tightly, feeling the rage rise up in her. Feeling the power of that rage. Two ancient lightbulbs exploded above her. Over at the operating table, the overheard light swayed. The instrument tray trembled. To her left, Clover and Ulysses' bodies swayed in a macabre syncopated rhythm.

Her concentration splintered when she heard the baby sobbing.

That's what it sounded like anyway. Picking up her head, she refocused on her surroundings, trying to locate the source of the sound. It came again – a pathetic whimpering. She turned her head toward Ulysses. Was it coming from him?

At the table, Ersen had exposed the bone in Trevor's forearm. He began to peel back the skin—

Trevor bolted upright on the table and screamed at the top of his lungs.

Ersen and Otis jumped back, both shouting out in terror. Jennifer looked over, at first overjoyed that Trevor was alive, then full of horror that he was going to feel what was about to happen to him.

"*What the fuck*!!!" Trevor shrieked when he saw his arm.

Otis stepped forward. "Oh shit. We thought you were dead, brah."

Trevor struggled to get up from the table, and Ersen

drew his massive fist back and punched him hard in the face. Trevor rocketed back onto the table, his head hitting the body block, out cold. Otis reached for some more tape and started binding Trevor to the table. Smiling happily, he spoke to the unconscious action hero.

"Yo dude, this is like that movie you did. What was it? *Edge Of Nowhere*, right? They tied you up on that rooftop, and then they dangled your ass off it. That was some dope shit right there."

Ersen sneered. "That probably wasn't even him. They have stunt guys to do all that." Ersen leaned over Trevor's face. "I don't know how to tell you this movie guy, but I don't have any anesthetic."

Otis smiled. "Dead men feel no pain, right?"

Ersen frowned. "I didn't see that one."

"No dude," Otis said, rolling his eyes. "That was a joke. Not a movie."

Jennifer was barely taking this in, as she tried to concentrate on the little sounds that seemed to be coming from Ulysses' vicinity. A muffled cry. A child?

No, she thought.

More like an animal.

It got louder. Muted in a strange way. Strange because it sounded as if it were coming from *inside Ulysses*. The cries gradually turned into a low growl. Jennifer looked over at the table; Ersen and Otis had not heard anything yet.

Looking back at Ulysses, the swaying of his body slowing down, she saw his stomach starting to distend obscenely. Her heart raced. She found herself breathing hard, struggling to get air through her nose with her mouth smothered by the tape.

Now there was something moving beneath Ulysses' skin.

Something was inside him. And it wanted out. Whatever it was, was stretching and poking against the inside of his abdomen. The growl became louder.

Angrier.

Jennifer remembered the Anubis myth. *A corpse giving birth to its own protector.* She thought of the exploded abdomen of the young woman in Angel's van. The bones broken outward.

She remembered something else.

She struggled to get her body angled on the cold table so that she could get her hands close to her rear jeans pocket. She strained, her veins bulging against the taut skin of her neck.

Trevor began screaming again. Looking over at the table, she heard Ersen say:

"Okay. I'm not good with the screaming."

"Watch this brah," Otis answered, ripping a long piece of tape off the roll and jamming it hard over Trevor's mouth.

Jennifer continued to try to get to her pocket. Trying to pull her bound hands from across her stomach to the back of her body was agony. Her shoulders screamed, her elbows were on fire, but she managed to extend her fingers enough to slide the scalpel from her back pocket. It was slow work, and several times her tenuous grip on the blade would slip, but at last it fell into her hand.

Turning over as far as possible, she bent her hand painfully back against her taped wrists, sliding the scalpel under the tape with her fingers. She glanced over her shoulder.

Ersen and Otis were busy trying to remove Trevor's radius bone.

She cut through the tape.

With her hands free, she ripped the tape off of her mouth and tried to slide herself toward Ulysses. Her arms couldn't reach.

Not wanting to take the time to cut the thick tape binding her ankles, she used all of her remaining energy to rock her body on the autopsy table, causing it to jerk on its wheels a couple of inches.

Trevor screamed from under the tape while Ersen, enjoying the suffering, laughed.

Getting within reach of Ulysses' hanging body, Jennifer swung at his engorged belly with the scalpel. She missed.

Rocking the squeaky table even closer, she was grateful that Trevor's screams from across the room, even muffled, covered the sound.

On her next swing, the blade came close enough to scrape Ulysses along the stomach, leaving a wide gash. The growl from inside became angrier. Taking a breath, she gathered all of her strength, and rocked the table one more time, landing right next to Ulysses.

Looking up at him, she whispered, "Sorry."

Swinging wide, she plunged the scalpel deep into Ulysses' abdomen.

The movement caught Ersen's eye. Glancing over at Jennifer and the hanging bodies, it took him a second to process what he was seeing.

Jennifer, extended off of the table as far as her body could stretch, had carved a gaping hole into Ulysses' midsection. Losing her balance, she fell off the table, her ankles still bound to the slab.

The rotten-egg smell of sulfur filled the room.

Jennifer stared up at the gaping, dripping hole now torn through Ulysses' belly.

The growl became louder. More like a roar.

Ersen and Otis watched. Frozen.

With a wet sucking sound and an exploding gush of dark fluids, a matted, damp, jet-black *dog's head* ripped itself from the hole in Ulysses' abdomen. It roared with a sound that made Jennifer cover her ears, and Ersen and Otis wince.

The feral black creature, *some kind of jackal*, Jennifer

thought, struggled spasmodically to free itself from the cavern in Ulysses' body. The creature had two sets of rage-filled eyes, one on top of the other. Its teeth were inch-long razor-sharp fangs in double rows in the top and bottom of its powerful jaws.

***

Marty drove past the building. The rain had turned the day dark. Parking at the fire hydrant on the wet, shiny Brooklyn street, he got out of his unmarked car and walked quickly, trying to dodge the drops. The heavy rain had turned into more of a mist, and it made for moody halos around the streetlights.

Marty approached the building and a bad feeling overwhelmed him. Something told him to unholster his weapon and keep it close. Having learned a long time ago never to ignore his gut, he reached behind him and pulled his gun, holding it with both hands and keeping it pointed at the sidewalk. Looking down, he caught his reflection in a puddle. He looked like a survivor from a shipwreck.

Rainwater was dripping from the handle of the front door as Marty gripped it and took a breath.

***

Jennifer, half upside down on the floor because her ankles were still taped to the gurney, cringed right underneath the creature as it writhed and twisted its way out of Ulysses' yawning abdomen. Ersen and Otis, across the room, watched in abject shock and terror as the creature finally unwound itself from the corpse and slammed to the floor with a heavy wet *plop*.

On all fours, the creature raised its head. Its black, wet, unblinking eyes, all four of them, scanned its surroundings. Its face was too big for its body; it appeared to be part wolf, part coyote, with a protruding forehead and its two sets of yellow eyes, which glowed fiercely. Its fangs dripped a viscous, stringy fluid.

The Anubis, covered in blood and gore, unfurled itself onto its hind legs. They all watched, helpless with fear as the creature began to grow.

The loud sounds of bones cracking echoed off the walls as its red, blotchy skin stretched, and its spiky fur spread across its belly as it grew to its full height of over seven feet. Jennifer tried to process the fact that while the head was an animal, the body was human in shape; rippling, thick muscles with heavily veined forearms, and at the end of its three-fingered hand, razor-sharp, two-inch claws.

Nobody dared move. Jennifer was so close to it that she could smell its putrid breath, and the clammy foul odor of decay that wafted from its fur.

At the table, Trevor stared in terror, his eyes wide, the tape cinched across his mouth. Ersen and Otis were trembling, unable to move.

Another wet, slurping sound came from the creature, and its snout *bloomed open*. Three black tendrils floated out from its hidden nostrils. The tendrils themselves opened and closed. The creature was sniffing.

***

Gun in a military grip, Marty quietly opened the front door, and silently slipped inside. The smell seemed worse now, the sickeningly sweet odor of something rotten. It was dark and except for the sound of water dripping somewhere, very quiet.

Marty advanced into the building, taking out his Maglite and crossing his wrists in front of him; resting the wrist of his gun hand on top of the wrist holding the flashlight. He swept the beam of light along the tile floor and the walls.

He stopped dead, hearing a skittering sound from behind him. Turning silently, he aimed the light behind him, and held his breath to listen – nothing. Maybe a rodent. This body harvesting "morgue" Burrows had told him about was underground, in the basement. There had to be a door that led to a staircase.

Quietly stepping into the main room, he looked up at the soaring ceiling, and again saw the peeling blue paint, and the yellow painted stars that impressed him the first time he was here, looking for Sean Burrows. Were some of those stars above him still shimmering? Could it be, almost a century later, that this moldy, once magical ceiling of the abandoned Loew's 46th St Movie Theater still sparkled?

The sheer vastness of the place daunted him. Did movie theaters even have basements? And how was he going to find it in the dark?

***

The tendrils of the creature hovered over Jennifer, moving around her face and up and down her body. Hearing its thick, wheezy breathing, she shut her eyes tightly and held her breath. The sulfur smell was overpowering.

There was an odd sound. A gurgling noise, like a stomach grumbling from across the room, and she sensed the tendrils moving away from her. Opening her eyes, she saw the tendrils were now pointed toward Ersen and Otis. Ersen had his hand over his stomach trying to muffle the growling of his hunger pangs. Jennifer was grateful for his intermittent fasting.

The Anubis' double sets of eyes focused on the two terrified men. On the gurney across from them, Trevor tried to press himself into the table, wanting to be invisible.

The tendrils suddenly snapped back into the creature's snout, and it stood up to its full height, the back legs like powerful tree trunks.

It started moving toward Ersen and Otis.

The steps it took were awkward and halting, as if it were still learning to walk; the feet leaving a trail of blood and gore in their wake as the creature made its way determinedly to the two body snatchers. It went down on all fours and moved faster.

Jennifer snapped out of her shock once the creature had moved away from her and used the scalpel that was still tightly in her grasp to free her ankles from the slab.

Ersen and Otis stepped away from the autopsy table as Trevor squirmed against his bonds. Ersen wielded his scalpel, while Otis brandished his bloodied knife. They tried to circle away from the creature, but the Anubis relentlessly, patiently stalked them.

***

It had taken Marty another ten minutes to realize there *was* no basement. There was no body harvesting "morgue" here – he had been played. Raffy Burrows had lied to him about the location, probably reveling in the double irony of sending Marty to the place where this investigation had begun, the abandoned theater that Sean Burrows called home. A house of make-believe. Burrows was perfectly happy to give up Ersen, but he was not about to betray the operation itself.

Marty was pissed.

***

Jennifer rushed over to the autopsy table where Trevor lay, only semi-conscious. Picking up his arm, she saw the bone in his forearm was completely exposed and sticking out from the skin; tendons and ligaments were already cut away from it.

Behind her, the Anubis closed the distance between it and Ersen and Otis.

Still holding Trevor's arm, his blood staining her fingers, Jennifer looked around frantically. She saw the instrument tray; there were forceps, a clamp, and a grisly-looking bone saw with chunks of flesh and chips of bone still attached. There was also surgical thread. And several pairs of latex gloves.

Trevor lifted his head, trying to see his arm. Jennifer ripped the tape from his mouth. He howled.

Jennifer checked behind her to see if the creature had reacted to the scream, but the Anubis was continuing its advance on Ersen and Otis.

Turning back to Trevor, an odd sense of calm descended on her. The medical training she had soaked up as a pre-med student kicked in. Snapping on a pair of gloves, she pulled up his shirt to examine the stab wound in his abdomen. It was deep, and still bleeding, but because it was lateral to his belly button, there was a good chance the blade had missed major organs. There was no way to be sure, but she felt that was less threatening than his arm trauma. Taking the roll of tape Otis had used on Trevor's mouth, she tore off a four-inch piece, and while pinching the edges of his stab wound together with her thumb and index finger, which caused another howl of pain, she slapped on the tape, hoping that at least for now the bleeding would ease.

"Trevor," she said evenly, "you've lost a lot of blood. I've got to try and reattach the tendons and get the bone back in place 'till we can get you to an ER."

Jennifer didn't mention the fact that she had no idea if they would get out of there alive, let alone to an ER. Trevor's wide eyes were focused on what was happening behind her. Jennifer turned and followed his gaze.

Ersen and Otis were stabbing wildly at the creature, which stood back up on its hind legs. The two men seemed tiny as the Anubis loomed over them, trapping them in the corner.

Hearing the desperate sounds of their shoes scraping over the stone floor as they advanced and retreated, and the steady rasp of the creature's breath, Jennifer knew that sooner or later this monstrous beast was going to turn its attention to her and Trevor. She had to stabilize him and get him the hell out of there.

"This is gonna hurt," she warned.

Trevor stared up at the ceiling and screamed as Jennifer snapped his bone back into the opening in his arm.

The Anubis roared at Ersen and Otis. Jennifer wanted to hold her ears against the inhuman cries coming from both sides of the room, but she needed both hands with Trevor. It was pushing her over the edge.

While focused on using the forceps to grasp the edges of Trevor's torn tendons, Jennifer was spared the sight of Ersen, in the corner of the room, trying to jab the enraged Anubis with his scalpel. The creature swiped its claw-like hand at Ersen's head—

And his face simply tore off, as if it were a Halloween mask.

The skin of Ersen's entire face, Mennonite beard, broken nose, black eye and all, smacked wetly against the wall, and slid to the floor.

Otis started screaming uncontrollably.

Trevor continued to scream as Jennifer pulled at his tendons. The volume was climbing. Jennifer was at the breaking point, trying to ignore the carnage behind her, and Trevor screaming in her face.

Finally looking at him, she said, "I'm sorry."

And hammered him in the face with her fist. Trevor again fell back on the table, unconscious. Glancing over her shoulder, Jennifer saw Ersen staggering, screaming, waving his arms. When he lowered his hands, she saw the whites of his eyes prominent over the exposed, raw, red sinew where his face used to be.

Horrified, Jennifer quickly turned back to her work, knowing she had to block everything else out in order to help Trevor. She had to move fast.

Otis couldn't stop screaming, his eyes clamped on Ersen's bloody skull and glistening muscle.

The creature turned to Otis, and with a lightning-fast strike of its powerful, clawed hand, tore open his entire body, from his neck to his belt. Otis looked down in helpless shock as the contents of his abdominal cavity spilled onto the floor.

He sagged to his knees, and for the brief, few remaining seconds of his life, tried to scoop his intestines back into his belly. He spasmed, and fell over on his face, dead.

The Anubis turned its attention back to Ersen, who remained on his feet, lurching drunkenly, clutching at his faceless skull. There was a blur of movement, just two powerful swings of the creature's arms, left and right, and Ersen's limbs flew away from his torso like an exploding ragdoll. Within seconds he was in pieces, scattered all over the autopsy room floor.

Jennifer, her hand shaking, her stomach lurching at the smell of human waste and the coppery odor of blood that filled the room, did her best to finish suturing Trevor's arm. When that was done, she looked at the creature and saw that its back was to her, allowing her to run to the other side of the room and grab a gurney.

Pulling the gurney to the side of the autopsy table, she got behind Trevor, and grabbed him by the shoulders. Grunting with the effort, grateful for all the experience she had moving dead weight, she managed to yank him on to the gurney.

The gurney's wheels squeaked when Trevor's body made contact, and the creature snapped its head around at the sound. Jennifer quickly pulled the gurney back into the shadows outside of the bright operating light above them, praying the Anubis couldn't see them.

The creature went back down on all fours and lumbered toward the light.

Jennifer held her breath and glanced down at Trevor, grateful that he was still unconscious. Or was he dead? She knew it was entirely possible. Her track record at saving people was not great. Could she even save herself?

The creature came closer. It moved through the surreally bright light. It paused, its head turning slowly left and right.

Jennifer waited in the shadows, hoping the creature would be satisfied with its two kills and move on. She once again felt the hot sparks of rage creeping over her body. Trying to take over. She certainly felt no grief over the fate of Ersen and Otis, but the thought that she could be snuffed out, just when she had figured out what was really going on in this hellish morgue, filled her with white hot fury.

"You're more powerful than you know."

She tried to concentrate - to channel the rage to work for her. The rusty fluorescents above her detonated violently in a spray of glass, sparks, and fluorescent dust.

The creature's head snapped toward her, and the snout bloomed open again, with a spray of droplets that landed on Trevor as he lay on the gurney.

Tendrils floated out of the creature's nose, like insect antennae. Twitching. Smelling.

Jennifer tried harder.

The giant operating light above the table ruptured with a deafening crash, and even the Anubis flinched as giant pieces of glass rained down on it.

Its tendrils seemed to have picked up a scent. They stretched into the shadows to the gurney. Toward Jennifer. She broke her concentration in order to jerk the gurney further back. She came around to the front of it and stood guard over Trevor. Her breath was coming in gasps. Jennifer cinched her eyes shut. The operating table levitated and flipped over. The surgical instruments danced on their tray. The tray flipped over violently, the scalpels and clamps and spreaders rocketing directly at the Anubis—

Embedding in the creature's side with a sickening squish.

Standing up again on its back legs, emitting a twisted roar that hurt Jennifer's ears, the Anubis towered over her. Opening her eyes, she could only look up in awe as the creature's bulk cast a giant shadow over her and Trevor. It made a propulsive exhaling sound, and the surgical instruments were propelled out of it, clattering to the floor.

It took two giant steps and was directly in front of her.

So close that its rancid breath moved her hair.

Jennifer had nothing left. She believed she was living the last moments of her life. Exhaustion replaced the rage as she saw Ersen and Otis' blood and gore dripping from the creature's giant claws. The tendrils reached for Jennifer. The sniffers moved up and down her face. It felt like spiders crawling over her skin. She fought the urge to bat them away with her hands.

She wondered if she were about to see her father again.

Jennifer looked up at the creature, waiting for what was surely coming. The least she could do was die with her chin up.

The creature's four eyes stared at her. Through her. Revealing nothing. The eyes blinked in calm unison.

Jennifer shut her eyes. Waited.

Scared.

There was a loud, cracking sound, and when she opened her eyes again, she saw the creature's chest and rib cage splitting open.

There were bones and some kind of folded fleshy tissue

inside, and to her horror, another pair of arms unfolded and reached out from the Anubis' chest.

These arms were smaller, not nearly as strong. Jennifer flashed on a dinosaur's arms as they extended toward her face, dripping some kind of thick sludge.

At the end of the arms were humanoid hands, with four thin fingers. The image of tweezers came to her terrified mind. The fingers lingered in front of her face.

Jennifer tore her eyes away from the fingers and found herself gazing into the creature's penetrating pairs of eyes. They observed her coolly. The Anubis breathed – a deep, wheezy rasp. Jennifer's legs were shaking.

The Anubis reached for her eyes with its smaller hand. Jennifer followed the fingers with her eyes. Frozen in fear.

One of the fingers gently touched her eyelid, and it closed her left eye. Then it gently closed her right eye.

Jennifer immediately remembered doing this same thing just hours ago – gently closing Ulysses' eyes as he lay dead.

Her father's face came to her; she had closed his eyes in the same way, with her fingertips, moments after he died.

Jennifer was strangely calm. She felt the creature's hand and arm withdraw.

Opening her eyes, she saw the Anubis staring at her as its small, withered arms folded back into its chest with another wet cracking sound. Unable to look away from its pinpoint eyes . . .

She saw the creature nod.

It was almost imperceptible, but she had no doubt.

The creature turned away from her, dropped down onto all fours again, and began its tortured walk back to Ulysses' hanging corpse.

Jennifer stepped out of the shadows and into the bright light as she watched the creature arrive at Ulysses' body, squatting down under the yawning, dripping hole that used to be his abdomen. It curled itself into a grisly ball of fur and teeth and claws, and somehow became smaller as Jennifer watched.

The Anubis slithered back up inside Ulysses, its now-smaller claws using his rib cage for leverage as it swung deep into the body, packing itself into Ulysses' chest. It seemed to become one with his chest wall and couldn't be seen anymore.

Jennifer blinked. Amazed to still be alive. As soon as the creature disappeared, she immediately doubted everything that had just happened. It had to have all been some kind of hallucination.

Trevor! Looking down at him, she swung into action. His pulse was incredibly weak. She got behind the gurney and raced out of the old autopsy room. Back into the dark, labyrinth hallways.

All she had to do was find her way out.

Running blindly, she used the nearly dead phone light with one hand while trying to steer the gurney with the other. Ahead of her, a figure appeared in the dim beam of her light.

Jennifer squinted into the darkness, shit, now what? Was someone really there?

It was an old woman. Jennifer recognized her as the first "ghost" she had seen at the morgue, with her prim business suit and jet-black hair set off by a white streak. Her right arm was still missing at the shoulder. Jennifer skidded to a stop with the gurney. She had to grab Trevor's shoulders to make sure he didn't slide off.

Without ever taking her eyes off of Jennifer, the woman, looking even more ghostly in the pale phone light, lifted her left arm and pointed. Jennifer was frozen at first – but understood. She pushed the gurney forward and ran in the direction the old woman was pointing to.

Just when she thought she was lost again, another

figure appeared in her light. It was the older man Clover had named Why Me. Staring at her balefully, he slowly pointed her in the right direction.

It happened over and over. Every time she lost her way, another figure appeared and sent her in the right direction. Sean Burrows, with his bullet-ripped chest. The young woman whom Angel had photographed, her broken ribs still bordering the gaping hole in her body, lifted her arm to point the way. The man with a bullet hole in his forehead whom Clover had named "Is That Thing Loaded" guided her.

The restless spirits of this morgue, the desecrated, whom she had unwittingly helped, were helping her.

Making another turn into the darkness ahead of her, Jennifer became completely disoriented. Her phone finally shut down. Not even able to see her own hand holding the cell phone, she shook it, immediately feeling foolish; what possible good could that do?

Bringing the gurney to a halt, she frantically looked around for another entity to help her, but there was only inky darkness. Madness kind of dark. Blinking her eyes, she couldn't tell the difference between when they were open and closed. It felt as if the black void had become airless. Her breathing was strained.

She heard something – a faint sound – growing louder.

A familiar sound.

The bellows-like in and out breathing of a ventilator.

Her head bent toward the sound. It was coming somewhere from her right, far away. She gripped the edge of the gurney and started moving forward, into the abyss of darkness in front of her.

The ventilator breathing became louder. It was calling her. Guiding her. She did her best to follow it, fighting off the claustrophobia of not knowing where the walls were, or – where the ceiling was. They could all be closing in on her, and she wouldn't know until it was too late.

The mechanical, relentless breathing became louder. Jennifer was getting closer, struggling against the feeling that with her next step she'd just fall off of a precipice. Closing her eyes, she took it slowly, concentrating on her breathing and following the sound of the unyielding machine.

Opening her eyes, she saw a dim spill of light ahead. She pushed the gurney faster, moving toward it. The sound of breathing was coming from somewhere near the light. She could see a bit more clearly. There was a turn up ahead, the hallway bent to the right. The light was coming from somewhere around that corner.

Running, she took the turn a little too fast, and the gurney bounced off of a wall. Trevor's body jostled, but he made no sound. She couldn't tell if he was breathing.

Approaching the light, she had the terrifying thought that they were both dead, and just didn't know it. Was the light up ahead *the* light? Was that where the spirits were guiding her? Were they about to leave this world? The light got brighter. The breathing louder.

The silhouetted figure of a man stood under the open trap doors. The same trap doors that had deposited Jennifer and Trevor in that hellhole, in what now seemed like a lifetime ago. The way in was the way out. They had made it.

Pushing the gurney closer, she saw the figure was standing next to some kind of a machine.

Thick, blue tubes connected the machine to this figure.

She stopped. It was her father.

The breathing tube snaked down his throat. His chest rose and fell in rhythm with the abrupt, machine-driven breaths.

Bathed in the light from the morgue above, almost like an angel, her dad looked at her. Without her even realizing it, their breathing synced up. His eyes were lucid and his face calm. She almost had the sensation that he was floating.

He held his arms out to her. Jennifer, her eyes filling, went toward him around the gurney. She was flooded with a feeling of comfort, as if everything that had ever bothered her was slipping away. *I must be dead, but it's fine. It's good. It's great!*

Holding her arms open, she moved to him. His lips smiled around the respirator. She was ready to go, to be with him again. Maybe with her mother too. Stepping into the pool of light, she was smiling, crying . . .

And he was gone.

***

The sun shone on Winthrop Street, the skies cleared of rain. It was an incredible autumn day, crisp blue sky, golden sunshine backlighting shrunken, brown leaves as they gently cascaded from tree limbs and onto the still wet streets. Passerby turned up their collars up to ward off the chill.

Detective Marty Bell walked past the police cars and ambulances that blocked the street in front of the morgue. Although he had forced the TV vans and reporter's cars to move, the press still jammed behind the crime-scene tape, shooting video and snapping pictures and doing standups with the entrance of the morgue behind them.

Marty had been on his way back to the station to possibly strangle Raffy Burrows, when he heard the chatter on his radio about something happening at the morgue at 599 Winthrop. The arriving day staff reported two people injured, at least three others dead, along with hanging corpses, body parts. Marty pulled a U-turn worthy of a Trevor Pryce movie and raced to the scene.

He cursed himself the whole way. If something had happened to Jennifer, he would never forgive himself for being two steps behind, and for being played by a body-snatching loser like Burrows. So Marty stayed outside of the morgue, pacing back and forth on the street. He would only be in the way if he forced himself inside.

Noticing a stir go through the crowd, he saw Jennifer being led out of the building. She was shell-shocked; her lab coat splashed with blood, squinting in the sunlight, just like he always did. They worked nights. They belonged in the dark. They were vampires.

She passed by the two coroners who had come in for the day shift, who had heard her cries for help under the open trap doors and called police. Jennifer nodded at them; but Marty could tell she was numb and still trying to process all she had seen and done that night.

Having had lots of practice, she had no problem ignoring the shouted questions from the reporters as a police officer escorted her to one of the ambulances where Marty waited for her. Watching as an EMT helped her sit on the tailgate of the ambulance, Marty felt tired and drained. He hadn't slept and wondered if he looked as rough as she did.

"You okay?" he asked.

She just stared at him.

Taking in the blood that covered her rubber gloves and her clothes, he looked away. He had heard the reports from the first responders: a forest of corpses in the basement of the morgue, dissections, body parts. It would be a scandal that would rock the city. However, all Marty wanted to do was ask her one simple question: *Did you see the body of my mother down there?*

But he didn't. It would be selfish. And how would she know? He'd find out sooner or later anyway. Maybe he didn't even want to know. The important thing was that no one else's mother would end up down there. Ever.

Looking at Jennifer, he spoke softly, asking the question that had to be asked: "Did you know about this?"

Looking at him numbly, it took her a while to find the words. "What do you think?" she asked. When he didn't answer, she turned to the EMT, who helped her into the ambulance.

Seeing her look over her shoulder as she got in, he followed her gaze, and saw what she did: a body bag being placed in a coroner's van.

Finally, Jennifer wept.

EIGHTEEN

This morgue was modern. Gleaming. Sterile white, and brightly lit to chase away all shadows. The floors were spotless. There were gleaming refrigeration drawers, glass cabinets, and brand-new autopsy tables that didn't even appear used yet.

Well-behaved corpses were neatly lined up, obediently waiting their turn for autopsy. Crisp white sheets were tucked around their bodies. Their toe tags had been computer-generated, not handwritten.

On the main autopsy table, under the bright-white light that gave everything under it a washed-out glaze, lay Trevor Pryce.

His pale body was naked, except for the neat white sheet pulled up to his waist, low enough to reveal a nasty, jagged scar below his belly button.

The right forearm also bore the scars of his ordeal. His

face was alabaster white, and his eyes stared up somewhere past the light, as if looking up at something fascinating, but that he couldn't quite understand.

If nothing else, it seemed like Trevor had found peace at last.

That peace was shattered when Trevor suddenly bolted up, and screamed in terror, his eyes wide and the veins in his neck straining.

"Cut!" a voice boomed out.

There was an explosion of activity as wardrobe and makeup people swarmed the stage. All of the other corpses stirred and slid their sheets off. A hip young costumer with streaks of purple hair gave Trevor a bathrobe, which he put on with a waggle of his eyebrows.

The morgue set, which sat on Stage 4 at Warner Brothers in Burbank, California, was ringed by director's chairs and busy crewmembers. A grid of hot lights hung overhead. Tables of food seemed to be everywhere. Walkie-talkies crackled.

"Ok that's a buy, this takes us to the apartment set."

The director, a young man in his early twenties, who looked even younger, wearing a Dodgers cap and a Dean Martin t-shirt, walked from his monitor at video village. Giving Trevor a fist bump and a big smile, which revealed a huge swath of gum above his teeth, he laughed happily.

"Dude you crushed it. Scene fifty-two up next."

Trevor was unsure. "Didn't you think the scream was too short? I could've—"

"It was perfect! We'll loop it later if we have to," the director assured him. Another young guy was coming toward them, and the director called out to him, "Josh, let's get him in the works for Scene fifty-two."

Trevor, frustrated, wanted to say something else, but the young helmer was already walking away.

Josh, the assistant director with a neatly trimmed

beard and tiny eyeglasses, smiled at Trevor. "Trev, you have a visitor."

***

Riverside Park sat on the edge of the Hudson, beneath the shadow of the Joe DiMaggio Highway, formerly known as the West Side Highway. The road stanchions had been painted a soothing green color, but the traffic racing by above could still be heard.

Nevertheless, Jennifer was glad to be there, in an outdoor café that overlooked a long steel and concrete pier that jutted out into the Hudson. It was a Saturday, so the café was crowded; luckily her friends had already gotten a table by the time she arrived.

It was a blustery day, late November, and probably one of the last weekends the café would be open. Soon it would be shuttered till next spring. Jennifer drank the last of her mimosa. It was almost time to leave; she couldn't be late for her lunch shift.

Her friends were laughing at a joke Jennifer had tuned out. Instead, she was thinking how grateful she was to be there, to be with them, to feel like she was once again joining the human race. The morgue seemed like a long time ago, although it had only been just over a month. Being with her friends, being anywhere else, felt like a miracle.

The body-harvesting ring had been exposed, but of course there were few perpetrators left alive to prosecute except for Raffy Burrows and some other funeral directors, hospital orderlies, and nursing-home administrators. Raffy had not anticipated that the main architects of the scheme would all be dead, and therefore his services as a snitch would really have no value. He was looking at a very long time in prison. Jennifer had cooperated with the police, but she knew they still had lots of questions. Questions about the corpses, how they were killed, and the condition of their bodies. Jennifer's answers had not quite satisfied.

At that moment, she wasn't going to worry about it.

At that moment, she was happy.

Putting down her champagne glass, Jennifer stood. "Gotta go."

Brenda pouted at her. A freckled redhead wearing a pair of heart-shaped sunglasses, she was one of the circle of people Jennifer had reconnected with. "Nooo! Not fair. You just got here."

Her other friends shouted protests.

Jennifer loved it. She shrugged with a smile. "Saturday lunch. Best tips of the week, can't afford to miss it."

"See you on Thursday?" Zach asked, shouting to her from the other side of the table. Zach's brooding good looks were offset by his completely absurd sense of humor. He was new to their group, but Jennifer had to admit she found herself looking at him a little longer than strictly necessary. Zach made her laugh every time they saw each other; it was just a matter of time before he asked her out. The answer would be yes.

Blowing kisses at everybody, Jennifer walked away from the table and to the ramp that led up to Riverside Boulevard. With any luck the M72 crosstown bus would be on time, and she'd be at the restaurant early. Putting her sunglasses on and zipping her jacket against her neck, she enjoyed the cool air on her face as she made her way up the incline, passing bicyclists and people chatting as they walked their dogs.

"Jennifer Shelby?" a man's voice called from behind her. Her heart skipped a beat. Who was looking for her? What now? The press had finally started to leave her alone, once her fifteen minutes had passed. She kept walking, hoping the person would just go away.

Instead, a man fell in step beside her. Stealing a

suspicious glance at him, she saw a pleasant looking guy in his late thirties, slightly balding. He wore a nice suit and carried a briefcase.

Smiling at her, he asked, "Are you Jennifer Shelby?"

"Why?" she quickened her step and didn't look at him.

The man laughed. "You're hard to find."

Glancing at him, she kept walking. "Look, I'm not talking to the press, I'm not selling my story, and I have nothing to say about Trevor Pryce or events at the morgue. Buh-bye."

Hurrying ahead of him, she reached Riverside Boulevard.

"Do you remember Ulysses Henderson?"

Jennifer stopped, turned, and looked at the man as he got to the top of the ramp.

"Of course I remember Ulysses."

"My name is Tom Ewell. I'm an attorney, and I represent his estate."

"*Estate?*" Jennifer repeated doubtfully. The man smiled again.

"That's pretty much everybody's reaction. Nevertheless, he remembered you in his will."

Jennifer stared at him, and her eyes filled. Not a day went by when she didn't think of Ulysses and how happy he had been the last time she saw him. How happy and how dead. She supposed that should give her some hope. Maybe there was peace in death? Some happiness on the other side? Sometimes there was precious little of it on this side.

Tom Ewell opened his briefcase, balanced it on his thigh, and removed a slim envelope. Coming closer to Jennifer, he spoke softly. "Ulysses bequeathed this to you."

Jennifer hesitated, watching the man for some sign of a con, some tell that this was a scam.

Instead there was a kind smile. "Apparently you meant a great deal to him." He waited for her to take the envelope.

She reached for it gingerly, as if expecting some kind of trap to spring. The lawyer didn't move; clearly she was supposed to open the envelope right then. Unsealing it, Jennifer took out what looked like a check.

"He wrote something about you finishing college and going to medical school."

Jennifer looked at the oblong paper in her hands.

It was a cashier's check made out to her in the amount of five hundred thousand dollars.

Her eyes had spilled over now, so she had to squint to read the amount again, to make sure she was reading it right. When she glanced up at Tom Ewell, he was already walking away, swinging his briefcase like he was happy to have just done a good deed.

Jennifer stood there, looking at the check, and sobbed.

***

Three thousand miles away and two days later, Trevor Pryce awaited his visitor in his trailer. It was a doublewide pop-out, as befitted a star of his caliber. Pop-out meaning that the side expanded, so that when it was all set up, the trailer resembled a mansion more than a vehicle.

Trevor, still in his bathrobe, was running his blender, making his afternoon apple-carrot-kale shake. He detested it but had to admit drinking this swill made him feel great. And these days he was all about feeling great.

Glancing at the walls of his trailer, there was plenty here to make Trevor feel great as well. Framed newspaper headlines and magazine covers, shouted such breathless headlines as *Action Star Slaughters Body Snatching Ring! Single-Handedly Saves Helpless Morgue Attendant!*

Next to those tabloid tributes was his framed commendation from the NYPD and a photo of the mayor of New York giving Trevor, his arm still in a sling, the keys to the city. The mayor had terrible breath and a severe case of dandruff, Trevor shuddered to recall. There were various other photos of him being fêted by the New York media for his heroic work. His cranky judge even dismissed the remainder of his community service. All in all, it had worked out pretty well, Trevor thought with satisfaction. Just one last loose end he hoped would tie off soon.

"Oh shit," he exclaimed, remembering something. Picking up a container of fish food, he hurried over to the fish tank that had previously been in Clover's office. The whole gang was there, including Ziti, none the worse for wear. Trevor lovingly tapped in some food and watched with a smile as the army of tropical fish undulated their little bodies toward the falling flakes.

He was still watching them when his trailer door open. *Finally,* he thought, turning.

"How'd it go?"

Tom Ewell entered the trailer, his suit replaced by a pair of torn jeans, brown moccasins, and a Hawaiian shirt.

"Perfect," he said with a smile. "I gave her the check and got out of there before she could ask any questions."

Trevor nodded, pleased, putting the fish food down.

"It was a pretty great acting exercise, actually," Tom went on. "How does a lawyer walk? How does he hold his head? When he speaks, does he—"

"Right mate," Trevor interrupted, peeling off a thousand dollars in hundred-dollar bills. "Spare me the Method. Did she seem happy?"

Tom took the cash and stuffed it in his pocket. "Actually, I'm pretty sure she was crying."

Trevor looked at him, considering that. Then nodded. "I made a woman cry," he said, almost to himself. "And it's a good thing."

He smiled at Tom. "That's a first."

John Gray

***

It was a Tuesday, which was a day off from the
restaurant for Jennifer. Taking a break from filling out her
school applications, she stood in this cemetery, looking
down at Ulysses' grave. She had paid for the headstone
herself. While the mayor of New York was throwing himself
in front of the cameras alongside that famous hero, Trevor
Pryce, she had had to fight with the city to claim Ulysses'
body. Jennifer was not about to let her friend get buried in
a mass, anonymous grave on Hart Island. She prevailed.

Jennifer went there once a week or so, just to have some
quiet time. Always feeling his presence, always believing he
knew she was there and that he appreciated it. Making a
point of never turning to her left to see the morgue building,
she hoped she would never have to lay eyes on it again. In
fact, after considering finding a different cemetery for
Ulysses, something out in the suburbs, or even on Staten
Island, Jennifer kept coming back to the idea that this was
where he lived, and where he had dreamed of seeing his
daughter again. This should be his final resting place.

Everything had turned out for the best in the end, she
thought, even though Trevor being hailed as a hero made
her a little nauseous. It amazed her how people immediately
read into the situation, especially the media, and had made
assumptions based on Trevor's movie persona. Those
perceptions caught fire and took on a life of their own. The
story of Trevor saving her life and exposing the body-
harvesting ring kind of wrote itself. As she had explained to
him when she visited him in the hospital, she was fine with
it, as long as it made everyone look at Trevor, and not at her.
And of course that was the kind of sacrifice he was very
willing to make for her.

When leaving New York, he had given her an open
invitation to visit him in Hollywood, to come to his sets, to

309

"party" with him. She liked Trevor, in spite of everything, and recognized that at the end of the day he was just another lost soul, whose fame and money really did little to mitigate his loneliness. It was doubtful that she'd ever see him again. In a movie maybe. To see him, to be around him would bring back too many feelings that were better left behind.

It was getting late, the afternoon sun low in the sky, and the chill had arrived. It got dark so early these days. Zipping up her coat, she glanced down at the Anubis amulet carefully hidden at the base of Ulysses' headstone, amidst the flowers and weeds.

Taking one last look at the headstone, she kissed her fingertips, and pressed them against Ulysses' name.

On top of the marker were two plain hot dogs.

Jennifer turned and walked away. Shrugging her shoulders against the cold, quickening her step. She had some plans to make.

Leaving the cemetery, she turned in the opposite direction of the morgue, and headed toward the subway. She stopped. *Fuck it,* she thought, *I'll take a cab.*

ACKNOWLEDGEMENTS

Like in every other aspect of my life, there are so many people to whom I am grateful; I would need another novel's worth of pages to thank them. Out of mercy for the reader, and to give me some cover in case I forget anyone, I'll try to keep it brief, beginning with the force of nature known as Maer Wilson, publisher and diligent, expert editor, and to whom I've no doubt caused some consternation - this run on sentence being a case in point. All mistakes are mine and mine alone. I also want to thank the wonderful family of writers at Ellysian Press, who made me feel welcome. Props also to M. Joseph Murphy for his sharp eye and great cover art.

Thanks to Craig Harvey and Michaelene Mary Taliano, who gave me an inside view into the workings of a city morgue. Any inaccuracies in the book have everything to do with making things creepier, and nothing to do with their expert advice.

Special gratitude to Harlan Coben and Lisa Gardner, who are not only great writers but superb humans. I've stol – I mean, learned, so much from them. I'm also grateful to Jay Bonansinga for his inspiration and encouragement. Thanks to Rhonda Hayter and Emily Murdoch Baker for their early reads and enormous contributions.

Special thanks to Gerard Bocaccio for his friendship, and willingness to help at all times.

And I always owe a debt of gratitude to that master of horror, Teddy Tenenbaum.

Much love and thanks to my awesome family. My wife Melissa, a brilliant writer who is always an inspiration, and whose honest criticism I've come to rely on ("What's with you and semi-colons?"). My smart and witty daughter Caitlin Gray who is always fun to bounce ideas off of and invariably comes up with great plot twists. Thanks to my brother Tom Gray whose unique sense of humor I always try my best to channel when I'm writing, and my sister-in-law Isabell Gray, who is no doubt relieved that her days of typing my manuscripts are long gone. And a grateful belly rub to Frannie and Ziggy.

A shout out to my true-blue managers, Rob Wolken and Dalip Sethi, and much gratitude to Richard Hoffman, publicist extraordinaire.

And to Peter Miller, gone but never forgotten.

And last but not least, to every single person who picks up this book and reads it - I am forever grateful to you, most of all.

ABOUT THE AUTHOR

(Picture courtesy Melissa Jo Peltier)

Brooklyn born John Gray is an award winning writer-director-producer of films and television, and the creator of the long running TV series, *Ghost Whisperer*. He has written and directed many feature films and movies for television, including *White Irish Drinkers*, starring Stephen Lang and Karen Allen; *Martin And Lewis*, starring Sean Hayes and Jeremy Northam; the Emmy® nominated *A Place For Annie*, with Sissy Spacek; the Emmy® nominated mini-series *Haven* with Natasha Richardson and Anne Bancroft; *Helter Skelter* with Clea DuVall and Bruno Kirby, and many others.

Gray has directed numerous episodes of broadcast and cable series, including multiple episodes of the NBC series *Grimm* and was also the producing director of the CBS series *Reckless*.

Gray's acclaimed short films have played and are

currently in film festivals all over the world including *French Kiss*, which has also notched 6.3 million views to date on YouTube.

He is married to writer-filmmaker Melissa Jo Peltier, and they make their home in New York and Cape Cod, MA.

The Desecrated is his debut novel.

Follow him on Twitter @JThomasGray, or Instagram @bayrdge.

Or visit his website at:

https://www.johngrayofficial.com/

ALSO FROM ELLYSIAN PRESS

The Clockwork Detective
R.A. McCandless

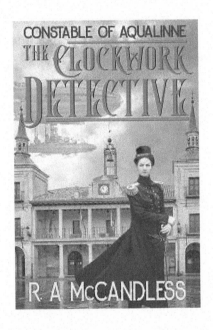

Aubrey Hartmann left the Imperial battlefields with a pocketful of medals, a fearsome reputation, and a clockwork leg.

The Imperium diverts her trip home to investigate the murder of a young *druwyd* in a strange town. She is ordered to not only find the killer but prevent a full-scale war with the dreaded Fae.

Meanwhile, the arrival of a sinister secret policeman threatens to dig up Aubrey's own secrets – ones that could ruin her career.

It soon becomes clear that Aubrey has powerful enemies with plans to stop her before she gets started. Determined to solve the mystery, Aubrey must survive centaurs, thugs and a monster of pure destruction.

"This is my kind of book: a wonderful, fully realized, utterly plausible Steampunk world with a dynamite plot, great characters, and the best dirigibles this side of anywhere. I hope there's more to come."— From James P. Blaylock, World Fantasy Award-Winning Author, Co-Founder of the Modern Steampunk Genre

Moonflowers
David A. Gray

I'm not like those other freaks. The kids who can look inside your head and bring your nightmares to life.

The weirdos who can steal your luck or make a thing true just by wishing it. The outliers born from the mess that followed Armageddon.

The ones you call Moonflowers, half mockingly and half afraid. They're the mistakes that humanity hates – and needs.

I'm not like them. I'm worse. And I'm the only thing standing between you and the legions of heaven and hell.

—Petal – The Armageddon-Lite Archives

Yonder & Far: The Lost Lock
Matthew C. Lucas

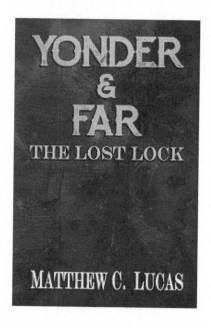

Fae Banished to Boston Town, 1798

In a shocking move, the Queen of the Fae has banished John Yonder and Captain John Far to the human world. Rumor has it that they have opened a law practice catering to the Fae. To what purpose, no one really knows.

John Yonder has accepted a seemingly simple case. He need only recover a lock of hair for a Fae courtier. She had given it to her lover, Wylde, who is also in Boston.

Yonder tricks a fortuneteller, Mary Faulkner, into assisting with the case. With a whisper in her ear, he tethers Mary's mind to Wylde's, creating a terrible, but potent human compass.

Following Mary's guidance, the trio sets out to follow Wylde. They set course into an uncertain and rocky future on land and sea, as pirates, slave owners, and a host of others hinder their path to Wylde, the lock of hair, and a possible return home to the Fae.

ABOUT ELLYSIAN PRESS

Ellysian Press has been bringing high-quality, award-winning books in the Speculative Fiction genres since 2014.

To find other Ellysian Press books, please visit our **website: (http://www.ellysianpress.com/)**.

You can find our complete list of **novels here**. They include:

Yonder & Far: The Lost Lock by Matthew C. Lucas

Fate Accompli by Keith R. Fentonmiller

Evil's Whisper by Jordan Elizabeth

Beneath a Fearful Moon by R.A. McCandless

Time to Die by Jordan Elizabeth

A Forgotten Past by Tiffany Lafleur

Aethereal by Kerry Reed

The Soft Fall by Marissa Byfield

Motley Education by S.A. Larsen

Moonflowers by David A. Gray

The Clockwork Detective by R.A. McCandless

Progenie by Mack Little

Time to Live by Jordan Elizabeth

Before Dawn by Elizabeth Arroyo

Redemption by Mike Schlossberg

Kālong by Carol Holland March

Marked Beauty by S.A. Larsen

Dreamscape by Kerry Reed

The Rending by Carol Holland March

A Deal in the Darkness by Allan B. Anderson

The Tyro by Carol Holland March

Muse Unexpected by VC Birlidis

The Devil's Triangle by Toni De Palma

Premonition by Agnes Jayne

Relics by Maer Wilson

A Shadow of Time by Louann Carroll

Idyllic Avenue by Chad Ganske

Portals by Maer Wilson

Innocent Blood by Louann Carroll

Magics by Maer Wilson

The **Ellysian Press Catalog** has a complete list of current and forthcoming books.

Made in USA - Kendallville, IN
42473_9781941637807
07.12.2022 1321